ORANGE ISLAND

I0799697

RED ROOK PRESS

This is a work of fiction. Any references to actual persons, living or dead, events, or locales are used fictitiously

Paperback: 978-1-972259-01-6
eBook: 978-1-972259-03-0

First paperback edition May 2026

Cover design: Anna Luis

Printed by Mixam in the United States of America.

Red Rook Press
Box 870244
The University of Alabama
Tuscaloosa, AL 35487-0244

ORANGE ISLAND

VANESSA FRANCES

DISCLAIMER

This novel is a work of fiction. Names, characters, businesses, schools, and incidents are the product of the author's imagination or are used fictitiously. Any resemblance to actual persons, living or dead, events, or locales is entirely coincidental. The author acknowledges that real-world entities and individuals may be mentioned for storytelling purposes, but all such references have been fictionalized for creative and artistic expression.

DEDICATION

To Florida, siblings, and standing water.

PROLOGUE

Orange Island, the earliest emergent landmass of Florida, dates back to the middle Rupelian period, approximately 33.9 to 28.4 million years ago, during the early Oligocene epoch.

Orange County, located in Central Florida and within what would have been Orange Island's former boundaries, boasts a rich geological heritage. Oranges were introduced to Florida by Spanish colonists and quickly became the county's main commodity crop; the dark-green foliage of orange trees filled the land, as did the scent of the orange blossoms when in bloom. Fewer commercial orange groves remained by the end of the twentieth century. The majority of groves were destroyed by the freezing temperatures that occurred in 1983, 1985, 1989, 2010, 2026, 2030, and 2037.

Rock Springs, part of the Wekiva River Basin, located within Orange County, stands as a testament to the prehistoric nature of the land, being a Pleistocene fossil-bearing area. Here, an array of fossils, including those of giant sloths, mammoths, camels, and dire wolves, dating back around 1.1 million years, were discovered. As time unfurled, Orange Island became a sanctuary, a bastion of life amid the rising tides of interglacial periods, a land of lotus-eaters.

As sea levels rise due to climate change, Orange County, with Orlando at its heart, may indeed become one of the last remaining bastions above the encroaching waters for the state of Florida, serving as a poignant reminder of the intertwined destinies of land, myth, and the ceaseless march of time.

ONE

My last memory of my sister Dove was at Disney World.

Her skin smelled like oranges, always oranges, citrusy and sharp. Distinct. Oranges were as much her as anything. On the days when she felt the furthest from me, and in all the years since, whether she was by my side or rotting in the Earth, citrus brought her back to life. And perhaps, in other ways, oranges had been a knell from the beginning. For Florida, for Dove, and for me.

Oranges stained everything about Dove—her breath, her teeth, her skin and her soul. If Dove were a place, she would've been an orange grove itself, able to withstand summer's exhaustive heat while extending her hopeful branches toward an impossible sky. There was a resilience about Dove I'd never mastered. I was still trying.

In the waterlogged heart of the Sunshine State, humidity led and illusion followed. And there I was, reaching for Dove's side.

Dove kept to herself most of that day, sipping from a plastic water bottle she'd filled with juice, marsh green eyes turning over between me and the passing cars in the parking lot. Detached and drifting.

She was distracted. I watched her glance over the crowd, her fingers drumming absently on the plastic bottle. She hadn't been herself for months, but on that day, the split between the Dove I knew and this one had never been more clear. She felt further away than ever. I didn't know then I'd be chasing her for the rest of my life.

We were a water-only household for the most part. With orange crop failures and rising temperatures, Dove's obsession with orange juice had become the biggest splurge in our weekly grocery shopping. My father always said there was something wrong with the orange juice these days, but Dove didn't care. It was all she drank.

"Too bitter," my father would say before sliding his open carton back across the counter. "It's not what it used to be."

Dove didn't mind. She didn't know any different.

I chalked Dove's mood up to problems between her and her boyfriend Carter. I liked him enough, with his silly questions and bug-eyed disposition. He'd made her happy, at least, I thought. Yet, there was a new shroud of darkness hovering around her over the last month. Something I'd never seen in her before. Something I was too young to understand.

I was ten. She was twenty-three. I couldn't imagine her world being any more complex than my playground arguments with Lauren and failed spelling tests. It had to be boy-stuff. Everything else, as hard as it had been, Dove had always handled.

She still made time for me, between her college classes and Carter, but it only went so far. Her attention had dwindled to little more than a cursory head pat before she disappeared into her bedroom. I heard her quiet footsteps down the hallway in the middle of the night, carefully weighted. She never lingered, always passing through.

So, when our father announced that morning, grinning and clutching crinkled bills, that he was taking us to a theme park, it felt like a miracle. I raced to my bedroom, dug through my things to find the princess crown I'd gotten at a friend's birthday party years ago, and shoved it into my hair. The comb scraped against my scalp, band cutting into my temples. It was too small. I kept it anyway. My father grinned as I sprinted from my room.

"Princess Savannah!"

Dove raised her eyebrows, but instead of interrogating his enthusiasm, she reminded him we had only so many gas rations.

"If you think this is worth it," she shrugged, folding her journal in her lap.

My father was undeterred. He always was. So unbridledly committed to his optimism, he tore through reality with a stake, striking it down until he'd forgotten what was right in front of him. Dove was our default realist. My father preferred his disconnect.

We loaded into the car, and I called shotgun. Dove resigned herself to the back seat, scribbling in her notebook.

Excitement burned in my stomach. These days, tickets to the park were impossibly expensive, entry costing almost $600 per person. Some friends at school casually mentioned their family trips to the park during our ten minute recess. Social skills were important, but so was not dying from a heat stroke. I was never sure how many of their stories were true, and what was crafted from regurgitated images online. In that moment, I didn't care either way. I just wanted to spend time with Dove.

We drove up to the booth and paid the $100 parking fee. I watched my father pull countless single bills out of his wallet and hand them over to the automated attendant.

The automated assistant, called an Augmistum, whirled, its metallic teeth chattering as it counted the money. It was as if it was grinding the paper into sand. I was surprised they took cash at all. Most places didn't.

Augmistums were hyperrealistic robots that not only served as attendants for the theme park but in service jobs or as personal assistants purchased by the elite. They were loved for their obedience, how easy it was to program them to be who you wanted. Augmistums were familiar strangers, close enough to make you comfortable.

I turned to Dove to gauge her reaction, fascinated by the Augmistum's clicking teeth and flashing green light, only to find her disengaged, staring out the window. Her eyes swirled across the steaming asphalt. Her lips pursed, she went back to her notebook.

"Have a mystical, magical, marvelous day." The Augmistum's gears turned its teeth into a poorly-attempted open-mouth grin.

My chest tingled. The Augmistum hissed.

My father's eyes went wild as he drove through the gate. He raced toward the Augmistum, who sped out before us to guide our car to an open spot, humming under his breath.

"Are you excited?" he gripped my shoulder, eyes locked on the Augmistum swerving between the cars toward the back of the lot. It moved like an insect carving through grass. Or a snake. "We're finally here."

I studied the wear lines across my father's forehead, the sunspots on his cheeks and below his nose, and the worn smile lines around his mouth. The heat and his work had always made him look older than he was. The weight of his arm pulled me sideways toward him in the driver's seat. I slumped over, trying to hold him up. His arm left a burning in my shoulder I tried to rub out.

"Yes!" I finally shrugged off my father's arm. The burn subsided, simmering and then disappearing. I looked out through the windshield toward the park, a place I'd only heard about in myth, from advertisements and the mouths of my friends. Characters waved on animated posters. An Augmistum stood by a cart full of water bottles. My eyes flickered from the mirror and back to Dove, who was still somewhere else. The burning returned, like a phantom, reacting to weight I was no longer carrying.

The Augmistum led us to a parking space near the back. My father pulled in and then slipped the key out of the ignition. The outside heat immediately became all the more apparent, pounding on my temples. I kicked my feet back and forth against the dashboard. The faint scratch of Dove's pen rose from the back seat. She stopped writing the second I turned to look. Dove grinned at me. The world expanded.

"What are we waiting for?" My father laughed, childlike, and swung open his door before running to open mine.

"Come on, princess."

I giggled, unclicking my seat belt and springing to my feet. The heat pulsed against my neck. I began to sweat, pushing my slipping crown off my forehead. I felt the two indents it had left in my temple.

Dove joined us, heading toward the line for the tram. She tucked her notebook into her bag, a deep frown across her face. Her eyes were rimmed with dark circles, sunburned skin cracked dry around her lips. She looked sick.

Everyone said Dove was a spitting image of my mother: dark hair, deep lips, and wide eyes. She was beautiful. Radiant. We'd lost my mother just after I was born, so Dove served as my only reference to what she might have looked like if she was still here. There was only one photo of all of us, my mother sickly in a hospital bed. I'd like to think she'd not like me to only know her that way. I had Dove as a stand-in.

My grandmother had told me I was an accident. Dove told me in this world, I was a miracle. Even if it took my mother from us. When I asked her how that could be true, she'd pull back my shoulders, pushing up my posture.

"Miracles are not always kind when they arrive."

I wish I'd asked her how she defined a miracle.

I'd not inherited much of my mother to look at my face. Maybe there was something to be said about Dove and my small ears. I was my father's mirror, freckled and perpetually red from the heat. Our noses were bent the same direction, twisted right.

I saw my mother on Dove. I wonder if she saw our father in me.

Wide-eyed, I'd watched Dove grow up as I learned to walk. She read to me, packed my lunches, and walked me to school for as long as I could remember.

Dad wasn't around because without him working we wouldn't eat. We'd lose the house, with its tattered furniture and ancient mattresses. We'd forgo our gas ration tickets. The AC would get cut.

But without Dove, we'd lose everything else.

Dove studied pharmacy and journalism, interning under a prominent professor at the College of Florida Orlando campus. She'd learned new words my father and I couldn't understand. She and Carter were out late and often. I vividly remember waking up from a dead sleep one night and seeing her outside my bedroom window in the rain, still as a corpse. She'd been staring at the empty road, soaked hair clinging to her head. I'd never talked to her about it.

The heat burned my arms. I regretted not asking Dove if she'd brought sunscreen. Dad would never have been that prepared. With Dove almost out of commission these days, my father's off-the-hip attitude had begun to fully determine our reality. I was seeing the consequences.

The three of us made it to the line for the tram, brushing behind the crowd of tourists and their Augmistums fanning them and providing water.

The Augmistums made me uncomfortable, *especially* as they had become more humanlike. They peppered their owners with reminders to hydrate, tracked the air quality, or informed them if it was a good day to go to the beach, depending on the heat index.

All the characters on TV shows had Augmistums, too. When I clicked through the channels after school, it was a coin toss between angry newscasters or teenagers taking trips to Alaska with their robot handlers in tow. Dove would catch me flicking back and forth between the channels and shut it off.

"None of that's real." She'd frown and hand me a book. "Don't let it fool you."

The Augmistums in front of us were like the ones I'd caught glimpses of on TV, but the people were much less glamorous. Many of them were covered in sunspots and had withered the same way as my father: too much time in the elements. The sun's relentless heat and the harsh realities of life always made themselves visible. Especially here. Floridians, if they'd been here for the long-haul, couldn't escape the marks the state left. You could always see them. If you knew how to look.

A horn blared as the tram pulled toward the crowd. Other children giggled and pushed against me. I felt their sweat, the heat of their breath against my back. My chest tightened. Something about the forced intimacy made my stomach hollow.

My father scanned the rows of people for an open spot. Sweat beads crowded on his forehead. The Augmistums called out the final boarding announcement. My father froze.

I felt a more familiar hand on my shoulder.

"Come on. Let's sit here." She led my father and me toward a row in the back of the tram with enough space for all of us. Dove smiled. I did too.

I clapped my hands and slid around my dad, staring at the sea of cars. The tram glided forward. The breeze dried the sweat off my forehead, cool and easy. I looked at Dove, her dark hair whipping around her face, sunlight catching the drops of sweat on her nose.

She caught me staring and winked. I grinned as she gestured forward, letting the wind wrap its cool fingers across my face as I looked beyond us. When I turned to her again, her eyes didn't waver from the parking lot. She stopped smiling.

My stomach tightened in excited knots, and I tapped my hands against my knees. I couldn't believe it. What would my friends say when I told them I'd been here? I wondered if my dad brought enough money to buy us an ice cream. Sweets were a luxury we'd never been entitled to outside of breakfast cereal, and only because it was cheap. I'd snuck to the kitchen time after time late at night, reaching into the fluorescent-colored boxes with my bare hands, rehydrating the dried grain in my mouth with spit and pulling all the sugar out into my mouth. I'd only dreamed of what ice cream might taste like. I hoped it was better than I imagined. It had to be.

The tram rolled to a stop.

"Please exit to your left," the Augmistum called behind us. My heart jumped in my chest, and I clambered for the door handle. My father grabbed my arm, pulling me back.

"What is it?" I asked. My eyes flickered across the rows of people getting off the tram and walking to the ticket center. The train to the park loomed above us, gliding across its elevated tracks.

"Let's just stay here!" my father said, grinning. "That breeze felt so good, didn't it?"

"But what about the castle?" I asked him, my throat tightening as the last few stragglers exited the tram. We were the only three left on board.

"We're here!" My dad smiled. "See?"

He stretched his arm toward the statue of a princess in the distance. It shimmered above the concrete. Heat radiated off the sides of the metal, making the statue distort and twist under the light. Another illusion. Sometimes, I swore as a kid I could see the cars breathe when it was hot enough.

"But—"

My father's smile wavered. "Come on, Sav, aren't you having fun?"

He ran his fingers through my hair and propped my crooked crown straight on my head. My face grew hot, my eyes welling with tears.

"Why can't we go in?"

My father swallowed, biting on his lip. I watched him fiddle with his wallet, looking around for more bills or a card, but I knew it was empty.

We could only afford to park.

"Final boarding, this is a final boarding announcement," the Augmistum called. The tram horn blared. We pulled away from the entrance and toward the parking lot. I watched the statue slip from view, a mirage sinking away with the heat.

My chest stung. Tears burned and left heat on the rest of my face. I watched the cars as we rolled past, the wind flipping my hair in front of my face until I couldn't see anything besides flashing light and the heat off the baking asphalt.

My dad swore under his breath. He cursed my mother, cursed the government, and I knew he was also cursing me, though he hoped I couldn't hear. He spit off the side of the tram, crossing his arms.

A hand came across my face. Dove used her shirt to wipe the sweat and tears off my cheeks.

"Hey, look here," she whispered, taking my hand. Dove lifted my fingers, holding them just off the tram, letting the air rush underneath them. I felt the force pulling my hand up, lifting it to float.

"You're flying," Dove squeezed my palm and then let me fingers go.

The tram glided around a corner, passing another going the opposite direction. I watched my father wave at the passing robot driver. He was back in his haze, somewhere else.

"Why did we even come here if he knew we couldn't get in?" I hiccupped between tears. "It's not fair."

"I know." Dove brushed her fingers through my hair. "None of this is. But it won't always be this way. I promise."

I coughed, wiping my nose on my shirt sleeve.

"How do you know that?" The rough fabric tickled my nostrils. I sneezed.

Dove smiled and pushed my hair back behind my ears. She took the crown off my head, resting it in her lap. The train horn honked, the sun beating against my exposed ears. I stared at the crown in her lap, seeing the chipped silver paint and missing rhinestones, the wear lines on the clips. Dove opened her bag and tucked the crown inside.

"Because it can't."

The tram pulled to a stop near our car, and Dove stood and led me off. My feet burned through my shoes on the asphalt. Our father reached out for her.

"Come on, you don't want to go around again?"

Dove shook her head.

"I don't."

She put her hand on my back and led me back toward the car, my father following close behind.

Three days later, they found Dove and Carter's bodies on the bank of the Wekiva River, my crown still buried in her bag.

TWO

Dove and Carter had drowned. That's what I was told. There was nothing else to believe.

My father didn't tell me about it. His grief and overwhelm left him pretending nothing bad happened; that nothing had happened at all. We learned to live almost as if Dove had never existed, at least, not really. It didn't work for me. She never went away, not for a moment after she left.

I'd found out after school. When I turned on the TV while waiting for my father to come home from work, after an Augmistum-centered reality show finished, there it was. Carter and Dove's ID photos were plastered on the screen, side by side. The news anchor spoke the word "drowned" with all the intrigue of someone reading off a grocery list. Forty-five seconds later, the segment was over, replaced by a commercial for blue jeans.

Unlike my father, I wasn't afraid, even then, to recognize something had gone awry and we were fundamentally changed. But I didn't cry. I sat, staring at the screen until my eyes hurt, and then I slunk back to my room, the TV buzzing. Dove's school photo blinked into view whenever I closed my eyes, burned into my brain.

My father was at our family dry cleaner, but I was sure someone had told him what happened. The police probably called before the story aired. I sensed he was avoiding me because he was more comfortable burying the past under layers of silence than confronting it, as if naming the tragedy would make it real. If he never acknowledged what happened, he wouldn't have to deal with it—or with me.

I wanted to scream, to demand answers from him when he returned, but I never did. I swallowed the impulse. I learned to deal with the aftermath in the news stories and whispers from classmates about my dead sister that formed the story as I understood it. I accepted the pieces that never fit together. I'd lived that way since.

Working was the thing my father did most. His routine had been the same my whole life: urgent morning alarm, rushed breakfast, out the door within fifteen minutes to the dry cleaner. It was his temple. He was always home late, wrinkles and the weight of exhaustion pulling around the corners of his face. I threw myself into work the same way as I got older, folding shirts and pressing jackets, anything to keep my mind occupied, to stop the thoughts of Dove from slipping through the cracks. The hum of the machines became a lullaby, soothing me into a state where I didn't have to think. I loved the machine noise. Sometimes, it was the only constant.

Perchloroethylene, lovingly called "perc," was recognized as a carcinogen over seventy years ago, but my father still swore by it, even using it illegally when legislation was passed. There wasn't a single other product he believed would get clothes to smell, feel, and sit on the body right. When cautious customers wandered into our family dry cleaner and spied the small warning label he kept in the corner, he'd smile as warm creases formed around his eyes.

"I promise, you have absolutely nothing to worry about. It's perfectly safe."

When they'd object, citing a story they'd seen on TV, he'd chuckle and place his hand on his chest. His brow softened. With his free hand, he'd reach into the old wooden desk at the front counter and pull the only family photo of my father, mother, Dove, and me from the drawer. The one of my mother, frail and deteriorating. I wonder who'd taken the picture. I'm sure he wouldn't remember if I'd asked.

"You can always go somewhere else, but . . . I'm supporting my daughters doing this . . . alone."

He'd point at my mother, pale and weak in a hospital bed. Her hair was matted down in knots. Dove stood to her left, thirteen years old, eyes wide. They were both turned inward to face a newborn me cradled in my father's arms.

"I do this all for them."

Patrons' eyes would flicker between the photo in his hand, his genuine expression, and the pesky chemical warning label, before finally laying their clothes on the counter. My dad, no matter how many times he gave the spiel, no matter how it evolved after it was only me he was supporting or how yellow and frail the photo became, always closed his eyes and bowed to the customer.

"Thank you for supporting our family."

I could never tell what my dad did or didn't feel about anything. He kept every emotion that wasn't joy separate from me and Dove. It made him impossible to mourn with. I couldn't share his grief, because I'm not sure if he had any. At least, none he'd allotted for me.

And if he did grieve my mother or Dove, he bore it alone, in the family dry cleaner for twelve to eighteen-hour shifts by himself every day. Dove said the only times she saw him take a break was the day I was born and then for Mom's funeral. And then, of course, the attempted theme park trip.

He hadn't been able to get away for Dove's funeral.

I'd watched him my whole life, standing in front of the whirring machines. He'd spent more of his life than he hadn't loading in solvents to pull stains from clothes, at all hours of the day, taking exhausted, heavy breaths as he leaned his body against the side of the machine. He never let me help him when it came to the real work. It didn't matter how often I'd asked. The only thing he'd ever let Dove and me do as we got old enough was work the front desk and check clothes in, under the condition that if anyone came in and asked about the perc warning label, we promised to come and get him from the back.

When I'd asked him about perc privately, he'd brushed it off.

"If it was so bad, wouldn't they have stopped me from getting it by now?"

That, I wasn't sure about. I could think of hundreds of things so dangerous or polluting that should be impossible to come by: processed meats, unlicensed animal breeding, corporate lobbyists, transfer and sale of carbon credits, the burial of natural gas waste, having more than three children . . . None of them, however, were.

Things that were banned, on the other hand: flying more than twice a year, unless, of course, you were wealthy enough to afford the appeals lawyer to make a business justification; resistance to automated technology in your workplace; abortion in all fifty states; attending protests without registering your face in a government-mandated and monitored "political activist" registry; and a myriad of other things I actually couldn't remember.

The way I experienced life had stayed, for the most part, consistent. I lived in the same house. My dad owned the dry cleaner. I had few friends, all of whom, besides my friend Lauren, also rarely left Central Florida. Since travel was so highly regulated, most of us had to find new forms of contentment in living vicariously through wealthy content creators or immersive virtual reality experiences. I remembered when Lauren and I had found an ancient video of Kiribati from the year 2011, the crystal-blue water still bordered by a white sand coastline. I had only ever known the island as having been lost to the sea, drowned in myth.

Florida, too, had suffered its fair share of sacrifice to the ocean. News stories broke weekly about families living on the coast retreating inland. Wealthy families began building transportable homes that could be positioned with helicopters in order to move them back from the receding coastline. *Even wealthier* families built new houses somewhere else once their current ones collapsed into the ocean. There were entire apartment complexes and buildings drifting out to sea, now home to the few remaining schools of wild fish.

Sometimes when I closed my eyes, I imagined ocean waves reaching greedy hands all the way to Central Florida and tugging my father and his machines out to the open sea, leaving me completely alone. I was trapped in our house, wandering the hallways, waiting for someone to come home. They never did.

These visions were most intense after I'd encountered a body of water. I tried to avoid them the best I could.

***

It was a particularly humid September afternoon, the glass doors of the dry cleaner beaded with moisture, dripping like sweat below the entryway. I pulled at the bottom hem of my shirt, wrapped it around my hand, and brushed the glass dry.

We hadn't had a break from the heat in months. The ache of humidity clung to every part of my body like a damp sweater day in and day out. You could swim in the air when it was this thick. Every year it got worse, records smashed, predictions falling short. The heat was an angry constant, Earth's fever intent on burning us up. It had done so to many people already.

It hadn't always been this bad. There was a time where Florida was the fair-weather friend to its northern neighbors, providing a temperate escape from the cold. I'd seen the photos across my computer screen textbooks at school, lounging men and women draped elegantly across folding chairs resting under the sunlight. They looked content, at peace under the blanket of heat. It had grown much too hot now to enjoy, like pulling a coat over a body drenched in sweat. Cursed by comfort.

I heard my father in the back of the store, loading and unloading clothes, the sound of the machines like clockwork. The rumble steadied my anxiety. I turned on the dated TV in the corner of the lobby and flipped mindlessly through the channels. A talk show featuring several celebrities discussed an apology video from their former friend trying to avoid cancellation. An action movie featuring billionaire Rodger Kettington, complete with so many quick cuts it made me dizzy. A reported rape case. Someone sobbing in a language I didn't speak. An ad for sustainable underwear.

I spotted a news alert in the bottom right of the screen.

"Hurricane Warning: Prepare and Stay Alert" the flashing text read in bright orange.

"Damn it," I huffed, folding my drawing paper and shoving it into the desk. The warning said that the storm would arrive in four days' time. The winds were going to hit Central Florida with 145 miles per hour of force.

They'd named it Barbara.

It was in moments like these I wished I had a SubcutaLink, a device implanted underneath the skin that provided real-time alerts to danger and information on crimes, politics, and impending natural disasters. People with SubcutaLinks tended to receive information roughly four hours ahead of the rest of us, which meant that by the time I made it out to buy the things my dad and I needed for the storm, the stores would already be crawling with Augmistums and people.

We couldn't afford an Augmistum or a SubcutaLink. There were barely enough food and gas rations for us to get by. Especially without Dove to help budget. On the rare occasion that I had to commute to college up north for an on-campus lecture, we risked eating from quartered cans of condensed soup for the following two weeks. My father worked more than anyone I knew. But it wasn't enough. He perpetually tried to convince himself otherwise.

By my senior year, I'd seen the College of Florida campus in person only seven times to save on gas rations. I'd spent college in my childhood bedroom. I interacted with my classmates on video calls, watching their pixelated heads bounce in our virtual classrooms. Occasionally, we'd get sent virtual reality equipment from the library, allowing us to simulate being in the classroom with other students. I'd always feel hollow after loading the headset in its return box to campus early to avoid the $1,000 fine if it was late.

Only the really wealthy kids could afford to live on campus full time, seen by us virtual students in the camera projected by our professors as they were lecturing out to an otherwise nearly empty hall.

Usually four or five students were in the classroom, spread out across the lecture hall. The professor's voice echoed against the walls, reverberating over the vacant chairs.

Dove had been luckier in that sense. She'd gotten an internship at the pharmaceutical school campus much closer to us. Carter owned a car. She'd had a place to go that wasn't the house or the dry cleaner, five days a week because she had a ride and a school sponsored reason. I'd always envied that.

"Dad," I called across the dry cleaner, walking toward the back door. My voice fought the whirring of clothes getting cleaned. It was unbelievably loud, the air hot and thick with the smell of cleaners. A single fan whirred in the corner, barely keeping up with the intensity of the heat. The chemical cloud weighed over the room.

"Dad!" I shouted again. The back door was open, letting in heavy, humid air. My eyes burned as I made my way over and stepped outside, shielding my eyes from the pounding sunlight.

I blinked, everything slowly coming back into focus. I saw my dad rubbing his hands together and staring out at the thin patch of forest behind the dry cleaner. The trees were nearly all dead; only low vegetation thrived, prickly fingers spraying through the grass toward the asphalt parking lot. He didn't stir when I joined him, watching the humid wind rustle through the bushes.

He still got like this often; quiet and hazy, temporarily in a world I wasn't part of. His jaw was slack, the whites of his eyes like thick-plated rings around the bottom of our identical dark irises. The air bubbled with heat so heavy I could barely breathe.

I placed a hand on his shoulder, rubbing a circle into the top of his back.

"There's a hurricane coming," I whispered, smelling the cleaners fresh on his shirt. "I need to get us some food and batteries. It looks like it's going to be bad."

My dad didn't move.

"Hey," I whispered again. "Dad?"

I followed his sight line toward the brush.

A cat with rich black fur was perched on a tree stump, piercing green eyes staring back at my father. It flicked its tail up and down against the stump, poised and steady, watching. She licked her paw. We never saw animals out in the daytime anymore, it was too hot. The cat seemed almost unbothered.

"Dad?" I asked again. "Did you hear me?"

My father blinked several times, wiped his hands on his pants.

"No, what did you say?"

"There's a storm coming. I need to get supplies before the store runs out."

He nodded, pulling his wallet out from his pocket, eyes still flickering back and forth between me and the cat. She lingered on the stump, unblinking. My father handed me a mix of crinkled bills and ration cards, then the keys to our car.

"Get the strawberry meal replacement shakes, too, if you can find them," he whispered, folding his wallet and placing it back in his pocket. "The chocolate one makes my stomach hurt."

The cat flicked its tail and hopped down from the stump, slinking back into the brush. My father watched her till she disappeared.

THREE

Hurricane Barbara roared with particular rage, rattling our windows. The shutters groaned. I was shaken, and though he didn't say it, my father was too. The whole house buzzed, sideways rain pelting against the walls. I swore I felt the house lean, the walls creaking like they may finally bend into the elements and snap in two. My father and I sat on the floor of the living room, legs tucked to our chests under separate blankets. He didn't stir when I shuddered at the thunder, but I watched as his fingers curled to his palm before fanning back out again.

We were lucky to keep our internet for a while, and I tapped through movies and articles on my computer between wind gusts. The house continued to groan. I watched as news reporters traipsed through flooded roads and streets, pointing cameras toward wind-torn buildings and screaming over the howling wind into their SubcutaLinks.

"We're hitting all kinds of records today," a heavily made-up woman in a dark raincoat yelled into her wrist. Her lipstick was smudged around the corners of her mouth, eyeliner running in ski slopes down both her blushed cheeks. Her smile didn't budge, revealing two rows of expensive teeth. They looked like they'd just been done. No stains.

"This could be the strongest storm to hit Central Florida since 2047!"

The shutters pulled on the side of the window, scraping against the wall. It almost sounded like the dry cleaner, low and mechanically repetitive.

That was the year Dove died.

The reporter held her grin. My chest grew heavy. It always did when Dove came up.

On screen, the reporter's fingers found their way toward her ear, and she nodded before raising her chin back toward her cameraman.

"According to David back in the studio, Hurricane Barbara *is* in fact the strongest storm on record to date!"

She smiled as another wind gust yanked her hair from her ponytail, sending blonde streams whipping all over her face. Her lipstick stained the ends of her hair to pale pink streamers. I was shocked she was still standing, struggling to pull the hair from her mouth.

I reached for a can of black beans and cracked it open. My crooked tooth butted against the bottom of my mouth, catching my lip in the crossfire. I flinched. Iron and salt filled my mouth. At least I didn't have to see the blood.

"Here are a couple things you should keep in mind over the next few days—"

The reporter's eyes flickered from the camera and back to the cameraman. Her face fell, jaw locking. All her new teeth disappeared behind her lips. After a moment, she cleared her throat, pushing her hair out of her face. Her dim smile returned. You could still see the pink on her ends.

"Back to the studio now to hear about the Hurricane Weekend Deals you can expect to see online. Trust me, you don't wanna miss it!"

She was shouting by that point, the SubcutaLink in her wrist pressed against her lips to capture her voice. The wind whipped both her and the camera man violently, the picture shaking. Her smile was the only thing still, until she gestured to the camera and the scene cut. I couldn't look away, hearing the distant and disruptive audio still rolling. I could hear the rain pelting against her skin. Soft and firm. The screen was black.

"Did we get it? I have to get this in my reel—"

The reporter's voice cooed through the speakers before abruptly cutting out.

Moments later, the picture returned to the studio where a manicured woman and an older man with just enough gray peppered into his dark hair sat behind a news desk. They both had perfect teeth too, with just enough stain.

"Stuck at home for the storm? Don't worry, we've gathered all of the best steals and deals of the Hurricane Barbara bonanza weekend, so you don't miss a moment of savings—"

I closed my laptop.

FOUR

Florida was an exceptional state. And not in the way people expected.

It had been ravaged not only by storms and conquistadors and tourists and political pundits, but also the elderly, the elite, the cold-intolerant, the tax evaders, the lonely.

Dove had always thought of Florida like a revolving door, so many people in and so many out that it was nearly impossible to keep track of everyone who wanted something from it.

It was a safe haven. It was a prison surrounded by water. It was land so alive that it fought back when tortured and demanded sacrifice the way only something wild could.

Florida was hated. Florida had cast the first stone. Florida was a purple state, a red state with blue enclaves hidden near the ports and core like quiet mirages against crystal water that turned murky the deeper you swam. Florida had grown more violent than most as the temperatures had warmed, taking humid afternoons and morphing them to wet-bulb risks.

No one had ever told me why my parents came here and if they'd meant to stay forever. I'd never asked. Dove had once told me in passing my mother was from somewhere else, far away north. She could remember the feeling of the state but never the name. Dove had tried to ask her. I cupped details about the outside world in small soundbites of my memory. Outside of Florida, the rest of the world might not even exist. Maybe it didn't.

Hurricane Barbara killed twenty-six people, and left hundreds wounded. Days later, the news scrolled their names across the screen in plain text before a medication commercial aired. There was no way to read them all. If I tried to play it back, I'd have to watch another ad.

My father and I spent the rest of the storm sitting on the mats sprawled on the living room floor, trading clinks of forks against tin cans of beans once the power went out. We didn't talk. The living room echoed with the sound of rain against the windows, the thrashing of the wind beginning to settle. When it did, I could hear him chewing.

Canned vegetables, fruit, and beans were the only rations left by the time I reached the grocery store. I grabbed them, along with one strawberry meal replacement shake at my dad's request.

I'd shoved as many cans as I could manage into a small cart, waiting for two hours in line for water. Weaving through the aisles, I passed the row of orange juice cartons. My fingers curled as I stared at the technicolor orange. They'd changed the art on the package. Everything had a stronger outlined than I remembered. I grabbed three cartons from the refrigerator, much more than we could afford, and beelined for the checkout, feeling Dove's hand on my shoulder.

The cashier had eyed me carefully as I pulled several wrinkled ration cards and cash from my wallet. The crinkled bills were worn at the edges by hundreds of exchanged hands. I swiped my debit card to pay for the extra orange juice.

"How many people live in your household?" the cashier asked me.

"Just two."

From a large cart behind her, she'd pulled three gallon jugs of water and heaved them onto the counter in front of me.

"Are you sure that's enough—"

"Next!" she called, waving me away with a dismissive hand.

We hadn't had to start drinking the tap water yet. For that I was grateful. I tried to be mindful of how often we did it, knowing the risk in how unclean the water was. We were getting close, the last few tablespoons pooling at the bottom of the final filtered jug.

The videos that had come out after the storm, to both TVs and SubcutaLinks everywhere, were brutal. Mothers whisked away from children in flood waters, animals blown backward against the sides of buildings, families huddled together in crowded shelters waiting for answers, waiting for anything.

Perhaps, only the passage of time.

It always amazed me how chaos could look so calm the moment you were removed from it.

We'd been lucky not to take on more damage. Our house was built long before storms had become as intense as they were now. Dove had pushed my father to make the walls and roof resistant to wind and water years ago, but he continued dragging his feet. The years went by and the gutter pulled away from the side of the house, cracking the wall in several places. Heat baked away the roof. Bugs desperate to escape the heat crawled through the cracks in the window screens, hovering around our antiquated air conditioner. My father continued his slow walk to adaptation, letting the walls mold.

A few years ago, the state stepped in and warned my father we'd be forced to shelter somewhere else if he didn't do something to fortify the house. He caved and bought simple storm shutters off someone online that was fleeing Florida for the northeast: a father with two young daughters. Neither girl could have been older than eleven. The man's hands shook as he pulled the shutters from the back seat.

"Will these work?" he'd asked my father. The shutters had some cracks, a slight film of mold across the top. One of his daughters peeked her head around the door of the car, blinking. The other's wary eyes were fixed on our twisted gutter attached to the overturned rainwater collector; neither doing its job. I looked up with her.

"Absolutely." My dad grinned, handing the man two ration cards and some cash. His eyes widened, not bothering to count what was handed to him. He thanked my father and drove off with his girls, towing a trailer full of their life's possessions off and out of sight.

The shutters were rusted in several places from years of humidity and water, but they were enough to make the house look more like our neighbors' with their up-to-standard shutters. My father installed them himself, hastily attaching them to our windows. He left the gutter.

Lauren had texted me that twenty-six people were killed. She'd gotten the alert on her SubcutaLink before anything had shown on my laptop and far before my father and I learned of the news on our hand-cranked radio once the power was out. I read her text as my father reached for the radio, knocking over a half-empty can of corn, sending kernels and wet slime across the tile. He clutched the radio in his hands as he walked across the house, tracking stray kernels all the way to his bedroom, and closed the door behind him.

Lauren and I had been best friends since middle school. Back then, her family wasn't as wealthy as they were now, but even then, her life felt larger than my own. Her world was open in ways mine never had been or ever would be. Lauren's parents worked in politics, and as their careers took off, so did their lifestyle—foreign trips, fundraisers at hotels I'd never step foot in, connections that made life feel effortless.

By the time we graduated high school, Lauren's future was set. She got to go to college on campus, living in a dorm with a view, while I finished my education in my childhood bedroom, writing my final papers in the same spot Dove had taught me to read in. Lauren spent breaks skiing in Alaska, one of the last few places with reliable snow, while I worried about the dry cleaner and whether another hurricane would put a tree through my window we couldn't afford to replace.

Over the years, as her family's money and influence grew, so did the distance between us. She talked about embassy galas and weekend getaways; I counted my ration cards in the checkout line. I struggled to hold her in my world anymore, the cavern between our experiences too wide to bridge. I considered responding to her text. Then my phone died.

Paper towels were expensive, so I cleaned the corn on the floor with my discarded shirt from the day before and threw it onto the growing pile of laundry in the corner of the room. The heap of clothes sat for days, sometimes weeks. An unspoken reminder of all the things that went unfinished in this house.

The living room felt empty without my father. It made me feel closer to the outside than the inside. The rain continued its retreating pelt against the windows, the wind waging one last push against the walls. Our hurricane shutters rattled, and water dripped through the worn edges. I spotted the black cat again through a gap in the shutters, barely snaking her way around the garbage cans. Her tail flicked out toward me for a moment before she disappeared.

Where had she hid?

Even with the storm, my routine felt the same. There wasn't money for us to do much more than this. It was all too expensive. Everything was. I'd gotten a menial scholarship for college. The rest of the funding came from high-interest loans I'd be paying back until my mid-sixties if I was lucky. The dry cleaner barely brought in enough to keep things running. At home, the roof leaked, and the shutters rattled every time a storm came through. It was consistent. All of it.

When the heat was bearable, I'd go for long walks around the neighborhood, winding my way through streets lined with faded houses like ours. It gave me a small escape from the suffocating stillness of home.

But even then, how many times can you look for something new in the same streets? I was walking in circles, everything familiar. I poured myself into anything that might take the ache the passing of time left in my chest. The hollow mundanity of what I expected for the rest of my existence stretched before me like a boundless cavern I didn't see an end to.

There didn't feel like a point. I tried to tell myself something could be different someday, but what? Nothing had any give. Nothing would break. Who was to say it wouldn't be my dad and me forever, watching the world unravel in a house that wouldn't stand it. I didn't feel like it was a choice I had any say in. Even if I did, I didn't know an alternative worth the risk.

And after he was gone, it would just be me.

I went to the fridge and pulled out an orange juice carton, quick to close it before too much of the cold rushed out. We'd have to throw everything in here away anyway with the power out. I cracked one carton open and drank straight from it, the citrus sharp against my tongue until I finished it. Then I opened another. It was more than I wanted, but I needed the taste, the familiar burn at the back of my throat, something tangible to hold onto. I drank enough to feel nauseous, but I let the feeling wrap me in an embrace like an old friend.

Dove went through orange juice like water. I still didn't get it. It was as sour as ever.

Carton in hand, I wandered down the hall toward my room but stopped short in front of Dove's old bedroom, digging my toes into the carpet. I hadn't been inside in a long time, more often *imagining* her behind the closed door. If I closed my eyes, I could picture she was still in there, as much a part of the house as the aching shutters and trellis of mold. I didn't want to disturb her. Dove's room was a temple, the idea of her presence perhaps still behind the door was enough of a force to keep me out. There were moments I'd caved, opened the door, stared around the corner, picked the pillow from her bed, and smelled the mildew against the faint orange. Maybe I'd imagined that, too.

I wandered into the room less these days. Doing so made me feel like I was further delaying the grief that never went away. Asking it to remain. I could pause it, but never absolve it. Returning to this room only made it worse in the aftermath.

But sometimes I couldn't help it.

Was I supposed to?

I took a deep breath, resting my forehead against the wood and letting my hand wander toward the doorknob. I hesitated, but turned the cool metal in my hand and pushed it open.

Dove's bedroom was largely untouched after she died. I had a suspicion my father occasionally came in here and dusted, the only chore in the house he did. I never asked. In the corner was her bed, still unmade and how she'd left it. Her bookshelf was lined with more books than I could ever imagine reading, her blinds open and letting the post glow of the storm hit the yellowing posters on the walls. There was a pair of discarded socks at the foot of her bed, and unfolded clothes hung off her desk chair.

Everything was perfectly preserved. Sometimes I'd stand in her closet, running my fingers across the fabric of all of her clothes. I'd put on and take off her jewelry, spinning her rings too large for my fingers around my thumb. I laid in her bed and cried.

I couldn't remember the last time I'd been here, imagining she'd enter at any moment, step through the door and ask me what I was doing in her bed. I'd laugh and roll over under the covers, burrowing myself in her white sheets like I was lying under a cloud. She'd ask if I'd brushed my teeth, if I'd made lunch for tomorrow. "Yes" would be the answer to both. And I'd waited so many times in that room with bated breath to give it to her.

I crept toward Dove's desk, running my fingers across the aged wood. Dove said this desk had belonged to my mother, the compartments and wood still original. It was beautiful. I'd seen Dove hunched over in her chair, furiously writing or typing into her computer at all hours of the day here, pausing only to massage the cramps out of her hands or ask me to get her an orange juice.

I ran my hands over the top of the desk and let my fingers wander to the small metal handles of the drawers. I'd never opened them. They'd been left closed for a reason. But, it didn't stop me from wondering. Given how much time Dove had spent here—in this room, at this desk. So much of her time was spent right here.

I set the carton down and leaned forward, kneeling before the drawer. Dove could be sitting in this chair, reading or writing, talking to Carter on the phone, begging me to leave her alone so she could finish her homework. I could see her dismissively waving her hand before she surrendered her frustration and rested her fingers on top of my head; fingernails rubbing into my scalp in slow, patient circles. I'd fallen asleep here while she did it, waking up only when she'd carry me back to my room to bed. By then, I wasn't tired anymore.

I played with the drawer handle and felt the texture of the metal against my hand. My throat tightened.

Gently, I pulled the drawer open.

Only one thing was inside: a dark green notebook with a brown leather clasp, and paper tabs poking from the top of the pages. I gently lifted the corner of it, finding nothing underneath. I picked up the notebook from the drawer. It was surprisingly heavy and coated with a thin layer of dust across the cover.

I set the notebook on Dove's desk chair and checked through the other drawers, finding all of them empty. I stared at the notebook, puzzled.

Why had it been the only thing left in the desk? I recognized the journal. It was the exact one I'd seen Dove writing in it countless times, pulling it away from me whenever I tried to read it over her shoulder. I assumed there must be secrets, crushes on boys, and interpersonal monologues. Maybe a non-stoic, mushy, and self-reflective Dove. A Dove I didn't know.

I opened the notebook and peeled back the first page, revealing Dove's loopy, narrow handwriting:

Property of Dove Alonso
Return if Found.

I stared at the notebook, running my finger across the loops and dives between the letters. Proof of life. At least at one point.

I started to flip cautiously through the pages.

"I need the can opener! Do you have it?" my father called from across the house.

"Coming!" I replied. At first, I moved to put the notebook back in the desk drawer, but then I stopped myself. I studied the worn leather cover, frowned, and shoved the notebook inside my hoodie before I closed the empty drawer, rattling the desk. Grabbing the nearly empty orange juice carton, I closed the door and left the room, rushing to help my father.

I kept the notebook in my hoodie until I had the chance to move it to my backpack. I hadn't opened it since I'd found it, but its presence in the bag lingered, tapping on the back of my mind as I carried it with me everywhere. For whatever reason, I couldn't make myself open it again, no matter how much I thought about it. This was all that was left of Dove. Her words, scrawled on these pages. Reading it would be like one last conversation with her. Maybe I just needed one more.

The dry cleaner has been quiet the last few days in the aftermath of the storm. Cleanup had started, crews in bright orange hauling down power lines and stray palm fronds from the roadways.

We'd had a break from the heat for a day or so. The relief was indescribable, the air light and cold. I'd taken a walk for the first time in months, letting the crisp air run over my shoulders, tilting my head back and breathing in air without moisture. I opened my bedroom window. It was gone as quickly as it came.

Several wealthy regulars bustled into the dry cleaner. The kind with drivers and multiple cars. They needed overnight cleanings for button-downs and dresses, racing to charity events in support of those affected by the hurricane. Others had business trips across the country. Others still were traveling all the way to Asia.

I'd always wanted to go to Asia and had spent hours on my computer, watching archival walk-through footage of different coastal towns and cities that had disappeared under water. Everything was bright and brilliant with color, from the clothes and the food to the public transportation and road signs. I'd always been envious of the trains you could take. I thought about it every time I handed over another gas ration for me and my father to drive to the store. I thought about it every afternoon I saw people walking thirteen miles home in the dead of the Florida summer to get groceries, some of them never making it back.

Asia was also a place Dove had promised we'd go together someday. I was really young, and at the time I'd believed every word she said was true. This included her promise that we'd take a trip together to see the other side of the planet before any more of these places were lost. As I got older, I knew she was giving me something to dream about. Something I could hope for, even if it never arrived. There was no way that would happen in this lifetime. I'd never be able to afford it. But to think about it, even if it was just a place to go when I closed my eyes, that was enough.

Besides, to go without Dove, it just wouldn't feel right.

FIVE

I finished my classwork early again at the desk of the dry cleaner, drawing slow squiggles across the top of my notebook. I blurred the graphite lines with the blue ones on the top of the paper. Both had stained my fingers. Boredom had a taste, and it was dry. My pen drifted off the paper, accidentally staining the desk. I rubbed at the mark with my palm.

The hum from the machines in the back was softer than usual with the lack of customers, so instead my ears filled with the noise from the street outside: rushing cars and horns like thunder. The business of the outside street was more foreign than the rumbling of the machines, with their familiar whirs I'd always been able to trace. I knew their patterns, when they would stop or start. When they'd screech in completion, when a part had come loose. The movement of people, rushing in all directions, was patternless and more terrifying than the constant mechanic rumble. Where people were going, and what they wanted, was unpredictable.

My mind wandered as I looked at the blurring television screen, even though my eyes hurt.

Lauren dragged me out of the house yesterday to retrieve dinner from our favorite restaurant, Lucky's. It was one of the last places to still have human waiters, a refuge from the ever-evolving Augmistum workforce.

Some of them were so lifelike that it was increasingly difficult to tell them apart from actual people. I found you had to stare deep into their eyes to confirm they were automated. The bloodshot lines running through the whites to the iris were the dead giveaway of a person. Augmistums were never tired. Most people were.

"It's awful, everything you see on the news now, you know?" Lauren sighed between handfuls of french fries. "I just tell myself, *Lauren, you have to be mindful and protect your peace because nothing else in this world is going to protect it for you.*"

Lauren's father was on the board of a major voting rights organization, something she was incredibly passionate about—the right for everyone to have a voice. She'd gone to the College of Florida on campus and graduated early, thanks to internships her father's connections secured. She was the first person I knew to have a SubcutaLink, and her family had been offered Augmistums as soon as they'd been made available.

Lauren rejected one for herself. She said digital slavery wasn't something she was comfortable supporting. She always tipped our human waiters.

Lauren showed me several photos from her recent trip to Japan on her SubcutaLink—vibrant cityscapes doused in more neon light than I'd seen my whole life and once-historical coastal monuments barely peaking over the waves. The Japanese coastline had changed. What coastal city hadn't? The scenes of Asia made me think of Dove and, consequently, the journal. My stomach hurt.

She flipped through the photos on her wrist absent-mindedly, giving me a quick half-sentence summary of each one before moving on to the next.

"You don't want to go there, Sav." She frowned, handing me a small bag of sustainable Korean and Japanese skin care products she'd brought back. "Almost everything beautiful is already underwater. You wouldn't believe how much better we have it, even if it doesn't feel like it."

I took a sip of my water. Some of the purification chemicals hadn't filtered all the way out. It tasted like straight salt. My tongue curled in my mouth.

"We can only do so much to change what's happening now." Lauren took a deep breath, closing her eyes and reaching for my hand. I let her do it, feeling the sweat of her palm. "And if I thought about everything wrong with the world all the time, I think I'd go insane."

A burn mark was on my sandwich bun. I picked at it with my free fingernail—a human error. I didn't see it at any other restaurant, not anymore. It was a bit endearing. At least honest.

"Some people do."

"My dad's seen so many of them." Lauren released my hand, wiping hers on the reusable napkin she'd brought with her. "It's getting so bad, everywhere. We just—" She stopped short and coughed. "We just have to keep advocating for people to do what they feel comfortable doing to make it better. But we can't just assume everything will always be awful. Things will change. People are always over-exaggerating how much we can really control."

Lauren took a deep breath, grabbing my hand again, and ran her index finger along the inside of my palm. I blinked. Her fingers were painted a loud shade of orange, more flamboyant than any fruit. Like oranges with the saturation dialed too high.

"Refuges like this are so important," Lauren whispered. "Every act of love for another human is a radical form of protest. It's so much louder than all the hate."

"Mmm-hmm."

"Sav, I love you." Lauren's eyes were full of tears. Her mascara ran down her left cheek. She snorted back her mucus. My lips pressed together.

"I love you, too, Lauren." Lauren's whole face lit up.

She sniffed, closing her fingers around the rest of my hand. "Doesn't that feel better?"

My eyes flickered between Lauren's softened expression and the glowing images of Asia on her wrist, of water spraying all over the disappearing coastline. I could see a building peaking above the waves of the Pacific Ocean.

"It does."

***

"I'm looking for Derrick Alonso?"

It barely registered someone had come into the cleaners. Time continued to blur together until days were incoherent. My eyes darted from the television and stirred me back to the dry cleaner.

I saw a tall man, a bit older than me, holding a baseball cap that he readjusted back on his head after wiping sweat with his hand off his forehead. He wore a fitted COF School of Pharmacy jacket.

"That's my father." I frowned, closing my notebook. "How can I help you?"

The man swallowed. "My name is Matis Wallace. I was hoping to talk to him about the room he was advertising to rent."

"A . . . room? I don't know anything about renting a room."

"I saw it here." Matis tapped on the top of his wrist, the SubcutaLink glowing through his skin as he scrolled through a list of rooms available in Orlando. He furrowed his eyebrows and tapped his wrist again. "Yeah, here it is."

He turned his wrist over, showing me the online marketplace listing that was, in fact, posted by my father. Matis scrolled through several photos of the listing. It was an empty room, one that I'd never seen before. But the walls were pale beige and the floor was identical to the one in our house.

"Wait—" I stopped him, reaching out and grabbing his wrist. "Sorry. Can you go back?"

Matis nodded and swiped one photo back. My throat grew tight.

In the back corner of the photo, two stacked boxes sat, and sticking out of the top of one I saw the tip of a silver children's crown and the strap of a dark green bag.

Dove's bag.

I went back to the full listing. It had been posted while I was out with Lauren. The blinds were open, letting the early evening sunlight into Dove's now-empty room.

"I'm sorry," I finally said, setting down Matis' wrist. "Let me go find my father. I'll be right back."

I slid from the chair and turned around, rushing toward the back of the dry cleaner with my heart racing, the second time in a few weeks I'd broken my father's rule of not going back there. The TV blared an ad for pet food that disappeared as I swung the doors to the back open.

"Dad?" I called out between the machines, poking my head around the corners of every space in the room. I heard the timer alarm go off and footsteps.

I rushed over. My father had a white shirt in his hands that he was gently putting on a hanger. The air was hot and dry. It was dizzying in here. His back was to me, but I could see the plaster smile through the back of his skull. It made the anger in me grow even hotter.

"What did I tell you about coming back here?" he called over his shoulder. The anger poured off me. It felt like venom in my chest, and I didn't want to hold it anymore.

"You're renting out Dove's room?" I retorted. I wanted to scream.

He froze, his shoulders rolling forward, deflating. Like he always did.

"There's a guy in the front asking to talk to you about it."

My father huffed, hanging the white shirt up. He didn't turn around.

"I'm sorry, Savannah."

I shook my head, grief and rage mixing together in a horrible, bitter pain in my stomach. "Why didn't you tell me?"

"You were out with Lauren."

"You didn't even think to ask me? To talk to me about it?" I felt my face get hot.

"I can't afford for us to stay in the house if I don't rent out Dove's old room. I didn't have a choice."

"But you moved everything out of her room without even telling me? Without asking if I wanted anything? If there was anything I could—"

My father turns around, his expression open, eyes soft.

"I'm just trying to take care of us." My dad's canned response for all decisions, good or bad, fell from his mouth like a perfectly rehearsed line. "I was able to get some decent money for the textbooks and some of her clothes . . . Renting out the space will help support us so we can stay in the area, close to the dry cleaner and your friends . . . I think it's what she would want. Don't you think so, too?"

My heart was racing, the chemical smell making my head spin. My vision grew clouded with fear and rage and anxiety all in the same moment. It was like I was experiencing Dove's death all over again.

"That room was all we had left of her." I held my jaw tight. "And you didn't even let me say goodbye."

I used every muscle in my body to restrain the tears in my eyes. I could still smell Dove's perfume, feel the covers of her bed against my skin. It was all disappearing now, like a meal cooked hours ago and with only the scent of the food lingering. Dove was a memory. Only a memory. She was not coming back. Ever.

My father grinned, like the words I'd said were unbound to the gravity they held.

"I saved you this."

He stepped farther into his office, kneeling to hand Dove's bag to me. I peered at some of its contents. I could see her wallet, several crinkled receipts among papers and pens, and my princess crown. I couldn't make myself go through all of it, the lump in my throat tightening. Tears burned hot in my eyes.

That was it. That was all that was left.

"See." My father pulled the crown from the bag and placed it on the top of my hair. His hands were hot. He smelled like chemicals.

"Princess Savannah."

Every muscle in my body burned. I wanted him to hurt the way I hurt about this. To realize that what was gone was irreplaceable. But I didn't move. I couldn't find my voice. Perhaps, that's where him and I were the most the same. I sat in the weight alone like poured concrete, letting it pull my arms down and roll over my shoulders.

"Didn't want you to forget our trip to the theme park, right?"

I bit firmly on the top of my lip, enough to taste freckles of blood rising from underneath my teeth. He continued to smile.

I told myself he was trying his best. That he didn't know better. That he meant well. That he lost my mother and Dove, too. None of the excuses I used to try and make myself feel better worked. I didn't believe him.

The hurt and rage didn't disappear, so I swallowed to keep them contained to my stomach. I festered. I wondered if repression could be a cause of death. I knew grief could.

"Thank you," I murmured, pushing my lips into a smile, eyes still burning with tears. Perhaps my father had gone blind to grief that was not his own because he'd lost the strength to carry any more. I believed it when I saw him shut off the news. I believed it when he grinned at my tears. I believed it when he used perc.

"The guy is waiting up front for you," I whispered.

"Wonderful," my father replied. "You know, I saw on his profile that he's also going to the College of Florida. The Pharmacy Campus. Where Dove was interning."

I nodded, swallowing back the burning in my mouth.

"Don't keep him waiting," I said, gesturing for the office door.

My father left me staring at the sterile fluorescent light, the crown fixed upon my head like a littered jewel.

I vowed to start reading Dove's journal.

SIX

But I didn't.

Dove's journal sat at the top of my to-do list every day for a week, scrawled and underlined and eventually moved to the subsequent day. I told myself I'd open it after I finished my homework, grabbed a protein bar from the pantry, rested my eyes, and scrolled through my phone, before I'd fall asleep and start over the next day. Eventually, the idea of reading through her journal felt almost more powerful than the act of reading the journal itself.

My anxious thoughts about the journal raced. What if Dove didn't intend for it to be read? What if it was something she'd kept for herself, while alive, to trace her thoughts, map out her mind in a private space?

Was I being selfish, trying to hold on to a part of her that wasn't mine to begin with?

I fretted over discovering Dove's stream of consciousness in her curled handwriting, detailing fights with Carter or Dad, her interpersonal reveling. These are things I would have longed to see as her little sister years ago but feared now. The collective weight of her empty bedroom and journal now carried an archival quality. It was the last relic of my sister. Something to preserve. To treasure. I was doing the right thing, leaving it alone.

Until Matis Wallace finally moved into Dove's old room ten days later.

Distracted that day, I dragged myself through homework assignments to ignore the sound of footsteps up and down the stairs as Matis carried his things into Dove's old bedroom. During a live lecture, I heard a banging sound against the floor, my computer shaking on my desk. I pushed my headphones farther over my ears. My eyes flickered to my bedroom wall, my jaw tightened. Another thud came from down the hall. I imagined Matis tearing up the floor, stocking Dove's closet with his clothes, covering the thumbtack holes in the wall from Dove's posters with his own inroads of individualism. A beeping alert rang in my ears.

"Please retain focus on the lecture," the automated response whirred. "Do not get distracted."

***

In the days before Matis arrived, the dry cleaner was just starting to see more business again, but the front desk work never became less mundane.

Everyday blurred into the next. I searched for anything to pull me away from thinking about the journal, let alone reading it.

I tried joining an online club for school. COF Shouts! was working on posters for a virtual climate protest, a loophole in not having to sign on to the "political activist" register maintained by the state because it was strictly online. When I saw the proposition, I was excited.

I offered to do some art for the group, eagerly sketching designs between classes while at the dry cleaner. I decided on sketching out a bear, the college mascot, with a wide open jaw, clamping down on the state of Florida and snapping it in half. The image was gruesome, but effective.

"Climate Change Will Bite Down on the Sunshine State!" I'd written in orange bubble text, sprawling around the outside of the drawing. The bear's paw was dripping with pen ink, encouraging the governor to sign on to the suggested emissions agreement proposed by several international committees. Finally, it would be a step in the right direction for the state in ensuring its own survival, or so it seemed.

I'd been inspired to create it in the aftermath of the hurricane. More videos of the disaster came out between ads for Augmistums or erectile dysfunction medication.

"Florida needs this agreement!" a red-faced woman shouted into the camera, her ocean backdrop interrupted by several downed trees and torn roofs, damage from the storm not yet removed. "Any one of us can look around and see how much we've already lost . . . Can't they?"

A branch cracked, coming down on a car behind her. The story cut to a commercial for dehydrated candy. It had an awful jingle, so annoying that I couldn't even hum it.

When I'd submitted my drawing to the leading organizers of COF Shouts!, they rejected the idea and told me it was probably best to delete the file altogether. The bear looked suddenly meek to me. Had it not been direct enough?

"We need to be careful here." A girl on the video call pushed her hair behind her ears, tugging on the frayed sleeves of a vintage pop-country star sweater. "We don't want to make anyone feel excluded."

"Excluded?"

"Yeah, like the people that don't agree with us won't be able to get behind something like this."

"Then, what should we be advocating for?"

"A climate recognition school holiday is what we're starting with," another girl chimed in, sharing her screen to reveal a bubbly poster asking for an extra day of Thanksgiving break.

"We really want to make sure the school provides people the opportunity to take up the space they need to process the state of the world."

"And, we're pushing for a new mandate that requests emissions to be cut by another quarter by 2100."

My eyes flickered between the girls and my outlined sketch.

"Will that . . . work?" Both girls blinked.

"Change takes time! We can't ask people too much before voting season. Poll turnout will *tank* this year if we get written off for being extreme and no one votes."

The power went out moments later, my father shouting from the first floor that he was going to go out and reset the breaker. My computer went black. Neighborhood dogs howled, and people clambered to open the windows for fresh air. A baby cried in the house across the street. I peered at my computer screen, the outlines of both girls still apparent against the black when I blinked.

I didn't go to any more meetings after that and buried the sketch of the bear in my bag alongside Dove's journal.

After the fallout with COF Shouts!, Lauren left on a two-week trip to Italy with her father for his job, occasionally sending back photos of the coastline or the flooded remains of what was once Venice. The ancient city was dwarfed by the ocean.

In one selfie, Lauren stood on the bow of a boat, capturing the tops of some buildings barely reaching over the water.

"So crazy," she'd caption the shots. *"Can you believe people lived here once?"*

I couldn't. The contrast was obvious when I compared the photos Lauren sent me with images of Venice from thirty years ago, when the water was rising, but not nearly this much. Older photos divided the past and present all the more obviously: beautiful streets lined with people, open-air vendors selling fish and clothing, the ocean reflecting light across the bridges. Now the ocean consumed them.

A selfie concluded Lauren's photo dump with a brief note about an Italian guy she'd recently become obsessed with. I'd lost track of all of the boy's names.

"Thinking of extending the trip. Can't afford to go home yet when things are just getting exciting!"

***

Another slam of furniture hit the floor in Dove's room, and in my surprise, I pushed my pen through my paper. I heard an exasperated laugh.

"Do not get distracted," the beep rang in my ear again, piercing and sharp. I pulled my headphones off. The lecture beeped angrily, but I stormed to the hall toward Dove's old room.

I knocked my fist against the door, and Matis opened it slowly, revealing a room full of unpacked boxes. He had a bed without a frame and a tidied desk stacked high with stray paper and textbooks. It was messy at best. He was grinning.

"Don't worry. It won't be like this for much longer. I hate when stuff is disorganized."

I didn't reply, my eyes flickering to my dad's stack of abandoned books in the hallway. Perhaps he didn't know the kind of house he was moving into. My father had made Dove's old room look neat enough to fool people about the rest of the house.

"Sorry about the noise," he chimed. "I think that's the last of the heavier stuff."

He nudged some stray papers off his foot, along with his COF School of Pharmacy ID card. I took a deep breath.

"I'm just trying to watch a lecture, and every time I look away from the screen—"

"The automated bot gets you. Yup, I remember."

I hated seeing him standing in Dove's old room. It was already a mess. Like everything else.

I frowned. "So you understand why I'd like a bit of peace."

Matis nodded. "Sorry about the commotion."

"Thanks," I replied, turning and starting to walk away from the room.

"What are you studying?" he asked as I reached Dove's doorframe. I stood still, contemplating if I wanted to reply. I wasn't sure if I wanted to punish him for being here just yet.

"Anthropology," I answered quietly.

"I took some anthropology classes as electives during my undergrad," Matis excitedly moved another box to his bed and off the floor. "They were always some of my favorite classes. You know—"

He darted from the door and back to his desk, sifting through the stacked pile of books. He found one and handed it to me.

"Have you read this one?" I peered at the cover.

The Collapse of Complex Societies by Joseph A. Tainter.

"I haven't," I replied, taking the book and turning it over, letting my fingers glide across the spine.

"It's really interesting. Taught me a lot."

"Thanks."

I dug my foot into the floor, studying the creases my toes left in the carpet. At least that was the same. The automated voice and beeping had left a distinct high-pitched ringing in my ears. I felt like Matis was attempting to make a peace offering, but it came off like pandering. I knew it wasn't his fault he unknowingly uprooted my last tether to Dove, but I couldn't help blame him anyway. Grief made me unreasonable. I wasn't ready to be any different. I wasn't sure I'd ever be.

"Your sister also went to COF, right?" A knot twisted in my stomach.

"Years ago, but yes, she did."

"Is her name Dove by chance?"

I frowned, crossing my arms across my middle. "Yes. Why?"

"I think I've heard your last name before, in passing at least. Your sister was really well liked on campus."

Matis leaned into the wall, palms open. I stepped back.

"Dove interned at the pharmacy campus in her senior year of undergrad for her degree." My jaw tightened, my fingers tensing around the book. "Studying under—"

My brain slipped, scavenging for the name of who Dove worked under at the Center of Research Development. It had been historically reserved for graduate and PhD students, but Dove had, as per usual, been an exception.

"Professor Powell."

Matis lit up.

"I'm one of Professor Powell's teaching assistants."

"Oh. Nice."

Creases formed across Matis' forehead, accompanying his smile.

"I'm in the doctorate in pharmacy program. I've been spending most of my time focusing on pharmacometrics. Have been there for a couple years now."

"Way over my head."

Matis laughed. I flicked the pages of the book he gave me.

"The work Professor Powell has done on climate resilience technology and medication is brilliant. She's been working on it for decades. We're actually in the final phases of development for something really exciting." The words started coming out of Matis' mouth and didn't stop. "It might actually change the response to human-induced climate change forever."

Matis talked to me the same way Carter always spoke to me in the few times we interacted: overly enthusiastically. And too much. Providing so much information meant everything became an accidental lecture. A constant stream of consciousness.

I remembered Dove gently tugging on Carter's hand in our kitchen, asking him to let me finish my reading homework. He'd been rambling to me about complex medication interactions while I was ten years old. It was something I had no hope of understanding. I probably still wouldn't.

"I actually think Dove was around when Professor Powell first started making breakthroughs in the research," Matis continued, pulling a book off his desk. He continued talking before I had any opportunity to get a word in edgewise. "At least, from what I've heard, she was one of the smartest interns Professor Powell ever had. I think that would've been right as Qucore finished the expanded wing—"

"Yeah, I was really young when she was working there." I closed my fingers even tighter around the book. I wanted this conversation to end. "I don't really know anything about that. Besides, she was out late and always tired."

Matis laughed.

"I bet. The progress they were making then, you only get that from giving it everything."

"Yup."

Matis stepped back into his room and kept shuffling through his books, undeterred by my disinterest.

"Where is Dove now? I'd love to talk to her about her work with Professor Powell at the time."

I blinked at him, fighting back a laugh forming in my throat. This felt like a sick joke.

"She died thirteen years ago."

Matis stopped fussing with the books on his desk, smile faltering for the first time.

"You're in her old bedroom."

His face fell.

"Oh. I didn't—"

"No, I know you didn't, but you asked."

"I—" Matis huffed, setting all of the books back on his desk and slumping into the chair. "I'm really bombing this introduction."

"A bit."

I turned the book in my hands over again. Matis had the curtains open, the light radiating through the length of the space. September was drawing to a close, but we were still under a heat advisory that had lasted for the entirety of the summer. I spotted a lone hawk out the window, wings billowing up and down as it pushed through the heat, across the skyline and eventually out of sight.

"I'm sorry," Matis said eventually.

"It's okay."

"It doesn't have to be."

"Okay, it's not. It sucks."

"I'm really sorry."

"Don't worry about it."

I took another deep breath, staring back out the window toward the glaring daylight.

Matis picked up his COF student ID, and twirled it between his fingers. He scratched the corner of the ID against the top of his hand. I felt a little bad that I'd been so harsh, but I knew if I wasn't, I'd fall apart. I didn't know what was worse.

"A lot of people speak highly of Dove on campus. She's a bit of a local legend. If you ever wanted to come with me to the lab, I'd be happy to introduce you to some people that have a lot of great things to say about her."

My jaw tightened.

"Is that why you wanted to move in here? Because you saw Alonso on the listing and you want to be close to some kind of . . . University mythos?"

Matis shook his head, putting up his hands.

"No, it was a weird coincidence. I mentioned I was moving to a new place to Professor Powell and she brought up the idea you all might be Dove's family after I mentioned your dad. I promise."

"And she didn't tell you Dove was dead?"

"No. She didn't. No one did."

I studied him for a moment, watching the way his eyes held mine. His expression was soft, open. I wasn't fully convinced, but I could only take him at his word.

I heard a beeping across the hall, followed by a yelling automated voice from my computer speakers. "Lecture time-out warning: Engage with content to continue or video will restart."

"Damn it," I huffed.

"Drag your cursor from the bottom to the top of the screen and then open a new note document," Matis said. "It bypasses the restart function if it thinks you've just been taking notes. Weird glitch in the program I found ages ago."

"Thank you." I nodded, and I meant it.

"I'm sorry about the noise."

"It happens. Sorry for being snide."

"It happens. Go finish your lecture." Matis cleared his throat "*Do not get distracted*," he half laughed, imitating the automated women.

"Yup. Noted. Thanks for the book."

Matis gave me a curt wave as I opened the door to my room, following the instructions he shared to reset the program. Just as I clicked open the new note tab, the lecture began to play. The warning disappeared from my screen.

He was right.

I plugged my headphones in. Before I slipped them on my head, tucked in the corner, Dove's bag caught my eye.

I took a deep breath and stepped over to the corner, seeing the silver glint of my princess crown at the top of Dove's bag and the corner of her journal sticking out of my backpack next to it. A unique twisting feeling spread in my neck, like a was being both held and restrained. Safe and made scared. I pulled Dove's journal out, holding it in my hands.

Property of Dove Alonso
Return if Found.

I ran my finger along her handwriting and willed myself to turn the first page.

It was a drawing that depicted a garden, with more flowers than I could ever name, leaves and petals reaching all over and across the dirt. Through the middle was a winding body of water, rich and blue, with orange trees lining the banks. Oranges were everywhere, pouring off the trees, falling to the ground, and rolling into the water. In the distance was a sketch of a building, house, or church, with muted brown walls, as if it was rising from the earth itself. It was both part of the scene and entirely separate, natural and foreign, barely realized from the Earth itself.

Besides the building, the water, and the oranges, the rest of the drawing was entirely in pencil, with shading on the different flowers being the only separation between them. It was beautiful but haunting, unlike anything I'd ever seen or even imagined. Like a dream.

At the bottom, in Dove's formal cursive, was one singular note of text.

"Fortunate are the gentle, for they will inherit the world."

SEVEN

With my back to the house, I stepped six paces forward. My eyes were closed at Dove's request. I felt shaky on my short legs, unbalanced in my body. A lack of connection between my brain and my limbs. Infantile and unsure, feigning being able to throw my weight around. I was six.

"Follow the sound of my voice!" Dove shouted. "Trust the senses that aren't your eyes," she called again. "Feel for the path."

I took a deep breath, holding my arms in front of me and moving toward her voice. The air was hot against my face, and I raised my shoulder to wipe the sweat beading on my forehead.

"You can do it!" Dove called again, but she sounded even farther away. My jaw tightened. The heat of the daytime sun turned the space behind my eyelids an unsettling dark pink. I could see the veins underneath my skin, webbed together. My heart was moving all that blood around. The realization of my body made me dizzy.

I pressed forward, reaching in front of me. My mind wandered. I wondered about cracks in the sidewalk, if a car was inches from turning down our street and running me over. I wondered if Dove was setting up to trick me. I wondered if she thought I was stupid.

These thoughts brewed in my gut, turning into an anxious rumble. I froze, reaching my arms out, but found nothing to press off.

This was the third time Dove had taken me behind the house to practice walking with my eyes closed, stepping farther and farther away from me each time. She wanted me to learn to trust my instincts, to not be deterred by my eyes.

"There are too many distractions in this life," she whispered, rubbing her arms over my shoulders. "If you don't know how to get by without looking through your eyes, you're going to fall for all of them."

It felt like a game at first, wandering toward Dove's embrace. I would open my eyes to see her smiling, like I was a champion. Her soft hair would brush against my forehead as she'd rest me on her hip and carry me inside. Dove would open the door, and our dark house would greet us, like I'd never opened my eyes at all.

This time was different. Dove had never stepped so far away, and the uncertainty of the wider world reared its ugly head.

"Savannah!" Dove called.

I walked toward her voice, eyes shut. Everything in my whole body was screaming to run, but I kept steady. I longed for that moment when my eyes opened and Dove would be there, pulling me close to her. I could feel her embrace already. I reached my arms as far forward as I could stretch them. My muscles burned.

"Savannah!" Dove called again. She had to be just paces away. I started walking faster, until I couldn't contain myself. I ran. My throat burned. The light taunted me behind closed eyes. The sun was so hot, and my skin buzzed. The air smelled of chemicals. I could hear the whoosh of cars in the distance. I was sure she was right here, testing me by getting closer to the road, wanting me to distinguish her call from the noise. This was my chance to prove to her that I could do it. That I knew how to trust my instincts. That I knew how to survive.

"Wait, stop!" Dove screamed, and my eyes shot open, burning in the light.

I stood at the edge of the sidewalk before the main road. Teetering over the curb, I stared out at the racing cars with their whirring engines, blowing my hair as they passed. Several cars honked, throwing off my balance further. I fought the urge to cry. My heart pounded in my throat.

"Get away from the road!" a gruff man screamed out his window.

Dove grabbed me by the arm and pulled me back. At my feet lay a dead opossum. Dove pulled me in close.

"Couldn't you hear me yelling?" Dove shook her head. "I was just on the other side of the house."

"I—" I peered out at the road and then back to Dove, my breath caught in my throat.

"I thought you were testing me," I whispered. "I thought I heard you over here. I thought—"

Dove shook her head and drew me into her. She wove her fingers through my hair, pulling my head into her side.

"I'm sorry, Savannah. I'm so sorry."

I couldn't take my eyes off the opossum, lifeless and still at the base of my feet, and finally, I started to cry over its small, mangled body. It, too, had mistrusted its senses. Strayed too far from what it understood.

Gone past where it should have.

Dove watched my gaze and lifted my chin. She wiped the tears from my cheeks.

"He got hit so you didn't get hit," she whispered. "He sacrificed himself to keep you safe. It was very brave."

I knew that wasn't true. I hadn't even known him. Why would he have done that for me, when I wouldn't have done it for him?

The opossum must have been there for hours, long before I even approached the road, beaten into the pavement by the sunlight.

The sentiment was nice.

I didn't argue with her, but I stopped looking down.

EIGHT

The quote in Dove's journal was almost biblical.

My father had never been religious, but he was American, so our house had one mint-condition Bible on the living room bookshelf. I don't know if he'd ever opened it. The spine was crisp, the pages neat.

I'd flipped through it before, squinting over the verses trying to make sense of them. It felt like I was peering into a forgotten history, a world running both parallel and perpendicular to ours now. Most of it didn't make any sense to me.

Dove had picked up the Bible occasionally, flipping through the delicate pages in the kitchen while she made breakfast. She'd sip her orange juice, tap her pen against the counter. Dove would hold it while scribbling notes into her journal before sliding it back on the bookshelf, half-reading, half-thinking. Outside of that, the book never moved.

Dove never talked to me about it.

Perhaps she was searching for something. I kept reading her journal.

This is the warmest winter I can remember. I think it's the warmest winter there's ever been. I guess in some ways, also the coolest.

The more I learn about Florida, the more I get, what it meant to people. Why it became the place I know now. How that fell apart. What the transformation meant.

Snowbirds once came here equipped with their winter coats in case of unexpected cold snaps, prepared for weather now a relic of another time. I can't imagine ever wearing a jacket again. Not now, when the air is a constant blanket. The thought of putting anything over my shirt soaked in sweat is more of a threat than a comfort. It never fails to fascinate me, how things transform and their meanings cease to be what they once were. What is warmth now? Not comfort, safety, or proof of life. It is only heat and consequence.

I'm sure this can't be the way we were designed to live, under the constant guise of heat advisories and gutted landscapes, indentured servitude disguised as poverty, always bracing, unprepared for what's next. Or maybe this is the natural consequence to a world pushed beyond its limit, ripe with fever.

My mother died of heatstroke when Savannah was born, in the middle of February. Maybe, by the time I read this again, that won't sound so impossible. I didn't believe them at the time. I thought there was no way she could've died in a way that was so preventable. We'd relegated the idea of the elements being able to have such a grip on us to the past or countries far away we couldn't name. We were civilized. We persisted. We created.

Stuff like that didn't happen here anymore, until it did. The problem with innovation is we reach for it to solve problems today, neglecting the possibility it might not work forever.

We want to make it happen in the moment. Even if we sacrifice everything beyond.

The future be damned. I don't know her at all.

People have told me I'm too young to remember the world from a long time ago, but I don't think I have to have been there to know now could never compare to what was.

Livable.

Open.

Warm, without burning. I find solace in the idea.

The old world.

Maybe someone will recognize it again someday. Things can right themselves from being misshapen. Just takes the right hands.

I can only hope whatever resurrection is coming is akin to the original and that in the reshaping we're not pushed out to sea.

Here's to it.

I read the entry four times through, following every curve of Dove's handwriting. I could hear her voice, closing my eyes to imagine her delivery of every line. The orange and soap rose from the page off her skin. I heard her fingers brush the pages. When I sat up, maybe she'd be sitting across from me, quietly wondering when I'd notice. Asking me what I thought about what she'd written. What it meant to me. I felt her pressure in every letter.

My bedroom was cold, a rarity.

"Fortunate are the gentle, for they will inherit the world," I tried to make sense of it. Whatever the drawing was, whatever it meant, it had been important enough to leave right at the beginning of her notes: a thesis statement or, perhaps, a word of caution.

The words read like a threat.

I wasn't sure.

The paper of the journal was worn, small curls forming at the corners. Yellowed with time. Yet, the memory of Dove was still so real. Maybe it was seeing her handwriting again that was pulling me back. Maybe it was because of how true her words were, like time hadn't passed at all.

What would she think of the world now? In the thirteen years she'd been gone, it seemed we'd only marched farther from that old Florida. I thought of all the books Dove read to me, about people, culture, and the way things were before they'd fallen from what we imagined the world could be.

The doorbell rang downstairs, followed by my dad's heavy footsteps through the living room. The house rattled. I could hear only muffled conversation from behind my closed door.

"Savannah!" my father called. "Can you come down here?"

I closed Dove's journal and tucked it in my bag, walking past Matis' open door. He would surely be at campus by now. I peeked my head around the corner toward his empty bed, backpack absent from its hook on the wall. I wasn't used to seeing Dove's room devoid of Dove's things and filled with a stranger's. The sight continued to make me uneasy no matter how kind Matis has been to me and my father about it. He hadn't asked me about Dove again since his move in, exchanging only kind hellos and goodbyes, and answering the occasional question for my science homework. I wondered what we actually knew about Dove, given what he'd said about the whispers on campus. I wondered what he'd think of what Dove had written but pushed it away.

She was my sister. These words were something only I could understand. Besides, he'd only known her in rumor. How real could that understanding be?

The truth was, I was skeptical of Matis. He was so open, so organized, carrying himself with a confidence that suggested he was moving toward something real. That very openness made me wary. I wasn't used to people feeling that genuine.

Seeing the contrast between the way Matis organized Dove's room against the chaos of the living room felt like standing between two worlds. In many ways, I was. Past and future, never more obvious. The constant was me.

Matis' was functionally organized. Like Dove had been. Like we were not.

My father was the furthest thing from functional since my mother died and even more so since Dove had. I blocked the disorder of the house out whenever I walked past it. It had become as much a part of the house as I was. Simply background noise. I didn't remember the house without it.

I could tell the front door was open by the time I made it downstairs because of the light flooding the living room. Our curtains were still drawn shut, my father's desperate attempt to keep the power bill from climbing in the pounding heat. It made our house feel like a clustered cave, shuttering the animals within it. Whether or not we were supposed to be here was another question.

It was already warmer than comfortable by the time I reached the living room. I eyed my father and a stranger through the doorway.

The stranger cleared his throat. He was sweating through his blue-collared shirt, hastily wiping the sweat pooling in the lenses of his glasses. He was a few years younger than my father, but the folds around his nose and mouth ran deeper than I imagined canyons did. A lifetime of frowning.

"Can I help you?"

"Hi, Miss Alonso, I'm with the Florida-sponsored Augmistum assistance program, and I was talking to your father about the possibility of adding an automated staff member to your workforce and the rebates from the state if you do so."

He pulled off his glasses and rubbed the sweat off his face, which was turning him a dark, flushed red.

"I'm not sure I understand," I replied. "The state *wants* us to hire an Augmistum?"

The man nodded, clearing his throat again.

"With the passing of Florida House Bill 76-B93, business owners most impacted by the current financial crisis are eligible for assistance if part of their workforce is converted to Augmistums. The Augmistum would also be provided to you by the state."

The man spoke without conviction. I was unconvinced.

"What would it need to do?"

He frowned.

"Whatever *you* need it to do. It can run payroll. Work the front desk. It's a"—the man flipped through a stack of notes on his clipboard—"dry cleaner that you own, yes, Mr. Alonso?"

My dad grinned. "The best in town."

"Perhaps it can work with the clothes, then, as well." The man shrugged, indifferent. "Clean the clothes, put them in bags."

"Clean the clothes?" My father frowned.

The man blinked, unphased. "Wouldn't that make your life easier? Give you some free time?"

My father wrung his hands together, and I could see the gears turning in his head. This man had handed my father an out he never wanted, and a realization he couldn't handle. He'd spent a lifetime dedicated to something so easily replaced. What would my father do with free time? I didn't know. I was sure he didn't either.

"What made you stop by?" I broke the silence, stepping farther into the doorway to catch a glimpse of his name tag.

Paul Smith.

There was no way that was his real name.

"I'm part of the citizen information committee. We're trying to let folks know these rebates are available."

"I think we're going to pass." I nodded, stepping in front of my father and reaching for the door. The paint was hot against my fingers.

"But thank you for coming by!" my father jumped in, cheerfully. His smile was oversaturated, like TV volume turned too high.

"Are you sure?" "Paul" continued, staring at my father. "We know with the storm, particular economic hardships are falling on business owners. And—"

He flipped back through the pages of his notes, eyes scouring them.

"—didn't you lose your older daughter several years ago? And your wife several years before then? I can only imagine that it's been a bit hard to run the entirety of a business on your own."

My father's smile held steady, but I caught a moment where his lip wavered.

"He has me." I frowned, reaching to close the door.

"Dove was quite the hard worker, though," "Paul" insisted.

I froze. "Paul" peered over his notes, directly at me.

"Top of her class at COF, the only undergraduate to work directly under Professor Powell, deeply involved in research well beyond her years. I'm sure she was an incredible asset to the business, and the family of course."

A new lump formed in my throat. "How do you know—"

"It's all public record," "Paul" replied.

"Paul" wiped the sweat off his forehead. If he were anyone else, I would've offered him water, but I didn't have the impulse to. I hoped he melted into the concrete. I hoped he turned to dirt.

My father's eyes glazed over. "Dove was something special."

"Indeed," "Paul" nodded. "Wouldn't it be nice to have something *remotely* as helpful at your disposal again?"

From the corner of my eye, sitting so perfectly still on the sidewalk beyond the front lawn, I saw the black cat had returned. Her green eyes blinked lazily at me and my father. She curled her tail around and tapped it in a slow rhythm against the ground. My eyes flickered to my dad, and I watched the exact moment he spotted her, immediately entranced.

"No thanks," I replied again. I could shove him off the porch. The ground was probably hot enough to sear his skin.

"Well, I appreciate your time. I'll be back in this area in a few weeks in case you change your mind and want help filing the paperwork."

"We won't."

"Paul" frowned, but there was a soft maliciousness around the corners of his eyes—subtle, but I'd seen it before, on the faces of men and women on the news, on the people that denied my father additional food rations. Manicured brutality. The unfeeling. The natural disconnect set in the faces of people trying to convince or deny you.

"We'll see."

I caught sight of the black cat again before I closed the door, watching as she leaped down the sidewalk and toward the bushes as "Paul" turned around.

My father didn't move, staring at the door, eyes unblinking.

"Hey, Dad." I nudged him. "You with me?"

My father nodded. "I need water."

I stared through the peephole and watched "Paul" walk down the sidewalk and across the road. He didn't turn back. I wondered if there was any chance he might be automated himself.

Could they make them sweat now?

I didn't know. There was a new lump in my throat.

I guided my dad to the couch and grabbed a cup of filtered water from the fridge. My eyes blinked back into the shadows of the house, enough light peeking through the blackout curtains to find my way to the kitchen and the refrigerator. I was thirsty myself, the heat persistent and unbearable. We'd left the door open for too long. Our ancient AC struggled to pull the temperature down within the house — just the limited daytime exposure dehydrating us in a matter of minutes. The house could sweat, perhaps Augmistums could too.

"It's really hot," my dad huffed, downing the water as soon as I handed it to him. He took a deep breath and returned the glass to me. His hand was shaking. I rushed him another cup from the kitchen and wrapped his hands around it to feel the cold condensation, the drops pooling on his fingers. He rubbed them together, the cold sinking into his skin.

"Really hot," I whispered, taking a sip of my own glass. A razor of light cut between the blackout curtains, splitting our living room down the middle.

The lump in my throat wouldn't budge.

NINE

Another announcement was made for people living near the ocean in Boston, New York, and Miami to move inland. This was the third time it had happened in the last four years.

I found this out over a lunch of lab-grown salmon Lauren and I split at the diner. Salmon had never been my favorite, but Lauren had offered to pay. I'd never noticed how off-putting the color was before now, but the vibrant hue made my eyes hurt. If salmon were really that pink in the wild, I was sure they'd get killed immediately.

Nothing that effervescent survives in nature.

Lauren received the alert on her SubcutaLink, tapping intermittently on her wrist between bites of salmon, the too-pink fish falling from her mouth in half-chewed specs. She wiped her mouth with her shirtsleeve. I set my fork down.

"They're telling people to move inward another three miles." Lauren coughed and flicked a piece of salmon off the side of her lip. It landed on the floor just beyond our table. It was so pink I could see it from my seat, like a blemish on the tile.

"And how long is that supposed to be safe for?"

She shrugged. "The article doesn't mention."

Lauren swiped through several photos on her wrist, a montage of several destroyed coastal structures followed. The article showcased families who'd lived on the ocean for generations, retreating from yet another home. A life of belongings shoved in the back of a van, a desire to take the paint from the walls probably never put to rest. How many times can you make a home before it's not home at all anymore? I'd only ever lived in one place, I couldn't imagine having to try and get attached over and over again. I think I'd let the sea take the both of us.

The final photo was of a metal pole staked into the ground, with several markings indicating rising water and historical floods. Just two inches below the top of the pole was the projected water level a decade from now. A woman stood beside it, the pole reaching under her nose, her eyes floating above where the surface of the water would be. She'd gone cross-eyed looking at it.

Lauren closed the article, and the woman disappeared, replaced by a photo of Lauren and her father standing beside a beautiful building in Europe.

"I'm sure it'll be safe for at least another couple years," she said, shrugging. "When my father talked to people in Italy about how they've responded to the rising water levels, they seemed to think we were definitely behind."

Lauren took another bite of the salmon. Despite her father's work being centered in the United States, she spent more time abroad than anyone I knew.

"How was Italy?" I finally asked her, though I didn't want to.

"Blissful." Lauren grinned. A piece of salmon was stuck to her front tooth. It looked like a fleshy gemstone. "I've been waiting to talk to you about it."

I'd spent every night of the last week digging into Dove's journal, scanning through the pages and trying to understand what she'd been up to. She'd been meticulous, writing every single day.

So far, nothing had been as haunting as the first page. A lot of the writing was straightforward, details about her life, scribbled "to-do" lists hidden in the margins of a stream of consciousness or brief philosophical exploration. She wrote about regular things, like her friends or how hard she was studying. Sometimes she talked about me, things I was reading, or what I was learning, or how she couldn't believe how fast I was growing. I'd learned new details about my mother, that she'd been a champion ice skater, born and bred somewhere in the cold. It made sense why the move to Florida had been so devastating. Her blood was too thick.

Sometimes Dove mentioned my dad, critiquing his "hand-wave" attitude the same way I found myself doing now. It was comforting to be the same age now Dove was then. I saw my reflection within the pages, looking back. Both more and less alone with her notes, all at once.

As soon as I'd gotten comfortable reading Dove's day-to-day recaps or quick expressions of longing or grief, the pages transformed into something else.

Each entry became a recount of different daily events, laid out in a bulleted list. Dove had intermixed the different items between local, national, and global happenings. Some personal details remained, scattered reflections on school or what she was doing, but the bulk of the entries had turned into a tabling of updates from around the world.

The journal read like a quick hit newscast, minus the pundits. Only the events as they happened.

- *Rampant famine for a sixth year in Sudan, 17,113 dead. Most are children.*
- *Globally, more farmers are migrating north in an attempt to promote crop growth and animal health. Intense heat in the southeast and southwest United States has turned many areas uninhabitable. Success of crop growth in Northern Canadian Territories and Alaska improving.*
- *Florida minimum wage raised to $23. Average cost of living up to $123,000 per adult.*
- *New strain of pneumonia has taken the lives of 11,000 in China.*
- *Nasal Implant for pollution filtering launches alongside SubcutaLink and updated Augmistums, all from Qucore.*

The lists went on. Everyday. Without stopping.

It was haunting to read about every tragedy that occurred before I'd been able to remember them. The losses. The disasters. The death. Dove had been militant about tracking all of it. I couldn't figure out why. She'd logged so many events within the bullet points, it would have been impossible to follow up on each of them. From what I could tell, Dove never returned with an update on any of the events she'd mapped out. The information was given and never brought up again. The journal served as record it had occurred. Not investigation.

Another new detail emerged on the pages with the bulleted lists. In the top right corner was what looked to be a part of a circle, and as the pages went on, the circle became more complete and eventually shaded in. I scanned several entries throughout the book and the pattern continued all the way through. Once one circle completed, usually over the span of several weeks, the beginnings of a new circle appeared alongside it.

When I crossed-checked the front of the book, I couldn't find any explanation from Dove about what the symbols were, only that they were on every single page.

I turned to the internet, hoping that maybe I could find some clue about what Dove was depicting or tracking. I searched for different types of circle patterns, modern and archaic, and waited as the screen loaded. The results were a maze of dead ends. Every search led to the same frustrating pop-ups, ads promising everything from "DIY Tracking Systems" to "Personalized Life Logs"—each one more insistent than the last.

I clicked past the ads, only to be met with subscription models that wanted credit cards before they'd even let me skim an article. "Just one more step!" the ads blared, urging me to unlock "premium content."

I tried typing a few different queries: "patterns in journaling" or "tracking systems for health," hoping to bypass the noise, but it was the same. A blur of commercialized nonsense, designed to get you caught in a never-ending cycle of sign-ups and service fees. It was maddening. The WiFi timed out, suggesting I had hit my maximum number of search queries for the day without needing to pay a premium that my father couldn't afford.

I'd never seen anything like them. I thought about taking a picture of and texting it to Lauren, but there was no way she'd know either. Besides, in the back of my mind, I really hoped that Dove had just left this for me. Whatever it was I was supposed to solve, she must have believed I was capable enough to do so.

Still, I knew there were things I didn't know. How could I? My world was the dry cleaner, the diner, our house, and the photos on Lauren's wrist.

I chewed on my lip. There was the bloody tang again. I had to stop doing that.

I stood from bed and walked across the hall toward Dove's room. Matis had a bad habit of leaving the door open. An invitation for conversation I'd been hesitant to take since our first meeting. I was so used to Dove's door being closed, it caught me by surprise every time I saw it. I'd walk past the room every morning on my way to the dry cleaner, overhearing whatever podcast or smooth jazz Matis was listening to. By the time I'd come back in the late afternoons, hauling my laptop and school notes back to my bedroom, he'd left for campus. I envied him for that a bit, the freedom, the ability to change environments and experience yourself in a new place. I'd never known anything like it.

I hesitated, then tapped on the doorframe. Matis looked up immediately.

"Do you know anything about this?"

Matis was hunched over his desk, laptop glowing against his face. He immediately brightened when he saw me. I apprehensively held out Dove's journal for him to look at, hesitant at first but pointing squarely at the circles. My heart pounded. Maybe this was a mistake.

I followed his eyes, making sure he didn't read anything on the pages. He didn't.

"No . . . but it seems like it might be some sort of counter or tracker. Hard to know what the time length or measure is without any kind of index."

We both looked at the circles, drawn tight and consistent across all the pages. I studied the marginal differences in Dove's pencil shadings, the slightest variance on each page. She'd been keeping tabs consistently on at least one thing in this journal, and I had no idea what it was.

"Thanks."

"No problem." Matis stared at me, without expectation. I could hear the power lines buzzing, cars rumbling in a steady rhythm. Dove's room was so much louder than mine, facing the louder side of the road. I wonder how she'd slept. The visual of her dark-rimmed eyes cut through my questioning. I needed to shake it off.

"Do you always keep everything so neat?" I asked Matis, gesturing around the room.

Matis shrugged, his brow furrowing slightly as he considered my question. "I guess it's just how I was raised. My parents worked hard and I saw how stressed they were trying to balance everything. I think I just wanted to make sure I wasn't adding to that chaos. If I kept my space organized, it helped me focus on what matters—school, work, the future..."

He paused for a moment, gaze drifting to the floor, a hint of vulnerability creeping into his expression. "I want to prove that their sacrifices weren't for nothing."

Matis was so nice. Nice to the point I was almost afraid of him. Where I could spot my father's disingenuousness in the corners of his mouth, Matis' warmth never flickered. He was a conduit for his hope. Probably because he seemed so much less afraid than I was.

"What do you want to do after all this? The lab, school . . ." Talking cut the tension down in my chest. My fingers tightened around Dove's notebook.

Matis drummed his fingers on the desk. "If I can find a way to create something good, to make things better for someone, it gives me a sense of control. It's the only thing I can do. That any of us can. Seek out what could be good and figure out whether or not it actually works. If you can systematize something righteous, things actually change."

Here we were, both navigating our own labyrinths of expectation, trying to build from the ashes. Only, one of us looked forward, the other back.

"Is that . . . Dove's journal?" Matis hesitated, I could feel it.

My throat gets tight.

"Yes. My father gave it to me." The venom seeps into my tone in a hundred ways I can't help, pulling the journal under my arm.

Matis nodded, the sting stopping him from asking any other questions. He'd been right to hesitate. Something in me felt guilty about coming off so cold, but it wasn't a part of me large enough to make a difference. This was about *my* sister. He was just a stranger living in her bedroom.

"How's school?" he asked me, as I started stepping back toward the hallway. His disposition never faltered, even when he was trying to save the interaction. I took a deep breath.

"Fine, just . . . boring. I want it to be over. Maybe start working somewhere that isn't the dry cleaner. Get out a little more."

Matis laughed.

"You might not love it as much as you think."

My eyes flickered to the watermark on the ceiling of Dove's bedroom, another thing my father neglected to fix. It almost looked like a tree, roots and branches snaking toward the corners of the room. I'm sure that meant the ceiling would collapse someday. Would Matis still be here? Would I?

"I'm sure I won't. But some money would be nice."

Matis nodded, folding his hands together.

"You know, if you ever do want to come to the Pharmacy campus, they're always open for people to work the front desk. Even if you just want to check it out."

I laughed. The sterile room echoed it back to me.

"I don't know anything about pharmaceutical work."

"You can use a phone."

"Sure. But for a much different purpose."

"Not as different as you think."

For a moment, Matis' eyes flickered back to Dove's journal. I wrapped my other hand around it.

"Maybe." I took a step back. Matis met my eyes again.

"Just think about it." He nodded. I closed my door, and Matis didn't.

***

"Italy was fun, mostly because I made it fun . . . " Lauren answered, wiping her hands across a napkin. "Had to make a lot of my own fun, considering my father spent most of our time there in meetings."

"Is Italy really concerned about voting rights in the United States?"

Lauren laughed.

"Come on, you know my father can work anywhere. But no, that wasn't the reason for this trip."

Lauren shrugged, taking another bite of salmon.

"There's some medical thing he's sitting on the board for now. They wanted someone with a"—she coughed again—"background in equal rights, economic fairness, etcetera. They're trying to recruit people from different backgrounds to champion insights, relevant thought-leadership, I'm sure you know the drill."

"Nope."

Lauren folded the napkin. I pushed my discarded salmon back and forth across my plate.

The TV in the diner glowed with an ad for the latest SubcutaLink, thinner and smaller than a single strand of hair and completely painless upon insertion. It had a higher processing speed than any computer over the course of human history. Two happy women on the screen cheered, using their SubcutaLinks to capture a photo of their champagne glasses filled to the brim with a vibrant, orange mimosa. An image of Dove, cross-legged at the dinner table typing into her computer with three discarded cartons of orange juice around her hands, clouded my vision. The commercial disappeared from my mind.

My eyes lingered on the TV without watching it. Lauren's voice faded into a background rumble. The women on screen clinked their glasses. I smelled Dove's orange juice. I felt myself nod to Lauren. She paid the check. I didn't argue. I couldn't.

Lauren leaned in close as we walked to the parking lot. She was laughing about something. I couldn't remember the last time I was this close to someone. In the heat, it wasn't comfortable.

The humidity was thick. I could feel the sweat beading on my forehead. I used to think I could get used to feeling like I was constantly wet and eventually I wouldn't notice anymore. Maybe it was because it was always getting more intense, crawling up like an escalator into the void. I guess adaptation was only natural to a point. Look at my mother.

My mind wandered to the sweat beads across the salesman's forehead yesterday, the paperwork, the coldness in his eyes. The way he knew Dove.

"Does your dad happen to know anything about this Augmistum assistance program that they launched?" I asked Lauren, wiping my head with my shirt. I smelled like salmon and sweat. "Something about Florida House Bill 76-B93—"

"Ah," Lauren interrupted. "The AAAP thing. Yeah, my dad thinks it'll help a lot of people, but you know how I feel about Augmistums. Apparently it received a landslide vote in the Florida House, which never happens anymore."

Was it this hard to breathe earlier?

"Someone showed up trying to get my dad to agree to get one for the rebates yesterday," I continued. "It was weird. He knew a surprising amount about Dove."

"Hm." Lauren frowned, stopping in the middle of the parking lot. She pressed her manicured nails against the top of her forehead.

"I wouldn't think too much about it. It's probably part of your dad's tax records or something."

"Sure, but, I don't know. They seemed like they were trying to sell him on the idea of something to replace Dove. Where did they get the money for this? Why start offering assistants now?"

Lauren shrugged. "Somebody thought it would make things more efficient, I guess."

Her father's car pulled up, mapped to autonomously drive her back to the other side of the city. She opened the door and I peered over her shoulder. There were several full bottles of water, fans, and a wide selection of sunscreens and sunglasses, more than my father and I had in our whole house.

"I'm sure you were on a list somewhere and it's on a need basis. I wouldn't worry about it."

"Yeah, maybe."

Before she got in, Lauren hesitated and then pulled out a small wad of cash from her purse. My hands tightened at my sides.

"What are you doing?"

Lauren's lips folded together, like they always did before she tried playing coy. She'd made the same face before splitting her chips with me in school, sliding me more than half of the bag and pretending to forget about them. It was her pitying face.

"I drove past the dry cleaner the other day, and I just... Maybe this would help make some repairs."

I froze. The offer felt like a bitter pill I was supposed to swallow without flinching. I was expected to take it, so she would feel good about herself. Her favorite charity case. It wasn't even the money, but the implication behind it. I felt foolish even bringing up the legislation to her, just further confirming we were poorer than ever.

"I appreciate it," I said, forcing my voice to steady, "but we're managing. My dad's actually fixing the roof next week."

Lauren seemed to sense my hesitation, and I could see the doubt on her face. She tucked the cash in her purse, as if it hadn't stung.

"That's great to hear."

The car system timed out, honking at Lauren to close the door.

"Okay, okay! I love you!"

"Love you too." I gave her a tight smile, watching her climb in before the door shut with a soft thud. I waved slowly as her window rolled up and the car sped out of the lot.

She'd never offered to drive me home. I'd never asked.

Lauren and her father had attended Dove's funeral, sending flowers and leaving promptly following the service in a sleek black car to the airport. I had feelings about Lauren's wealth I was never able to place. It wasn't jealousy, because the truth was, I didn't want her life. I knew that because she *did* have her life, people like my father and I would always have ours. What I hated more than anything was acknowledging what I wished would go unspoken. It made it harder to forget.

As soon as I walked back home, I pulled Dove's journal back from my bag, my eyes scanning over the next page and the slightly fuller circle in the top corner.

- *A third Category Five Hurricane bashes Florida's west coast.*
- *The last African elephant dies in the Smithsonian National Zoo. 360 people are in attendance and the event is live streamed.*
- *Just eight public schools remain in Alabama after the dissolving of the Department of Education. Parents are forced into private education or homeschool.*
- *Professor Powell of COF receives sponsorship by Qucore for new medical-climate research on campus in Orlando, supported by TA Carter Lehman and intern Dove Alonso.*

I stopped reading, blinking and rereading the last line over and over. There it was. The entrance of Dove into her own recounting, complete with a smiley face. If I'd learned anything about her entries so far, if she'd included it here, it's because it needed to be there. She wouldn't have done it otherwise. These entries weren't about her, they were about everything. This was listed here because, perhaps, it was about both.

Something tugged at me.

I closed the notebook, leaving it on my bed and walked back out into the hallway toward Dove's room.

Matis was crouched over his desk again, headphones on. I tapped on the doorframe. He didn't move. I tapped again, this time more persistent, and he swirled around, grinning.

"Hey—"

"I want to go to campus with you."

Matis blinked back his surprise. I held his gaze for as long as I could, stern.

As I said the words out loud, the persistent nausea in my stomach disappeared for the first time all day. I forgot the fluorescent salmon. There was no interruption begging to be felt.

This was the chance for me to get the moment of release I'd been begging for. It was just going to require a little work. I had to find out anything I could about the last few weeks of Dove's life, and that meant being in the place she had spent the most time in. If I did, maybe all of this would finally stop. Maybe, just maybe, hiding behind that urge to understand, if I found it, would be closure. Release. A way to move on.

I looked up at the tree shaped watermark on the ceiling. The house rumbled as the AC groaned in the heat.

"Okay," Matis said. "Cool."

From Matis' computer, I heard the audio playing from the same SubcutaLink commercial that had been on inside the diner; the upbeat music, the woman's cheerful laughter, the clink of the mimosas.

I could almost taste the orange.

TEN

I saw a glimmer of old Florida only once, years ago, when my father took me with him to get supplies for the dry cleaner. It was shortly after Dove died, when the two of us weren't talking much. We were co-existing, crossing paths in the kitchen or when he'd ask for help carrying something to the dry cleaner. Our hands brushed as I grabbed the other side of a box, helping him inside.

We interacted more through the walls. I heard him rattling through the silverware early in the morning, making his cereal and slamming the front door closed. There was always the low, constant murmur of the morning talk shows accompanying his coughing, cleaning his bowl. I was sure he heard me turning up the volume on the TV when he was in his room. Perhaps we were both calling out to the other.

It was surprising he'd asked me to come at all. I'd gotten used to him disappearing for work or errands, leaving me alone to wander the house or stand under the full daylight outside until my skin turned red. I liked to watch the color change. It reminded me I was real in the time I felt the most untethered. Something could change.

I'd been occupying myself with books from Dove's shelf, reading them in the light between the curtains in the living room. Accompanied by the quiet thunder of cars passing, the hum of the air conditioner, I found my peace. I searched for refuge in other things I could control: the books I read, trying on Dove's old jackets, allowing my face to burn in the sun. I knew Dove would hate it. In a way, that made me want to do it more.

It was a different world to be in motion with my father in the car. Places both new and unfamiliar moved by so fast from the passenger seat. The sidewalks that took me hours to traverse disappeared within moments. Buildings once distant inched closer and then sank into the horizon. Observing the world was softer beneath AC, more easily digested, with less bite. There was a layer of separation, even if the space you were occupying was the same. I loved it. I loved it most when we went fast enough for things to get blurry.

North of where we lived, there was a smaller, wealthy community, with tall brick walls and a black gate. At the front of the wall, I saw oak trees by the dozen. I'd never seen so many my whole life. I don't think I'd ever seen one at all.

The trees were sequestered here, too expensive to be maintained elsewhere. The remains of wild Florida were pay-walled and protected by a different tax bracket.

I pushed my face on the window, sweat streaking the glass. Tall and unwavering, the trees were miniature castles, conical branches reaching toward the sky.

They were draped in Spanish moss, sunlight peeking through the gaps to the road and wavering in the wind. If I squinted, the moss almost looked like floating dress silhouettes braced against the light. They spun and twirled just the same.

"Roll down your window."

I half-heard my father when he said it, his voice barely audible over the rattling AC. His eyes were focused on the road, unwavering.

"You should smell it."

I clamored for the button on the door and lowered the window. Wind whipped into the car and rustled the papers my father had in the back. The buffeting hurt my ears.

I leaned forward, breathing deeply, hearing Dove's voice in my head telling me to close my eyes. To feel beyond what I could see. To understand.

So I did, letting the breeze form my associations instead of my vision. My body started to relax. The air was warm, wild with energy. Moisture blew across my face, and the smell of the earth greeted me as intended. Knowingness of my surroundings I didn't need to see in order to feel ran over the bridge of my nose and down the sides of my face. It was as much part of me as I was part of it.

There was a current here, a charge, something I couldn't observe back home. The street we lived on, without a single tree, the sky blurred with power lines well over a hundred years old, coupled with our family's grief, was nothing compared to this. The feeling of lightness. Of lift.

If this is what Florida had been, even twenty years ago, I couldn't imagine what we'd decided was more worth it.

It was magical. It felt like a precipice. It felt real.

I realized maybe I did want to see it. Not limit my senses the way Dove had asked me to. I was hungry for *real* Florida, all the way to my bones. I wanted to sink into this ecosystem hidden from me, understand what even Dove had often lacked the words to describe. Maybe I could.

My eyes shot open, but we'd driven through it all. There were no more trees. The whole of old Florida, disappeared into something I only held the feeling of. My rough association, limited to my less expansive senses. The road changed back into cars and billboards, suntorn benches and dead air. The angles of light cut the sun in jagged edged shadows instead of through gentle loops of moss.

It was gone before I even knew how to miss it.

ELEVEN

• Critical 2.5c warming threshold passed, record number of deaths due to heat stroke and exhaustion. New predictions for 2100 suggest further extreme heat events will make parts of Asia and Africa uninhabitable for over 600 million people.
• A second mass migration from the southwestern United States is causing resource and housing concerns in the Pacific Northwest.
• Referencing the 2020 COVID-19 pandemic, College of Florida announces "cost-savings" degree program to be completed fully remote, while spiking on-campus tuition.
• One gallon of milk crosses the $10 threshold.

Matis' car was filthy for someone who kept their room so clean. Crumpled paper greeted my feet in the passenger footwell as I swung inside, along with used napkins and lab paperwork. Bird poop was on the windshield, a strangely comforting sign of life splashed against the concrete backdrop of Orlando rolling in front of us.

Despite October's arrival, the heat was as brutal as ever, if not worse than September's. I felt the weight on my skin, like it was working with gravity to pull my flesh from my bones. Summers always made me feel older. I could see the wear in my face by October; new lines spread around the creases of my eyes, dark spots swelling like oil spills across the bridge of my nose left over from healing sunburns.

There was plenty I could do to fix all of it, tailored skin grafts to make the face more resistant to high UV exposure, surgeries to pull back and accentuate your bone structure by halving the amount of skin on your face. Lauren's mother had that one done last year, and she came out of the operating room looking even younger than Lauren. Her age didn't reveal itself until she opened her mouth.

"Have you been to the Center of Research Development before?"

Matis' question rattled me from my intense focus on the heat from the sidewalk.

"No, I haven't."

"Ever?"

"No. Why would I?"

Matis nodded, and pulled out of the driveway. My stomach lurched. I was so rarely in the car anymore that I couldn't help feeling a bit motion-sick. I tried to look at the skyline, but the daylight was so bright I ended up squinting toward the buildings that loomed in the distance. Maybe that only worked if you were on the ocean. I didn't know.

"I think you'll be impressed," Matis continued, fiddling with his SubcutaLink and turning on the jazz station he always played in his room. Warm piano filled the car. I relaxed a little.

Matis merged onto the 408 bridge beside the Orlando Executive Airport. COF's Center of Research Development was in Lake Delta; a hyper-planned pseudo-city thirty minutes from downtown Orlando. It boasted flying, automated taxis that would take you from one side of the community to the other, a myriad of eco-friendly restaurants with evolving menus to fit the season, and forty-four miles of walking and biking trails under the cover of heat-resistant awnings. They were well over fifty years into the development plan, with the sole mission of creating an idyllic place to live and die. It was an interesting agenda.

Publicizing green living had become a status symbol among the elite; lining their roofs with solar panels and eating vegan food before climbing into their private jets and purchasing enough carbon credits to take multiple international trips a year. The facade of environmentalism wasn't cheap, but it did get you into *Homes & Gardens.* I found myself thumbing through the pages of one of the latest editions at the dentist office, printed on "thirty-five percent recycled paper," advertising several social media influencers' second and third home upgrades with solar panels and natural swimming pools. My card declined at my teeth cleaning. I was still paying the office back.

"I thought the rock ledges of the pool really complimented the trees in the back," one of the influencers explained, her manicured finger pointed at the towering pines. A status symbol.

"Having them next to the water just made it so rustic."

"It doesn't matter what we do as individuals if corporations and greed still have the government in a choke hold," Dove had explained to me one night after I'd cried over my father forgetting to rinse out a plastic jar of peanut butter and put it in the correct bin. The small tragedies that waged war in my heart. We'd received a lecture at school from an Augmistum sponsored by one of the largest oil companies in the country reminding us "the power we have to control pollution starts at home." They'd been running the same campaign with the help of education lobbyists for nearly one hundred years, a fact I learned after my emotional breakdown over peanut butter.

"Limit your travel, eat a low-meat diet, and remember to exercise your political rights through voting!"

The Augmistum had high cheeks and pale white teeth, and handed each of us a piece of paper detailing the right way to recycle.

I came home and stuck it to the fridge. Dove promptly took it down and pulled my soapy hands away from scrubbing the peanut butter jar.

"Stuff like this is important," Dove whispered, toweling dry my hands. "But it's not as important as making sure the people at the top pay attention and recognize that resources are finite for us and them, even if they don't believe it."

I sniffled.

"Besides," Dove whispered, tossing the soapy peanut butter jar in the regular trash can. "I can guarantee you, *they're* not recycling."

When Dove left the kitchen, I went back to scrubbing the jar.

In Matis' passenger seat, I was overwhelmed by the amount of cars on the highway, even in the middle of the day. There were more people on the roads than I'd ever seen closer to home. I was certain when Dove had been commuting this way all those years ago, there hadn't been nearly as many people. For all of the disasters Florida had undergone in the last twenty years, more people than ever were moving here. They wanted to take advantage of the taxes and the "future coastal property" economy; purchasing land inland in preparation for it potentially being seaside by the time they retired. It was a gamble. Driving more definitely helped their cause.

The buildings off the highway were scattered in different shades of browns, grays, and the occasional technicolor. Housing developments, the rare brick and mortar clothing stores, and electric car chargers. There was a field of solar panels.

Accident attorneys and theme park billboards dotted the highway so organically, it was as if they'd always been part of the skyline. It was hard to imagine it any other way. There was enough mildew on them that they blended right in.

"It's been a really exciting time under Professor Powell," Matis shared. "We've been using pharmacometrics and systems pharmacology to predict how patients may react to a drug in both virtual environments and with Augmistums. It's been yielding incredible results. Qucore has been helping secure the data collection."

"Qucore invented SubcutaLink, right?" I recalled, remembering the note in Dove's journal.

Matis nodded.

"They sponsor a ton of research work we do at the campus. Like I said, they have their own wing and everything. That's where the majority of my work with Professor Powell is."

"And what exactly is it that you all are working on?"

Someone laid on their horn in the left lane, raising their hands and screaming toward the car in front of them. I flinched, waiting for the other driver to pull out a weapon. Road rage gun violence deaths had been through the roof all summer. Politicians were blaming the tourists. I was sure it was the heat. It made all of us crazy.

"It's a medication for heat-intolerance." Matis tapped his fingers excitedly on the dashboard.

"With climate change, the number of heat advisories is skyrocketing. It's causing people to miss work, higher resource allocation for cooling and dehydration, and obviously—"

"People are dying," I finished for him.

"Yeah." Matis cleared his throat.

"That's why what we're working on is so important. If we can help people become more resistant to temperature increases, we could not only be saving tens of millions of dollars, but also millions of lives."

We exited the highway, and ahead in the distance, I saw a pocket of surprisingly dense forest.

Ever since that day my father and I drove to pick up supplies, I daydreamed about the Florida woods. I didn't need to travel across the country to understand that it was one of a kind. I knew it, instinctually. I'd seen the pictures of the west coast, the remaining California redwoods that towered over brooding dark green brush, what was left of the ancient forests of New England and Appalachia. Florida was still in a league of its own. From the dense humidity of the swamp rose an array of trees; mangroves crouching over the side of the water, and palms waving long fingers toward the arms of the live oaks. Where the tropics and the continental meshed into murky waters that were never short on life, that was what made Florida woods so special—it was a constant convergence point.

"How long has Professor Powell been working on this?" I asked, not taking my eyes off the wooded area until it became a dark green spot in the rearview mirror.

"Almost two decades." He said.

I rested my head against the window, feeling the prickle of heat in tandem with the cool glass.

"It makes sense I guess, to start investing in resilience at this point, if nothing's going to stop."

"And it doesn't mean that we shouldn't be pushing for things to stop either," Matis continued. "Anything that can help reduce the consequences is better than doing nothing."

I nodded, looking at the spine of Dove's journal in my backpack. I felt it would've been wrong to come here without bringing it with me. Lately, I hadn't been going anywhere without it. It felt nice to carry something of hers, as if in some strange way, she was watching over me.

"I figure you're not coming here to ask about a job." Matis reached and turned the AC down a bit, just enough to feel the absence of the cold. "And that's completely fine. Whatever your reasons."

I watched his eyes flicker over to me and then back to the road. He chewed his bottom lip when I didn't immediately reply, as if he shouldn't have said anything.

"Who knows," I folded my hands in my lap. "Maybe I'll become an expert in this stuff."

"Never too late to start."

We took a left turn and arrived at a well-manicured stretch of road, lined with a covered bike path and rows of well-tended flowers. I couldn't tell if they were real or not. Ahead, I saw a tall, angular building, with raised glass accents and solar panels across the roof. We drew closer, and I stared through the windshield toward the deep blue "COF" on the front of the building. A small natural pond was near the front doors, and several people sat under the awning, eating lunch. An industrial-size, bladeless outdoor fan oscillated across the seating area. I saw an Augmistum walking between the tables and inside, holding several bottles of COF branded water. The scene was surreal, but familiar, like I'd dreamed this. I couldn't believe this was how some people experienced school; as I thought about my small desk at home, facing the wall with a fraction of a window, and my professors' faces blurring on my lagging internet.

Matis pulled the car into a student parking spot and grabbed his backpack.

The research building wasn't nearly as tall as the skyscrapers in downtown Orlando, but for some reason, it felt all the more imposing. Heavy. The building had gravity and was pulling me into orbit.

"It's really a special building, so many people dedicated to doing the work." Matis grinned, reaching for the car door.

I peered down at Dove's journal peeking out of my bag balanced between my feet. I'd arrived. Unclicking my seatbelt, I watched Matis' reflection in the car window as he got out, his face elongating and disappearing into the COF blue.

TWELVE

The only time Dove had ever *really* snapped at me was when I drank her orange juice. It had been particularly hot that day. I'd been left alone at home with an otherwise empty fridge.

I never liked the protein shakes my father bought, only drinking them when we were scant on options. My father bought things that would be filling, but never nutritionally dense. I'd go months without seeing a single fruit or vegetable in the fridge, but there was always bread. Some new protein bar. More often than not, my father spent the ration cards for necessities on something else. I often wondered how much cost really had to do with it. I don't think it was malicious, only distracted. The outcome was the same.

This time, no protein shakes were hidden in the door of the refrigerator, only two small cartons of the orange juice Dove drank religiously.

I'd never tasted orange juice until that day, which I thought was funny as a Floridian. I knew how important the fruit had been here, but with how rare the commodity was now, I'd never been able to try it. I wasn't sure how Dove managed to scrounge together enough money and ration tickets for it every week, especially with how much she drank, but I guess when you wanted something bad enough, you'd do anything for it.

The single container was tucked near the back of the almost empty fridge, cold against my fingers as I pulled the carton into my palm. A small straw was on the side, and I tore it off, pressing it into the sealed hole in the top of the box.

I raised the carton to my lips and took a sip.

It was tangy, and tingled against the roof of my mouth when I drank it. But, like my father said, too sour. Without knowing why, I sucked down the entirety of the container, crushing the empty box flat in my hands and discarding it in the trash can.

Hours later when Dove returned, I heard her open the fridge and then slam it closed. I hid in my room until I heard her feet pounding up the stairs to my door. Dove swung it open, eyes wide.

"Did you drink my orange juice?" Dove her voice was sharper than it ever had been, a frantic grimace across her face. She looked exhausted.

"I . . . yes." I swallowed, still tasting it in the back of my throat. I sank further from her, retreating into my bed. She was different. She never spoke to me like this.

"I asked you not to do that."

"I know. I'm sorry. There was nothing else."

Dove took a breath. Her face was wet with sweat. Her knuckles were dry, the skin curling up on the top just like paper.

"That's mine, Savannah. That's the only thing I've ever asked you not to touch. Explicitly."

"I know."

She pressed her lips together, reaching her hand to the doorframe. She was steadying herself. For as warm as it was, she almost looked cold.

"Don't touch it again."

"I won't. I promise."

Dove closed her eyes, exhaling.

"I'm going to the store. I'll be back."

She turned around and walked out of my bedroom, and I heard her walk to the front door and lock it. She returned several hours later with two large cases of orange juice, and when I saw them in the fridge, one case was already missing three cartons.

I never touched it again.

THIRTEEN

The Qucore Pharmaceutical Innovation Lab was an immense, modern wing tucked at the back of COF's Center of Research Development. The lobby was crowded with Augmistums, TAs, and professors moving through the extended, sterile corridors between rooms. Clumps of students hovered together over tables, taping on their SubcutaLinks or staring into their screenless laptops, their coursework loading directly behind their eyes. It was like watching the videos I'd seen of honeybees come to life. Everything and everyone had a place here. Nothing was cluttered, it would only get in the way.

As we stepped into the building, past the lobby, the noise began to dissipate. Beyond the sound of footsteps clicking against the cold linoleum floors, the rest of the building was silent. Several unoccupied chairs formed half-ovals around empty tables. All of them were so clean it was impossible to believe anyone had ever sat there. It was pristine. Almost inhumane.

"Wait here for a second," Matis instructed, reaching into his pocket for his ID card, which he scanned on one of the doors ahead of us. He placed his index finger on a dimly lit blue scanner until it clicked politely. The glass doors slid open.

"I'll get you a guest pass."

He stepped into the closing doors, leaving me in the hallway. I'd never seen ceilings this high, windows tall and open enough to let sunlight from outside stream across the floors. Churches were my only reference point, sprawling glass, vaulted ceilings. I was sure I could fit at least three of our houses in here, laid across the floor like children's toys.

The air inside was cold, soothing over the burned bridge of my nose. You could almost believe it wasn't boiling outside in the confines of this illusion. I was standing within a mirage, a Garden of Eden, immune to desolation if only through an impenetrable wall.

I felt wildly out of place, gravitating toward the wall like a bug or vine. Clumps of people parted around me in different directions, heading for the staircase or the elevator, none making eye contact. A girl in a dark blue College of Florida sweater bumped my arm, frowning before rushing toward the glass doors. Several Augmistums also made their way toward the ID scanner, twisting their artificial fingers around and resting their fingernails against the scanner, where their identification chips were.

I couldn't imagine Dove spending so much time here. She probably stuck out like a sore thumb. Dove was open in a way it felt like nothing else in this place was. Everyone here was bullishly navigating the building, interactions with others the last thing on their minds. I wondered how she'd felt the first time she'd stepped in here, if it had felt as surreal. If it had felt like a second home. No matter how different from home it was.

I wandered back toward one of the immense white walls, where I spied a large glass case. On the marble wall behind it were several hundred names, listed in alphabetical order.

At the top of the list, in elegant script, *"A Thank You to Our Donors."*

My eyes skimmed across the list, until I reached the "M" section:

Theodore and Carmen Mills

Lauren's parents. I frowned.

Why would they be donors here?

Maybe her father was out for another tax write-off opportunity. I didn't know.

When I drew closer to the glass case, I peered inside and saw an immaculately detailed miniature model of the state of Florida, all the way to the sunken Florida Keys and remains of Miami, the feeble Panhandle. Across the model were scaled down versions of houses and apartment complexes, broken up by patchy sections of forest and roadways. The coastline had been dragged in farther by the creator, the state beginning to look less like a hockey stick and more like a tattered rectangle, and all of the edges softened and sunk by the ocean. Several wind turbines were scattered throughout the model. Solar panels topped nearly all the houses. New green spaces I knew didn't exist were dotted all along some of the more residential neighborhoods. It was both different and the same as the place I'd lived all my life.

My eyes wandered through the diagram, eventually following the highway from the Center of Research and Development all the way to what should have been our neighborhood. The roads were largely unchanged, but the scene was entirely different. It had been replaced with a new park and several sleek, white office buildings. In fact, most of the older part of Orlando's downtown was absent from the diagram, only several housing complexes and apartments remained. Even the dreamy, expensive neighborhood where I'd once been in awe of the oak trees was nowhere to be found.

Near the interior of the diagram were several larger buildings north of downtown Orlando that I didn't recognize, boxlike and plain, tucked within what appeared like an immense orange grove. The miniature trees sprung from the model, detailed with hundreds of orange dots barely visible to the eye.

I'd never seen a *real* orange grove before, only the lab-created plants hidden inside man-made facilities, fully dependent on intervention to survive. The grove within the model was wild, scattered in nonuniform patterns and rows, stretching for what must be at least sixty miles north of Orlando, filling all of the empty spaces between the apartment complexes and houses the creator had left behind.

At the bottom of the case was a small placard, black with gold lettering.

The 2100 Florida

Would it really be only forty years until that was all gone and replaced? Would there be even less?

I didn't want to think about it.

"Having a god's point of view always puts things into perspective, doesn't it?"

A woman, groomed and poised, approached me, her hair in a loose ponytail around one of her shoulders. Her nose curved downward in a steep slope, angling her nostrils toward the earth. She was wearing a crisp, white lab coat, *COF* embroidered on the right side of her chest. There was a smudge on the lens of her glasses.

"I don't really feel like a god when I look at it," there was a birdlike quality to this woman, pointed, direct. "Just distant."

"Why distant?"

The woman would not look away from me.

"This isn't anything like what I know."

She turned, eyes running the length of the model.

"Qucore commissioned an artist to create this for the lobby," the woman continued. "I think it's an interesting part of the decor."

She stepped away to the other side of the glass, eyes scanning the diagram as if soaking it in. She had eyes that didn't match the otherwise closed nature of her face. They were wide and observant. They must have belonged to a different person, and hers had ended up with someone else. I imagined they were stolen and swapped. I'd seen plenty of videos of them doing that to Augmistums. At this point, it couldn't be much different for us.

"Gives us something to work toward," her face went still, focused on the model.

"It's missing a couple of things," I replied, thinking of the dry cleaner and my father's crowded house. I stared at the Astroturf park in its place. I think I'd be the only one that would miss it.

"It's not completely to scale," the woman replied, indifferent. "Artistic impression, maybe. But, I'd also prefer if it was a little more accurate."

She looked at me and I finally saw the name tag clipped to her coat pocket: *Professor Elaina Powell.*

There she was.

"You have the same face as an old student of mine." Professor Powell tilted her head, studying me. She moved like an owl, meticulously scrapping every detail she could. "Are you an Alonso?"

"Yes," I pulled my bag up my shoulder. My chest was tight. "I'm Savannah. Dove Alonso was my older sister. I don't ever get told we looked anything alike."

Professor Powell lowered her gaze. I felt her take in the whole of my face.

"It's your bones. I can see her in your jaw."

Her stare was so persistent that I could feel where her eyes were tracing, stitching information for her mind. She could understand everything just by looking. I was taller than her, but the knowingness in her eyes still made me feel small. I wanted her to look away, so I could breathe.

"Dove was an impressive mind," Professor Powell continued. "We lost her too soon."

"This place meant a lot to her," I shared.

Professor Powell pursed her lips. "She had a great career ahead of her. What she was able to accomplish and understand at her age was incredible. I do wish what happened hadn't been her path."

I felt the weight of Dove's journal resting inside my bag, leaning into my hip. Professor Powell's eyes returned to the 2100 Florida model. My fingers wrapped around the strap. I finally took a deep breath.

"There's true innovation coming from this lab that simply wouldn't have been possible without Dove's contributions. Real, influential work. Oftentimes discovery is an inconvenient truth. Dove didn't shy away from that."

Professor Powell laid her hand on the wall of the model. The glass came away clean when she removed it, still perfect.

"I think it would have meant a lot to her to know that."

A smile curled the corners of Professor Powell's lips.

"Dove mentioned you and your father a lot. He owns a dry cleaner, correct? Somewhere—"

Professor Powell pointed at the model, vaguely gesturing to where our house and the dry cleaner would have appeared in the model.

"Here?" I nodded.

"That's where it's supposed to be."

"Like I said, it's not entirely accurate. Who knows what will really happen. At the end of the day, we're not supposed to be gods, no matter how we try."

Professor Powell stepped back from the model.

"Are you a student now?"

"No, I'm actually visiting with Matis Wallace. He just moved in with my father and I."

"Yes, I remember him telling me that. Good on him for taking you by."

I noticed Matis passing through the glass doors. His eyes widened when he noticed Professor Powell, and I watched him straighten his backpack across his shoulders as he got closer, fiddling with the yellow guest badge in his hands.

"Good afternoon, Professor, this is Savannah—"

"Alonso. Yes. We were getting to know each other."

Matis nodded and handed me the neon yellow guest badge, and I slipped the lanyard over my head. It was itchy on my neck.

"I was going to give her a quick tour of the lab if that's all right."

Professor Powell nodded. "Of course." Her eyes flickered back to me, wide and birdlike. "Stay as long as you'd like."

Professor Powell gave us a curt wave and walked back toward the glass doors without turning back. Matis let his posture drop, stretching his hands.

"She's incredibly intelligent; I can't even begin to tell you."

I watched Professor Powell's form disappear, sinking into the walls of the building itself.

"She looks at things like she's trying to absorb them."

Matis shook his head, taking his ID back out of his wallet.

"It's because she is."

***

Matis guided us toward the glass doors, then let me scan my guest pass against the ID tracker. The computer took my fingerprint and asked me to speak my name into a small microphone tucked in the corner of the system. I hesitated, but Matis shrugged.

"You have to."

"Savannah Alonso."

The doors slid open.

The lab smelled of cleaning chemicals, the air so dry it prickled against my skin. Several lab spaces were tucked throughout the hallway, bustling professors and students rushing between lab equipment and computers sequestered behind the glass. Everything was new. There were computers I'd only ever seen advertised on my dated laptop — sleek screens with data I couldn't comprehend. Everything looked impeccably clean.

"That's where they're working on the virtual trials for the medication we've been working on," Matis explained. "Our algorithm makes it possible to test the chemical construction of the medication on an immense amount of unique genetic variables, like age, weight, geographical location . . . Dove was on one of the founding trial teams for the testing. She helped develop the system they're still using today. She and Carter helped set it up. Carter coded most of the database himself. Dove helped to streamline the first digital drug trials using the algorithms built by Professor Powell and Carter."

Several students inside the lab stared at us as we passed before turning back toward their computers. In the back of one of the rooms, I saw a girl with long dark hair, and for a moment, I swore it was Dove. I imagined Dove's shoes clicking through this hallway, pulling her dark hair into a ponytail, jotting notes. Entirely in her element.

I didn't know anything about this, but I knew Dove. I knew that whatever was happening here had to be important. She wouldn't settle for anything less.

"This medication is going to help people in warmer climates have a better tolerance for rising temperatures," Matis continued. "It's revolutionary. We could be helping people jump over at least a hundred years of evolution. The number of lives that could be changed once this becomes available for people. It just—" He took a deep breath. "It just makes me feel really lucky to be able to do something like this. Especially when so much feels so—"

"Awful."

"Awful."

We neared the end of the hallway, coming upon the emergency exit doors and a large lecture hall. Peering around the corner, I could see it was empty. Several lights were on over the podium on the stage and the projector screen was pulled down. Something had ended.

"That's where Professor Powell does her lectures, and where they host the donor events when they fly in to see how things are progressing."

"The donors are the people on the wall in the lobby, right?"

"Yes, but there are others that have opted to stay anonymous. The larger donors specifically tend to not like the publicity."

"Matis!" a short girl called out into the corridor, staring at Matis and me near the end of the hallway.

"Could you come help us with this?"

"Sure, give me one minute."

The girl nodded and disappeared back inside one of the classrooms. Matis reached into his backpack and handed me several crumpled bills and a COF ID card. I flipped it over to reveal a copy of his ID.

"I have my own ID. Why are you giving me one? And why do you have two?"

He laughed.

"I always keep a spare. You'll need it to catch the university bus that runs back toward downtown. It should be able to drop you off walking distance from the dry cleaner. You can't use your undergraduate ID for it."

"I can't take your money."

"I'm offering it to you because I can't drive you back and I'm not going to make you wait in the lobby until I get out of here. You can tip the Augmistum if he's gruff about letting you onboard."

"Do they even care about money?"

"They're modeled off humans, aren't they?"

His eyes were kind. I didn't feel like I was being studied. This time I was only being seen. Part of me still hated it. More of me wished I didn't.

I folded the bills and tucked them into my pocket, staring at Matis' ID photo. He was much younger, but his smile was the same. Consistently genuine.

"Was it what you thought it would be?" Matis whispered.

I heard distant shoes clicking into the hallway, several doors opening and closing with quiet conversation.

"I don't know what I expected it to be. I knew I had to see it."

Matis nodded. "Come back whenever you'd like."

"Thanks."

Matis tapped on his wrist, pulling up his SubcutaLink and then a bus schedule.

"The next bus will be here in a few minutes. Head out these back doors and take a left. You'll see the blinking sign."

"Thanks, Matis."

I pushed open the heavy metal door and turned to wave at Matis, feeling the scorching sunlight on my face as soon as the sun greeted my skin. I missed the cold air the second I left it behind.

I wondered if Dove felt that way too.

FOURTEEN

"Another two hundred people were reported dead as the death toll from severe drought in Oklahoma continues to rise."

A TV was on inside the bus, tucked above the driver's head. The audio was barely loud enough to hear over the rumbling of tires against the weathered road closer to downtown. I tucked Matis' spare ID in my wallet, resting my bag in my lap.

Professor Powell's looming gaze wouldn't leave my mind. I ran my hand across my jaw.

Had she really seen Dove in my face?

There was something both comforting and intimidating about Professor Powell, the way I watched her analyze everything within seconds. If she could see Dove in my face when I never had, what else did she know about my sister?

My eyes flickered back to the TV. The heavily made-up woman from the hurricane newscast was back in the studio, glazed over eyes staring directly into the camera. Her lipstick was smudged, fading into a gradient toward her mouth. There was a stain on her shirt, and a bumpy, halfhearted nature to her high ponytail. A surrender. All of her looked rushed, disheveled. I wondered if after the hurricane fiasco, she'd been demoted to daytime desk duty. The light in her eyes was stripped, her skin cakey with makeup, blotchy under her hollowed eyes. She looked more human.

"Additional resources are being allocated by the federal government from Colorado and California in an effort to help combat the eight-month-long drought devastating the plains and southwestern United States, though officials from both states say they don't have water to spare."

The bus hit a small bump in the road, my bag bounced in my lap. The Augmistum driver accelerated. Turning back, I saw an abandoned Augmistum arm in the road. Even the weight of the bus had not misshapen it, still in its perfect, almost human condition. The skin on the arm was pristine, uncut. I wondered if it had been lost, or if it was just litter.

I reached in my bag, gently running my finger over the spine of Dove's journal. I swore, if only for a moment, it felt alive with heat. Maybe it was my own, absorbed from the light radiating through the bus window to my hands. Maybe Dove was breathing through it.

The news anchor brushed the top of her head, attempting to flatten the bumps of the ponytail, to no avail. Someone must have shown her in the monitor. Her lips tightened as she scanned the teleprompter.

"A candidate has announced his presidential run for 2064. This is unprecedentedly early, given voting for the 2060 election is this November."

The anchor laughed, but the tension remained in her face, like someone had taken a rod to stake up her smile.

"Former Lunar Tech Dynamics CEO, heir to the Oyster Oil fortune, and award-winning actor Rodger

Kettington announced his campaign at a press conference on Tuesday. The former Republican will be running as a Democrat, citing the party change with a renewed interest in reinstating Social Security, something Republicans have actively opposed for the last several election cycles."

The video cut to an older man, gripping the podium on stage in front of a crowd of several hundred people. A woman half his age with too-white teeth had her hand wrapped tightly around his arm, steadying him from leaning backward. His thirty-something cane.

"It's time to support our aging population again—" Kettington coughed into the microphone. "With bi-monthly Social Security payments for up to five years."

Cheering ensued.

"That is why I'm running to be your—" Kettington coughed again, hurriedly taking a sip of water from the cup in his wife's hand. "Sixty-third president of the United States. And this time, we won't let *hate* win. I'm looking at you, Republicans! The future is coming, and you're gonna hear us."

Kettington reached a shaky hand into his suit jacket pocket and pulled out a pair of dark tinted sunglasses. His wife slid them up his nose, gesturing toward the camera for him to wave in the right direction. A large projector screen behind him flashed to a "Kettington 2064" banner, followed by several photos of him at PRIDE events, meeting with prominent international dictators, and walking around his forty-bedroom mansion on the *New*-New England coast. His wife's lip curled and she leaned forward to kiss the wrinkled skin on his forehead.

The crowd roared.

Kettington had another coughing fit.

I wasn't sure he'd even *live* long enough to run in 2064.

I didn't know who I was going to vote for next month. Let alone in 2064. I thought about my "COF Shouts!" poster folded at the bottom of my bag and the girls who were pushing voter registration as the ideal path to progress. I hadn't seen a single prominent candidate running off climate change, or the wealth gap, or war or infrastructure or any of the other nightmarish things I'd only just started learning about by reading Dove's journal. What she'd laid out the details of, even back then, had been horrifying. I didn't think she could've imagined what would become of things. Or maybe Dove had been so meticulous about tracking it because she *could* imagine it.

I held the bag close to my chest.

Lately, when I wasn't absorbed in the events she was logging, my fingers continued to wander over those shaded circles. I still couldn't make sense of them.

I'd thought about asking Professor Powell. Maybe she could decipher them for me. But something in my gut twisted at the thought. There was something about her that made me particularly uneasy, no matter how important she'd been to Dove.

The TV cut back to the newsroom, where the anchor sat still as a statue. Her smile was more strained, but someone had fixed her lipstick and the bumps in her ponytail.

"Kettington is also a longtime donor to the COF Center of Research Development in Orlando, animal lover, and fitness enthusiast," the anchor said, nodding.

Kettington—

I closed my eyes. I saw the donor wall I'd seen inside the research center, and sure enough, I remembered his name several spaces above Lauren's parents.

Clearly, the research being done was important enough for even the wealthiest to be concerned with it. I wondered if he'd seen the 2100 Florida model and what he thought of it.

Was it accurate to someone who wanted to become president?

"And finally today, here's how one small town came together to help eight-year-old Jacobi afford his first round of chemotherapy—"

FIFTEEN

• Wildfire smoke disrupts bird migrations for the ninth year in a row.
• 900,000 new cases of Dengue Fever reported in Bangladesh.
• Breakthrough research at COF finds resistance to temperature increases may be possible through oral medication. Initial virtual trials successful.
• Deadly drought kills nearly 200+ people in Idaho.
• Sacrifice Zones rise in number around the Gulf of Mexico, including Cedar Key and Crystal River on Florida's western coast.

It had been three days since I'd slept. My bones ached, body stiff, but my mind was wide awake. I couldn't stop combing through Dove's journal, studying every page.

The journal wasn't all preventing me from sleep. Professor Powell's rounded eyes peered over all my dreams lately, her pupils blinking over half-submerged landscapes or above barren crop fields. Her gaze became the whole sky. The rest of her body never formed, only those two birdlike eyes, unwavering against whatever nightmarish landscape lingered below: a burning city, the whole of Florida sinking into a deep and impossible swamp.

I flipped my comforter down and it fell to the floor, the humidity in the room heavy against my oily skin. The small box fan in the corner wasn't cutting through the weight of the air, and the moisture stuck, stagnant. I was as much outside as it was within. There was no escape. My ceiling, was for now, at least free of the water spots in Dove's.

I returned to Dove's journal, my unsettled fingers rolling the corners of the pages. Studying her anecdotes was somehow more pleasant than sleep. When I wasn't reading the journal, I wanted to be. Everything she detailed, no matter how dark, had become an escape, but not exactly in a pleasant way. The way the information hit my brain was intoxicating. I had to know what the next one said, let it possess me. Even if the information made me feel sick. To have it was better than the absence.

Something whispered at the back of my mind, that I felt in the quietest parts of my bones, that Dove wanted me to read this. To see the tragedy. To know. This logging was for me. Why, I still didn't know. But the belief gnawed in my stomach, grazed it's fingers against the back of my neck, turning my head to the past. I couldn't look away.

The tragedy I understood least was hers.

I poured over every entry like they were written in secret code, trying to figure out what Dove meant. It was part of the fixation. The shaded circles tormented me, pulling me deeper into a maze of confusion. It wasn't just her words, but the spaces between them, the symbols left behind. I dug into every online resource I could find on encryption, codes, and even messages in art. I scanned obscure forums, read theories about hidden messages, just to see if anyone else had cracked the puzzle I was holding in my hands. There was nothing that made sense.

I told myself that if I could just figure it out—if I could just connect the dots—this might make sense. Maybe it wasn't too late.

***

One night, I wrote down the patterns I saw in the events, common themes, the way she'd written particular letters. I even sketched some of the circles, but the more I looked at them, the more I felt like they were taunting me, dismissing my ignorant attempts to draw closer to Dove's meaning. The journal asked me how well I knew my sister. I was afraid of the answer.

I was searching for more than just answers. I was searching for a way to fix everything, to bridge the space between Dove's world and mine. A tether to the past that could propel me to the future, to the right choices. To anything. I wanted someone to tell me what to do, what was right. Sometimes I felt like that's what the journal was punishing me for most.

I flipped the journal back to the first page:

"Fortunate are the gentle, for they will inherit the world."

The loops and lines of her handwriting were much softer here, gracefully curved that the quote could have been a typed font face. There was a more deliberate and accurate appearance to her handwriting further in the journal, less graceful and more utilitarian, every bulleted list less rounded than the last.

I'd finally reached my first fully shaded circle. It was so perfect, it could've been printed to the page. I ran my finger over the writing. The heat of my hand combined with the moisture of the room smudged the ink, turning the circle into an incongruent blob. The tip of my finger stained black and I rubbed it against my thumb. Both fingers turned a loose shade of gray, like graphite. I closed the journal, finally returning it to my bag. I still wasn't tired. The night would drag on with me, whether I was reading the journal or not.

For the first time in a long time, I heard crickets. They chirped in clustered chords outside my window, ringing from all directions. You didn't hear animals often, unless you were tucked in the few rural areas. Morning doves and hawks, that I could vaguely remember the cooing or screeching of from childhood, had retreated to their habitats far away from the people. As far as they could get from us, as much distance as they could find, they took. I didn't blame them. Why stay somewhere without a place to hide?

The crickets were a surprising, yet comforting, change. Near my window, I heard the chirping sounds increase, though when I peered out to the bare sidewalk and empty road, I had no idea where they could be hiding. Maybe they'd burrowed in the decaying tires my dad had left in the backyard. They'd found home in the uninhabitable too.

Suddenly, the front porch light switched on and I saw my father step outside, staring into the dark. He was still as a corpse, waiting for something, or maybe, anticipating it.

I backed away from my window and turned out of my bedroom, stepping quietly so as to not wake Matis, whose door was still wide open. Coming around the corner, I saw my father in the doorway, the back of his silhouette outlined by the painted light brushed in from the porch. He leaned against the doorframe, unmoving. In front of him, sitting still and slowly blinking its large green eyes, was the black cat.

"Dad?" I whispered, inching closer behind him. He didn't reply.

An eerie feeling I couldn't name washed over me. My chest tightened.

"Dad, can you—"

"Shh . . ." he whispered. "I don't want to disturb her."

I reached the doorway, peered over his shoulder and toward the cat. She was slowly blinking at my dad and then at his feet; watching a cluster of ants make their way toward a crack in our wall. They disappeared behind one another, in perfect formation.

"Are you okay?" I lowered my voice. "What are you doing out here?"

My dad's eyes were glassy, the warm light from the porch making his pupils flicker like a candle.

"I knew she was here. I had to see her again."

He turned, smiled wide, and looked at the black cat, who bounced her tail and stared at where the ants disappeared.

"She always knows when I need her," my father continued. "That's what's so special about her."

The cat blinked at him, her nose wiggling as she sniffed the night air.

"I didn't know you liked cats so much." I crouched, getting on eye level with her. She turned, acknowledging the motion. Slowly, I reached my hand out, gesturing for her to come close and let me scratch her head. She did not move. Her eyes locked on mine, coy and observant.

My father laughed.

"You don't recognize her?"

I frowned, stepping back from the cat. She was undeterred, setting her sights on my dad.

"What are you talking about?"

He turned from the cat, to me. The joy on his face was both profound and terrifying, eyes wild, as if he discovered something both brilliant and abhorrent.

"This," he said, grinning, pointing at the cat, "is *Dove*."

My stomach turned over. "What?"

My father reached for me, forcing my shoulders forward to get closer to the cat. She did not move.

"See her fur, the eyes? The way she's always looking, always waiting for me." He laughed, lips quivering. He was loose, coming undone in his reveal, like he'd been holding this information, like some mystical secret.

"That's Dove, through and through."

I swallowed the lump in my throat, looking back at the cat. Her fur was jet black, absorbing almost all the light from the porch as it shined on her back. It was the cat's eyes that were the most jarring; fixed and green, blinking, with an uncanny knowingness so honest, they were nearly human.

For a moment, I let myself believe him. This cat *was* really Dove, circling the house to watch over me and my father, reincarnated like a guardian. I thought about her keeping a careful distance, never too close, never asking for attention, but preserving space with each other, asking for nothing in return. She wanted to make sure we were okay. She wanted to be sure. Just like she'd always done.

My face grew hot. Tears fought to escape my eyes. My nose burned. I wanted to cry. I wanted to believe in this daydream. I wanted to scoop the cat into my arms, bring her inside to the couch and sob into her fur. I wanted her to claw into my wrist until she drew blood. I wanted to smell the orange juice. I wanted to hear her heartbeat roar in my ears. I longed for signs of Dove's life where I knew there was none. My father was content to pretend. I wished I was too.

I looked back at him. So at peace. So deeply in love with the idea Dove was here with us, that her absence had been nothing more than a bad dream.

A stray ant, separate from the long line of them, rushed across the sidewalk toward the wall. The cat studied it, head tilted, but let it pass. It too disappeared in the crack in the wall with the others.

"Maybe it is," I whispered to my father, placing a hand on his shoulder. "Just maybe."

He didn't answer, mesmerized by the cat under the porch light. She beat her tail against the ground, eyes flicking to me momentarily before she returned her attention to my dad. His smile widened.

"See?"

I rubbed my hand against his back and stepped away from the doorway. The air felt no different inside. I walked toward the kitchen, reaching for a glass of water. On the counter, I saw a manila folder, tucked underneath a stack of mail like it had been taken out and forgotten, mixed within the rest of the clutter. It had to have been taken out recently.

Curious, I moved the paper fliers for Pre Black Friday sales, an internet bill, and several postcards for Roger Kettington's 2064 presidential campaign, and picked up the folder. Flipping open the cover, I froze. It was Dove's autopsy report. I'd never seen it before.

A pang of guilt struck me; my father must have pulled it out, probably on one of his late nights alone, sifting through the same words as if searching for something the police had missed. Or maybe he needed it to feed some threadbare hope that things had unfolded differently. I could picture him, hunched and exhausted, clinging to that impossibility. Dove's loopy handwriting etched across my vision, scowling at my ignorance.

Grief was vicious like that. It sank into you, twisting around your heart. It grew with your heartbeats, hungry for pumping blood. Life is what makes grief possible. Death only enables it to exist.

I heard my father gently cooing to the cat on the porch. I looked at the folder in my hands. The paper was frayed, yellowing at the corners, the script on the front small and professional. I took a deep breath and opened it.

In neat, sterile writing, I saw what I already knew, but never admitted to myself. It's different to have something told to you versus seeing it through your own eyes. Maybe I too had clutched to the hope someday I'd wake up and Dove would walk through the front door again, apologize for the scare, for being gone so long, for making me do all of this alone. She'd put something in the oven for dinner, scoot her chair beside mine and ask what I'd been learning. She'd ask if I could help her wash the dishes. Maybe we could go to that neighborhood together, and I could see the oak trees this time, eyes open.

Autopsy determines victim's cause of death was suicide.

I hadn't prepared myself to see it written so matter-of-fact. I stared, trying to make sense of the words, like I didn't know what they meant. Like I could twist them into something else. The weight of my father's presence on the porch crept into my mind. I felt him there, detached from the world. From me.

I wondered what he'd do if I brought this up. If I asked him—really asked him—why he didn't talk to me about any of it. Why he buried the truth so deep, kept so much of Dove's passing hidden, tucked away in manila folders and scattered scraps, separate schedules and distance—always projecting from a half-step away.

"Dad?" I called.

The only response was the sound of the cat purring, the soft hum of the porch light flickering in the distance.

The silence stretched too long before my father finally spoke, his voice low and distant, like it wasn't even meant for me.

"I'm gonna check on the dry cleaner," he said, his words laden with that same routine.

He didn't look up from the cat. His hand patted the animal's back, trying to soothe some deep, unreachable ache.

I opened my mouth, but I couldn't find the words I wanted. My throat tightened, and all that came out was air. He wasn't going to let me in—not now, maybe not ever.

"Okay," I said.

Without another glance, my father stood up, gave the cat one final scratch behind the ears, and walked into the dark.

SIXTEEN

• Another fifteen of the world's wealthiest made their way to the moon today. Recreational space travel causes a decrease in air quality worldwide.
• Wildlife Conservationist Deccan Graham dies by self-immolation, citing David Buckel (2018) and Wynn Bruce (2022) as inspiration. Graham's essay on the collapse of the United States was the most read article on the New York Times website in 2046. Attendees of his funeral were asked to place themselves on the mandated "political activist registry."
• Excess microplastics have been found in terrestrial, air, groundwater, marine, and freshwater systems, stronger filtration systems required globally.

I couldn't pull the report on Dove's death from my mind.

"Do not get distracted."

The automated voice whirred in my ear, so persistent I spent most of my exam grinding my teeth. I had seventeen minutes left to finish and fifteen questions to go. The pulsating headache didn't help, all the text on my laptop screen blurred together. My chest tightened, the weight of the clinical words from Dove's report had lodged themselves inside me, pressing against everything else. The examiner's neat sterile handwriting branded itself across every thought.

"Do not get distracted."

For the first thirty minutes of the exam, I'd stared out the window, counting the number and color of cars that passed. Fifteen blue. Seven red. Over time, the automated voice became a background meditation to the words of the autopsy swirling in my head until I hardly remembered I was taking a test at all.

***

Dove and Carter had seemed distant those last months, burned out and drained, but never hopeless. Dove had made plans, kept up with her routines; there'd been a spark of her usual defiance even as things grew tense. But she hadn't given up. She wouldn't have done that to us. To me.

My brain swam with everything I'd read in Dove's journal, the tragedy and horror mounting heavy on my skull. I'd gotten far enough that there were three full circles in the top corner of the pages, and the frequency that a new circle emerged was shortening. I studied the bullet lists on every page, scanning for new insights from Dove about what to do with what she'd left behind and how to interpret it. I continued to come up empty handed. I rattled the information off in my head like a choir chant, a guttural hymn that rumbled from my head into my bones. It became an oath—or maybe an omen, to try and understand. To know.

I thought about all the places the people driving those cars on the road could be going, what disasters they might have encountered. I thought about how many of them might have lost people they loved in those tragedies Dove recounted across the pages of her journal.

How many of them would lose those they loved in future tragedies?

How preventable would it all be?

How many people like Dove were out there, doomed to not escape it?

It felt insane that we weren't all standing on the roofs of our houses, screaming at how far we'd strayed from empathy. Why weren't we all asking ourselves about the absurdity we were tolerating and what we were holding out for? Why couldn't we all find that anger within us?

The time I spent not reading Dove's journal felt wasted, devoid of importance.

If I wasn't taking in the information, analyzing the weight of it, the impact, what she'd charted would go to waste.

Dove's journal was changing me, in ways that I wasn't sure I understood. I didn't feel motivated to focus on school. What was any of this insight good for? What was I going to do with it?

Sure, it might get me to a job. Maybe in a few years I'd make enough money to move out of my father's house and rent a shoebox-size apartment. Or, a room in somebody else's house like Matis. Perhaps I'd have to move out in forty years when our house and the dry cleaner were demolished and turned into sterile modern homes and manicured parks. By then, there's a chance I will have saved enough money for the down payment on a cardboard box. Maybe they'd let me pay rent on the astroturf.

Then again, what was learning everything in Dove's journal good for? What was I going to do with *that*? Torture myself with the fact I felt so utterly powerless?

But, what could matter more than trying to understand how we'd gotten here?

"Do not get distracted," the bot whirred again. "There are ten minutes remaining for this exam."

I slammed my computer closed, deciding I'd take the F. I couldn't sit in this room anymore.

Matis' door was open, but the room was empty. I'd seen him a little less than usual lately. He was spending even more time at the Center of Research Development, leaving before I woke up and returning long after I'd tried to go to bed. A trend for the inhabitants of that room.

Matis had given me his spare ID so I could go back to campus, but part of me didn't know if I could handle another encounter with Professor Powell. Those bird eyes. Being studied. I didn't know if I could handle it. Professor Powell had the kind of gaze that made me want to disappear. Most people didn't see you anymore, they just looked. It was safer for me that way, the disconnect of understanding. In someways, it gave you more control, because they weren't interpreting you. There was freedom in that.

The other part of me was desperate to go to campus and experience Dove's presence again, to stare at the 2100 Florida model, to feel the cold air conditioning against my skin. To be something.

I was a dog staring at a bone getting pulled farther out of reach. I didn't know if I could jump any higher.

My phone rang. Lauren offered to take me to Lucky's.

I told her I didn't have any money. She offered to pay. The last week of eating canned beans and fruit had started to wear on me, so the "yes" slipped out before I realized I'd said it. I grabbed my bag and some water, and started walking.

The dry cleaner had picked up more business lately, meaning the poignant, etherlike smell of the perchloroethylene had gotten stronger. My father had been in a fog every night since we'd stared at the black cat together. I wondered how much the perc had to do with his disconnection. Had I been unfair to him? How much autonomy did he really have left?

The break from the house and the dry cleaner felt heaven-sent, and when I stepped into the diner, the persistent tightness in my stomach started to untangle.

I hadn't heard from Lauren in a few weeks. She had been accompanying her parents on another circuit of fundraisers and philanthropic events.

Major campaigning was underway as the 2060 election grew closer, and her father was determined to achieve the highest voter turnout since 2020. Growing up, Lauren's house had always been filled with these conversations, her father hosting endless dinners with people I'd only seen on TV.

"This is the largest election by population of all time, you know," Lauren said, sliding a menu across the table to me. She had a tendency to make me feel like I was at a press conference.

Watching her slide into the seat across from me, I thought back to those weekends when we were younger, playing hide-and-seek around her house. Back then, her home had seemed almost enchanted, with its grand, spiraling staircase and endless rooms. There was a library with floor-to-ceiling bookshelves, each filled with old, leather-bound volumes; a sunroom with rows of expensive plants. I remembered trailing behind her, peeking into rooms we weren't supposed to be in, marveling at the sheer size of the place. My barefeet left smudges on the marble floor. I remember her mother had always hated that.

My eyes drifted to the diner menu, but my mind wandered. The shaded circles. I wondered if Lauren could know something, if there was something from her travels or her father's work that might give me information. I felt like I was just getting was desperate. In a way, I was.

"Do you know anything about circle symbols or codes for tracking? Just like, really primitive kinds of drawings."

Lauren looked up at me, eyebrows raised.

"Do you have an example?"

I hesitated and wary of betrayal, I swallowed.

"No."

She shrugged, not invested. "It could be something like lunar cycles. Or maybe it's for dates, anniversaries, something like that."

"Okay."

"Why do you ask?"

I felt stupid for even bringing it up.

"Just something from a book I was reading."

Lauren gave me a skeptical look, but didn't press. "Fun!" She shifted her gaze back to the menu, more interested in the food than the conversation.

I let the silence stretch between us, keeping my thoughts to myself.

While we stared at our menus, Lauren's car parked itself near the back of the restaurant, and I turned to watch, taking in its sleek, handle-less design. It was a newer model than I'd seen her ride in before, with a darker tint on the windows. The car's smooth, rounded sides reminded me of a perfect paperweight. You can hold down whatever you liked with it.

I thought of our first "big adventure" together back in middle school when Lauren and I had played in her dad's electric sedan and we'd pretended to drive off into the sunset, caught before we'd left the driveway.

But it was different now. Lauren was different. I guess I was too.

"You know, if we get everyone registered, and encourage people to show at the polls, it's really going to help bolster political awareness," Lauren was happy to change the subject back to voting. "It'll empower people to push for change."

My eyes didn't leave her car. Her words barely registered.

"Is that new?" I asked, gesturing toward it. "Yeah," she replied, tapping the top of her SubcutaLink and locking the doors. "It was a gift for my dad and he didn't need it, so now it's mine." Lauren grinned. "The updated self-park is pretty convenient. I can have it drop me anywhere I want and it will find a parking spot wherever one's available. It can even read tow zone signs."

The car made a quiet beep before shutting off the headlights.

"You know, they use a lot of the consumer research from that stuff to refine how it's used by the military and stuff." The words came out before I could stop them. A month's worth of exposure to Dove's journal crawled out of my throat. She'd written about the surveillance technology that helped cars self-operate in an entry I'd read a day or two ago. I was bubbling over with information. It burned in my brain, falling out of my mouth.

Lauren's eyes widened.

"It's actually kind of awful," I continued. "And then that data gets sold to private military contractors, and then further tested in other countries, before they apply the findings to people in the US."

I felt high as I said it, let the horror out, but the hit lasted for only a moment. Now, we both sat with what was once crawling to get out of me. There was a dullness in Lauren's eyes. She looked numb.

The bell on the front door of the diner chimed, and a rush of cold air hit my face. I swallowed my dehydration. My stomach hurt. I couldn't help myself.

"So we get to benefit from all the cool new consumer technology, but it actually comes from some pretty dangerous places, even if we inherently aren't using it for evil purposes."

When was the last time I drank any water?

"I didn't know that," Lauren replied, setting her bag on the table. She wouldn't look at me. She shifted through the contents in her purse, shaking her head. "That sounds bad."

"Mmm-hmm." I nodded, studying her face for a reaction. Nothing. She opened the menu and scanned through the drink options. We'd been here hundreds of times. There was no way she didn't know what she wanted to order. The dismissal stung.

I looked at the menu, pretending that I wouldn't just ask for a cup of water and a sandwich. I decided since Lauren had offered to pay, I was going to get a side of fries. I wasn't used to feeling this kind of resentment; this anger that she didn't see what I was seeing. Lauren had always been able to float above this sense of doom that rot most of us. Something in me wanted her to understand. At least acknowledge.

After a few minutes, a waitress approached our table. I didn't recognize her. Most of the people that worked at the diner had been here for longer than I'd been alive. She had perfectly curled blonde hair, full lips, and an all-American smile. She pulled out a pen and paper from the pocket of her apron, tapping it on her side.

"Can I get the chicken pot pie?" Lauren asked her, staring at the menu. She still wouldn't look at me. "And some lemonade?"

"Of course." The woman jotted it down before turning over to me. "And for you?"

My eyes floated over the length of her face. She had beautiful skin, beige and lightly blushed. Her nails were a shade of red nearly identical to the booths at the diner. Something felt *deeply* wrong, but I couldn't put my finger on it until I looked into her eyes.

No veins. No blood.

She blinked, almost human. But I couldn't unsee it. "Are you automated?" I stared at the waitress.

"Yes," she responded, politically, a crime for Augmistums to not disclose their status. "Today is my first day."

Everything I'd tried to shake off coming to the diner came rushing back. There was that ache; in my brain and my bones.

I set my menu on the table, staring at Lauren. "You see this, right?"

Lauren's eyes flickered to the automated waitress, never to me.

"Maybe they need extra help," she said, shrugging.

"This place is never busy." I frowned. "You can't use that as an excuse."

"I'm not making an excuse." Lauren shook her head. She studied the same menu we'd seen hundreds of times. "It's not like either of us own the place. It's not our fault. It's just the way it is."

"What?" The frustration made my head spin. "You've always told me the only reason you like this place is *because* they don't have any Augmistums here. What happened to that?"

Lauren's table tapping continued.

"I don't know. I'm finding out at the same time you are." She turned back to the waitress. "Why did they bring you here?"

The all-American smile returned to the Augmistum's face.

"The Florida-sponsored Augmistum assistance program. The owners are entitled to three government-sponsored Augmistums under the jurisdiction of Florida House Bill 76-B93, so I—"

"I'm not hungry." The feeling of betrayal in my stomach outweighed the desire for food and I stood up from the table.

"Savannah, come on." Lauren reached for me. "This isn't a big deal—"

"Big deal?" I almost shouted. The three other patrons across the bar turned to me. At least they saw me. My heart pounded. "You know that's the program that's been soliciting my dad—I *told* you that. You've always been so adamant against these things."

Lauren's eyes flickered to the ground.

"I don't think that people getting a little help is fatalist," she whispered. "It's just a waitress."

"Right." The room spun, my hands scavenged for the back of the booth. "It's about what it *means* for them to be here. Can't you see that?"

Lauren stared at me, in both concern and pity.

"Can you please sit down? You've been off all afternoon. Is something wrong?"

Instinctively, I pulled my bag in closer, the weight of Dove's journal knocking against my hip. Lauren's gaze followed the movement, her eyes narrowing slightly, but this time I couldn't meet hers.

It wasn't just that Lauren was noticing, she'd always noticed. It was the passive way she looked that made it all worse. The way someone acknowledges roadkill. Looking when it's already too late.

"I've got to go."

"Savannah—"

It didn't even matter where I was going. I just needed to leave. I needed the space to breathe—away from her, from the fruitless urge to make sense of something that I didn't know how to. The pressure of Dove's death, the unanswered questions, the journal with its cryptic entries, were a suffocating fog. Each page I read, every new entry I uncovered, seemed to pull me deeper into something I couldn't grasp. I was drowning, and the more I tried to swim, the more I sank.

I headed toward the diner doors. The heat outside pushed back against my chest, dirty air burning my lungs. At least it was real. Honest. Walking in the heat was the most honest thing I could do. In the brutal sunlight, I could almost feel something. My skin prickled with the burn of the sun, and as the heat pressed into every exposed inch of me, a reminder of my own existence. To be human in a world that wanted us out of it.

I stepped across the sidewalk, the concrete unforgiving beneath my shoes and then stopped.

I waited a few seconds, just listening, holding my breath, wondering if Lauren would come running after me. I didn't want her to, at least, not really. But I was afraid, too. Afraid of being alone with what was crushing me.

But there was nothing.

For a second, I almost wanted to go back inside. I could sit down with Lauren and pretend nothing had changed. That everything was normal, that I wasn't carrying this weight around, this unbearable thing inside me that I couldn't let go of. But I didn't. I stood there, the ache in my chest spreading.

I couldn't.

Down the road, I saw the COF bus for the Center of Research Development pulling toward the stop. Several students stepped off and a small line of people began to board. Like ants.

I reached into my pocket and pulled out Matis' spare ID and ran toward the bus. I panted in the heat, the sunlight stinging every part of me. I could hear my heart in my ears, a drumline, an inquiry. My chest burned nearly as much as my skin. An invisible hand pushed me onboard before my feet had time to catch up.

The AC rushed brushed my face. I was the last one on and I snagged a window seat, staring out toward the diner at Lauren's parked car. I could see the back of her head through the glass. She nodded toward the automated waitress, taking the lemonade from her and opening a straw, undeterred. Lauren briefly glanced toward the door I'd walked out of, before taking a sip.

SEVENTEEN

Dove put her hands on my shoulders, holding tight to one of my arms and extending it toward the bushes. The plant was a bit taller than me, the leaves running over the top of my head. I could feel it on top of my scalp. I reached out my hand, then hesitated.

"You can touch it," Dove whispered, gesturing toward one of the lower branches. "Just be gentle."

I couldn't have been older than six; interactions with nature were such a luxury that they never ceased to fascinate me. I'd admired the drawings of deep green leaves in picture books, studying the patterns that made them all different, alive.

The idea of an innately wild place, untouched by people and pollution, was as mystical as stories of dragons and faraway kingdoms. Both found home in my imagination, something I had to create just for myself.

Dove found a quiet, grassy area a few miles from our house, but to get there we had to take a short bus ride. She'd carried me to the bus stop while Dad was at the dry cleaner. The spot was hidden behind an abandoned furniture store, stray vines running in tangles over the side of the structure, in the shadow of the Orlando Executive Airport.

I'd never been on a bus before, and I was intensely curious about my new view, much higher up than our father's car. From this height, I could peer between the buildings, glimpsing at streets and rooftops that were usually hidden. The city stretched out in layers I hadn't known were there, each one hinting at a new place we might be headed. The world grew deeper. Home became even smaller.

"This used to be a garden," Dove whispered, pointing toward several clustered apartment complexes. "You could walk around for hours besides hundreds of plants, and in the springtime, it was full of roses. Mom used to take me."

I tried to imagine that—a lush garden, vibrant and flush like Dove's face in the summer. I imagined the close-knit clusters of bushes, ripe with flowers or maybe fruit. It was an impossible image, and it hurt my head.

"Where did it go?" I whispered, watching several families unload bags of groceries from the cars, hauling them toward a dull brown apartment building.

"They needed the ground for something else," Dove replied, peering at the families walking in and out of the doors, or gathered on their small outdoor patios. "That's part of nature too."

I'd never thought of nature as everything, not just the trees. It was the black asphalt of the roadways, the whir of cars and buses, the dense burning smells in the air and the constant heat. It was all of us. The way we pushed or pulled against the world around us. The way we changed it. Every force, every act of kindness and compassion, all of that was nature too. Everything.

I hesitantly reached into the bush, letting the lower leaves tickle the surface of my palm. I expected the plant to recoil at my touch, but it didn't. I'd always assumed trees must be so fragile that the smallest interaction with a human would destroy them.

What else could explain why there were so few around?

"See," Dove said, grinning. "Isn't that amazing?"

The leaf was mostly rounded, small inlets lining the border. I studied all of the micro indentations, where it was smooth, where it was sharp. I wondered how something could be so functional and simultaneously, so vibrant. The green was overwhelming, rich and enveloping. I stared into the bush, seeing hundreds of leaves beyond me, none of them identical. They were like fingerprints, each different from the last, all growing from the same place.

I leaned farther in, my small fingers still grasping tightly around the leaf, till I pulled the branch too far forward and tore the leaf in half. I started crying.

"It's okay," Dove whispered, taking the torn leaf from my hands. "You pruned it a little. It might grow back even better."

The AC in The Center of Research Development grazed across my neck, the cold plastic chair soothing my legs.

The 2100 Florida Model

My eyes stuck to the model. It was particularly quiet, so I pulled one of the chairs from the study tables and sat beside the glass display case. The chair squeaked against the pristine floor as I pulled it forward, getting as close as I possibly could.

It was dark by the time I got off the bus, the parking lot thin with a few cars. This far from the city, if it was clear, I realized you could still see the stars. Not only that, but there was rustling in some of the bushes, signs of small and scattered life. A mosquito landed on the top of my shoulder before I walked toward the sliding front doors, and I didn't swat it. Could I fault her for trying to survive?

There were plenty of beautiful things to admire about the 2100 Florida model, whether it was the wind turbines or hydroelectric plants, the carefully crafted green spaces and parks, and the sheer amount of trees. Though Professor Powell had claimed the model wasn't entirely accurate, I hoped that the artist was right about the greenery. The lushness was enough to make anyone take notice. I craved a world like that, dense with life.

I'd been hurt by the exclusion of our house originally, but now I wasn't sure. My father and his perchloroethylene, our dated car and hand-me-down hurricane shutters all seemed like relics.

It was hard to tell. Maybe we did need a restart.

"You should have told me you were coming."

I turned and saw Matis walking out of the Qucore Lab, tucking his ID in his pocket. He held a folded lab coat, backpack slung over one shoulder. He was exhausted, eyes rounded and puffy, but he smiled when he saw me sitting there. He pulled a chair away from another table and dragged it over beside mine.

"It was kind of a last-minute decision." I tapped my finger against the side of the glass. "I promise if I'd known I was coming, I would've told you."

Matis waved his hand. "You don't owe me an explanation."

We sat in the quiet for a moment. I was almost alarmed by the building's silence, no rolling cars along the road, no rumble from an outdated AC unit, no whirring machines. It was eerily peaceful; a sterile hearth. The 2100 Florida model was the most vibrant piece in the whole room.

"Why do they have this?" I asked.

"It's part of Qucore's eventual investment into Florida." Matis set his backpack on the ground. "The goal is to ensure this *is* Florida by 2100. More climate resilient technology. Infrastructure that can withstand stronger hurricanes. Green spaces. Native plants. It's a reminder about why our work is so important." Matis leaned in closer to the model, eyes wide. "All of this becomes possible if we have people that can withstand what's coming. And we're so close."

"Really?"

Up close, Matis' looked tired. "The trials have come back perfect. This is over ten years' worth of data proving that we've created something that works."

"That's great."

He folded his hands in his lap, looking out across the model and back toward the Qucore wing.

"I think Dove would be really amazed at how far all of this has come." Matis grinned.

I studied the top of my sneakers, running my hands on the chair.

"They're launching the initial rollout within the next few weeks. It's going to focus on those most vulnerable to extreme heat, so people that work outdoors, the elderly, and—"

"Poor people," I finished for him. "Right?"

"Yes." Matis leaned in closer, watching me. "Does that bother you?"

"Not in principle. I just...worry about people being guinea pigs."

"None of the trials have come back poorly," he assured.

"I know, I just—"

I rested my chin on the top of the glass, counting the carved blue waves in the rising ocean. The Florida model warped through the curved corner of the glass, giving the state elevation it didn't have.

"Have you heard about Florida House Bill 76-B93? The one where the state is providing low-income business owners with subsidized Augmistums."

Matis nodded. "Yeah. Why?"

"Someone came to the house the other day trying to get my dad to sign up for the program."

Matis tapped his fingers against the glass. "That's also the Bill Qucore is hoping will get the medication to vulnerable communities faster. If we have government support for the distribution, more people will be able to start taking it."

My eyes skimmed over the top of the artificial tree line. The glass made them morph in a bell curve.

"What do you think about it?" I asked, peering deeper into the model. My breath fogged the glass.

"What do you mean?"

"Do you think . . . it's weird? This specific focus on these communities. When has the state ever actually cared about making sure we had actual resources? I couldn't even get enough water for me and my father during the last hurricane. It just—I don't know, it seems disingenuous."

Matis scooted closer, mirroring my vantage point over the glass. His ear brushed my cheekbone. "I think maybe people are realizing that if we don't support the people that need help, there's going to be no hope for anyone. It's a call for compassion. At least, that's how I see it."

"Seems a little late."

"There are still good people in the world, Savannah. We're not entirely fucked."

My face felt hot. "Are you sure?"

"What would I be doing this for if I wasn't?"

My eyes flickered toward where home should be—to the absent dry cleaner, the empty roadways, how thin this Florida was from above, the ocean leaping above a sunken Miami. It was so hard to be sure what was a blessing, what was an omen, especially with disaster after disaster. My mind slogged across pages and pages of Dove's notes, all of the darkness she recounted, everything I knew now.

Was there really enough good left worth hoping for? I trusted Dove, and she hadn't thought so. At least not enough to stay.

Matis nudged my leg. I stared into the model, studying the thousands of tiny orange trees.

"Do you really think Dove would've been here if she didn't think it was worth it?"

My eyes fell to my bag on the floor, to Dove's journal. I couldn't bring myself to tell Matis everything I'd read, what Dove knew. I couldn't make him also take on the weight of that grief, of the rage and fear I knew lived on those pages, not when I knew what his work here meant to him.

"I don't know."

Matis hadn't seen the darkness in Dove's eyes, the weight she carried from this place. Of course it had meant a lot to her. It had meant *everything* to her. But had it been worth it? Had *anything* been worth it?

The neat, arid handwriting stung behind my eyes as I closed them.

Autopsy determines victim's cause of death was suicide.

Maybe Dove had given up.

"Why does everything about the world feel so dark?" I finally whispered. My vision blurred, tears hot in my eyes.

"I didn't know Dove." Matis moved closer to me, lowering his voice. "But if she's even half the intelligent, compassionate, and dedicated person that people have made her out to be, I know how much it would mean to her that we see through what she started."

I sat up from the glass and turned to him. My palms were sweating against the glass. I felt the ball of anger and grief I had spent a decade swallowing back growing stronger. I could've screamed. I wanted to shrink myself and live inside the model. I wanted to destroy it. I wanted to dig up all of the trees and swallow them whole. I wanted to string a hammock between them and sway in the wind. I wanted to pull off all the leaves. I wanted to see if they changed colors when the air finally got cold and what happened when it finally did. I wanted all of it, and nothing.

I took a shaky breath.

"I want to believe that the work you're doing here is worth having to live the rest of my life without her."

Matis placed his hands around my shoulders, pulling me from the model. The sweat from my palms left a mark on top of the glass, and like Lauren's marble floors, like burnt sandwiches, they were signs of humanity. Signs of life.

The 2100 Florida model was blurry where I had leaned on the glass, just distorted enough to see a difference.

Matis took my hands between his, and though I almost recoiled from the touch, I didn't. He held the spot between my index finger and thumb and rubbed it slowly.

For the first time in weeks, I felt a release.

"Everyone is going to be thankful for Dove. I promise."

EIGHTEEN

• *Birth rates fall globally by 27%.*
• *Spray from the oceans releases record PFAs, prompting additional reconsideration for living near the coasts.*
• *Development of Harmony Grove begins in Florida.*
• *Youth-led climate protesters in Florida forced to register for the political activist registrar.*
• *Southeast loses 530 million labor hours, amounting to about $30 billion, due to extreme heat impacts on productivity.*
• *Melting permafrost in Fairbanks, AK, causes multiple structures to sink.*

I'd started reading Dove's journal more intentionally. With less fury to binge it. It helped the insomnia, my brain able to unwrap itself. After my talk with Matis, I didn't want the journal to pull me entirely out of reality. I tried to quench my desire to know and understand the pages without letting the weight sink me into a state of paralysis. I was still learning. The information was getting darker the further I read.

This was the first time I'd picked it up in several days. I'd finished my classwork as the sun disappeared and the afternoon rain ceased. The house was serene, the road outside surprisingly quiet for just after rush hour. The low light reminded me of waking up early in the morning for elementary school and watching Dove walk briskly inside after another late night at the research center. I'd wait all morning for that moment, to see her step through the door and feel her arms wrap me in the tightest embrace.

Tonight, my windows were wet on the inside, the ancient insulation of our house not nearly enough to keep up with the constant moisture. Everything was particularly sticky. The house creaked with the weight of the rain.

I pressed the eraser side of my pencil on the condensation on the window and drew a smiley face. Another water droplet ran the length of the window, and sliced the drawing in half, before racing to the bottom. I retraced over the smile trying to reinforce it, using my finger instead of the eraser tip. It held, at least, better than before.

I felt steadier than I had in weeks. I caught myself drifting from the present less. When I felt like I was floating, I could ground myself in the room. I counted my books. I listened to a song. I stood in the hallway and listened to Matis type. Anything to turn outward instead of in.

I focused on my schoolwork or the customers at the dry cleaner. I'd kept the news off the TV. Conversations with Matis, when I passed by his open door, became an escape; watching him lean over his desk, tapping into his SubcutaLink or flipping through the pages of his textbooks. I listened to him tell me how things were going at the lab. I was happier.

I still hadn't told him about the details in the journal. Burdening him with that while work was so busy seemed unfair. At least, that's what I told myself.

I wrote an apology text to Lauren, telling her that I was sorry. She sent one back, short and sweet, followed by a photo of herself on some beach, her skin tanned and glowing against the backdrop of crystal-clear water. I replied with a thumbs-up instead of ignoring it.

I filled my time with distractions. The dry cleaner was busy, my exams kept me occupied, if only for a little while.

The uneasiness—the deep, gnawing feeling that I couldn't shake—was still there, the uninvited guest. If I didn't let my mind linger, focused enough on the mundane, assimilated to the noise of daily life, I didn't have to face it. My sunburn was finally healing.

I tried to close the gap between myself and my father, the quiet distance between us growing more pronounced with every passing day. Sometimes I caught him staring out the window, his eyes distant, as if he was seeing something I couldn't. Other times, he would busy himself with small tasks, checking the locks, adjusting the blinds, watering the plants, looking for the black cat. He moved through the house like a ghost, walking the path he'd worn between the kitchen and the porch, rarely stopping to speak.

Every time I opened my mouth, the words I wanted to say fell flat. I'd ask him if he needed help with something, but he'd just nod or mumble an excuse, retreating to the porch to watch for the cat again. He was still a world away.

For now, I let it go. Maybe this was just how it had to be, our separate ways of surviving the impossible.

It felt better this way, in this new form of stasis. I felt more functional, more present. But the uneasiness always came back. A shadow I couldn't outrun.

I watched another water droplet roll down through the smiley face I'd drawn on the window.

There was something about this particular entry in Dove's journal that made me feel more unsettled than any of them had in a long time.

Harmony Grove. . .

I reread the line again.

This was the first time in a while I'd seen something in the journal I didn't recognize or couldn't immediately research. There was no other context for it. When I typed *Harmony Grove, Florida* into my computer, there were no results. I tried variations—*Harmony Groves, Peaceful Grove, Harmony Grotto*—but nothing of interest turned up besides hotels that had closed decades ago and tourist attractions long sunken into the Gulf of Mexico.

In the top of the page, more circles were drawn like on the others, shaded from top to bottom. The rest of the page was in all ways of the journal, unremarkable.

I frowned and flipped the page in anticipation of Dove jotting another list, but there wasn't one.

Across the next two pages of the journal was a drawing. It featured several landmasses and winding rivers, and a surprising amount of trees. Near the edge of the delta were several large brown rectangles I could only assume were buildings, buried in the distance of the lush green she'd sketched out.

I'd never seen anything like this, the richness of a natural landscape so vivid, surreal. The trees extended and interlocked their branches together, only a faint sliver of sky barely visible above the overarching canopy. Dove had shaded parts of the river in the bottom of the drawing; a stunning shade of crystal blue that faded into the black swamp water, cutting through the length of the woods. The black water crawled to the other side of the page, disappearing off the edge of the paper.

The drawing was untitled and descriptionless, a jarring break between all the pages of tragedy. I ran my fingers across the two pages, feeling the texture from the colored pencils as Dove had pulled them in through the binding and across the other side. I could fall all the way in to this drawing. I lifted the journal from my desk and brought it closer to my eyes, taking the color in as deep as I could, when I saw it, labeled in faint pencil right through the center of the water. You could just barely make it out.

Wekiva River.

My stomach dropped.

Staring me in the face, a sketch of where they'd found Dove and Carter's bodies. Here was my portal, a waving flag, or eyes of a siren. I'd spent the majority of my life avoiding even the thought of this place, but here it was, laid out in immaculate detail from corner to corner.

Why had Dove drawn this here?

I knew that Wekiva was important to Dove. She and Carter went often, long before she'd died. She'd come home and show me photos she'd taken of the trees, the water, or the rope swing hidden above a former swimming spot. It was where she went when she wanted to be at peace. The land had been preserved as a state park for nearly one hundred years, and as the coastline disappeared and the subdivisions expanded, it had become one of the rare untouched spots in Central Florida. I was sure that was why Dove loved it so much.

You weren't technically allowed to swim in the water anymore, or traverse through the deeper parts of the woods beyond several designated paths and kayaking routes. Allegedly, the state was wary about any of the forest getting damaged by an influx of foot traffic or the discarding of trash and cigarettes. There wasn't much land left you could gamble on people treating well. Who knew if that was actually true.

Too much had already been destroyed by growing demand for tourism in untouched spaces. It was because of this that the spots that were still wild were highly protected, stowed mostly away from people, only admired from a distance.

Dove and Carter had always gotten away with going deeper into the park and disappearing beyond the patrol of the park rangers. I knew that much from her photos. There was a point in time I'd thought her trespassing had caused a park ranger to take her life. But there had not been a single wound on her body when they found her that would indicate that was true.

Maybe Dove wanted to die where she'd felt the most at home, the most safe, the most free.

Looking back at the drawing, I noticed the sheer volume of trees that Dove had sketched around the river. There were more than could ever have been growing around there naturally, and they didn't look like mangroves or the other trees I'd seen in books or in the ancient videos I'd found online about Central Florida swamps. It could have been the way Dove had drawn them on the map, but I wasn't sure.

It was also the way they were spread out, in neat and even rows, lending space for clear paths around the river and toward the several large rectangles I assumed were buildings at the end of the river. It was as if the trees were meant to guide your eyes all the way toward the buildings. Wild woods couldn't grow with that kind of intentionality; even I knew that.

Something about the drawing felt eerily familiar. My eyes flickered away from the journal and back toward the window, studying the streaked remains of the smiley face. Now it looked more like a lone, open parenthesis, containing all the sky above it.

I reached back for the journal, turning the pages all the way to the front. I'd almost forgotten the massive garden Dove had drawn on the first page, full of flowers and hundreds of orange trees. In the distance, the muted brown, windowless building that I now recognized as the same as from Dove's drawing of the Wekiva River.

"Fortunate are the gentle, for they will inherit the world."

I flipped back and forth between the new drawing and the one in the front of the journal, confirming my suspicion. The buildings were identical, down to the shade of brown.

What were these buildings doing by the Wekiva River?

There was a loud bang from downstairs and I sprung to my feet, rushing toward my open bedroom door. Rounding the corner, I saw my father, collapsed on the tile floor, completely motionless. He'd hit his head on the corner of the kitchen counter, and a gash bled above his right eye and down to the tile, staining it real salmon pink.

"Dad—" I raced over, propping his head on top of my thighs. His eyes fluttered, and he mumbled something incoherent. "Dad, can you hear me? Are you okay?"

I pulled the corner of my shirt and pressed it against the gash on his forehead, the blood soaking through the fabric almost instantly. I balled up the shirt and pressed on the cut, trying to stop the bleeding.

"Savannah?" he mumbled, his mouth opening to speak in babbles.

"What happened?" I whispered.

My father blinked around the room and then flinched at the light streaks peeking through the gaps of the closed blackout curtains.

"I—it's so hot."

My father was laughing, both his arms shaking and twitching involuntarily. He stared at me from the floor, eyes wandering like they were drinking in the entirety of the room for the first time.

"I was on my feet for too long. I must have—can you bring me some water?"

I nodded, gently lowering his head back down and racing to the kitchen. We were on one of our last clean bottles of water, I realized, both my father and I had been too busy to take our ration cards to the grocery store. I poured the remaining water into a glass, and it didn't fill it even halfway.

I heard my father's shaky breathing from behind the counter and apprehensively filled the rest of the glass with tap water and rushed to him, lifting his head to my lap and helping him take a sip. His shakiness began to subside.

"Are you okay?" I blotted the top of his forehead. "Do I need to call someone?"

He shook his head, taking the cup of water from my hands and taking another sip. "Too expensive."

I helped him hold the cold cup of water against his exposed shoulder.

"Would you also grab me one of those strawberry protein shakes we have left?"

"Let me help you to the couch first."

I heaved my dad's arm over my shoulder, steadying him as I walked to the living room and lowered him to the couch. The slack of my back never got any lighter, no matter how much older I got. He took a deep breath and closed his eyes. His whole face was a stark shade of white, paler than I'd ever seen him.

For the first time, it really hit me that if I lost my dad, I'd be completely alone. No one was left but us.

Sure, Matis was here, but he wasn't family. No one outside of my father could talk to me about my mother, about Dove, about me. And even though he didn't, the space held between us was irreplaceable. His departure would leave me sitting in it alone, forever.

The grief my father gave me in his distance, walls tall and draped with aloofness instead of resolve, was no less painful, but familiar. It was something I understood. The absence of it was uncharted territory.

I grabbed the last strawberry protein shake and carefully pulled off the seal.

NINETEEN

"2064 presidential candidate Rodger Kettington announces his call to merge the Department of Defense and the Department of Energy if elected," the newscaster's dull voice echoed from the TV.

I rubbed my eyes. Kettington's team must have had a gigantic budget for him to be promoting an election four years from now this early. The way his face seemed to peel off his bones was making me increasingly uncomfortable every time I saw him.

My father was asleep on the couch. I couldn't bear to leave him alone, so I settled in front of our ancient TV, turning the volume down to a barely audible whisper. Matis wasn't home yet, his hours at campus getting later with each passing week.

I didn't recognize the anchor on the screen, her makeup neat and perfect, eyes square to the camera. The woman who'd covered Hurricane Barbara had quietly disappeared from the network.

"Kettington cites the basis for his plan as part of his American Revitalization program, which also includes his reinstatement of partial Social Security. He's been pushing campaign advertisements heavily on various SubcutaLink AI and virtual reality platforms, after several hundred thousand requests for modules to tour his mansion on the New-New England coast.

Gen Beta voters have been part of the largest push for Kettington's virtual reality house tours, seeming to reflect fondly on his guest appearance on kids' show *The Zany Zonkers*."

The program cut to a brief clip of Kettington waving his hands in a vocal booth and then to a blue dog he played on the show.

The animated dog version of Kettington on the screen counted to three on its hand before spinning in a circle and falling to the ground. Several flashing cars drove across the screen, followed by incoherent dialogue.

I never watched *The Zany Zonkers* but remembered friends of mine talking about it in the school cafeteria. Dove had also been adamantly against me watching shows with any kind of sponsorship, which were most things on television. *The Zany Zonkers* had become a bit of an internet joke for featuring advertisements every forty-five seconds. Several child psychologists had to come forward with studies on the impact of persistent advertising on children in order for the show to adjust to showing ads every two minutes instead.

Though I'd never watched it, I could still hear the jingles sung in school, over and over again in my head.

"Step into the future, where laughter's the trend, With Joy Pods by Farmer Spend, your joy has no end!

Giggle beams and happy dreams, beamed straight to your head, Say goodbye to reality, and embrace the joy instead!"

I hummed the melody to myself, tapping quietly on my knees.

Lauren had a pair of Joy Pods. The plastic clips broke after Lauren tried to push them on top of my ears one afternoon after I'd pestered her for hours, begging her to let me try. Her parents didn't bother fixing them or getting another pair. I remember trying to glue the pieces back together, but even still, the blue power button never turned back on.

"Qucore received additional emergency funding to help finalize the testing on their heat intolerance medication being developed in Orlando. That funding will be directed to the Qucore Pharmaceutical Innovation Lab within the COF's Center of Research Development."

The story cut to a bald man standing behind a small wooden podium. "We're elated about the work being done in Orlando that's going to change how the entire nation is able to prepare themselves for warmer temperatures. Resilience is the next important hurdle for mankind's journey in adaptation. Our commitment to fostering adaptability encompasses not only innovative solutions but also a shared responsibility to build a sustainable and climate-resilient populous for generations to come."

The newscaster grinned, and cut to a segment about the latest advancements in animal Augmistums, which could be used for both protection and home surveillance. The anchor demonstrated with an unassuming white and brown dog, rubbing the top of its head with a rubber hand and then going to strike it. The dog suddenly bared a multitude of sharpened metallic teeth, lunging for the hand and pulling it toward the screen.

"And what do we think about that, folks?" the anchor chirped. The dog Augmistum pulled a finger off the rubber hand. They weren't yet commercially available. The station cut to an ad for psoriasis medication.

My dad rolled on his back, and I flipped the TV off. With the blackout curtains pulled, the room dissolved into complete darkness against the night. Dove's drawings, the technicolor flowers and deep water, haunted by the brown buildings in the distance, loomed in my head.

Through the small, uncovered sliver of the window, I saw a streetlight flicker once and then burn out, turning a deep shade of purple. My father stirred on the couch, quietly snoring. I took a deep breath and closed the curtains and to the couch, wrapping myself in my bedroom comforter, listening for my father's paced breathing. The house was quiet. No wind. Only the humming AC.

When I closed my eyes, I saw it again, the flowers, the river.

All of it.

And it didn't go away.

TWENTY

"I've only been to the Wekiva River once."

Matis studied the map in Dove's journal. I watched as his eyes skimmed around the edges of the drawn woods and over the winding Wekiva River. My fingers curled apprehensively over the other side of the pages. I fought the urge to pull the journal into my chest, knowing that I needed him. I needed to be brave. This was the closest I was to getting real answers that I'd been. Maybe part of me was just afraid Matis seeing the drawing would make it disappear. So far, it had held.

"I was young at the time. My father held me on his shoulders so I could see the fish. There was an early Augmistum model in the gift shop. I don't remember much else about it."

"Do you know why Dove might have drawn it in here?" I whispered, my eyes flicking over to my father sleeping on the couch, head still wrapped in a bandage. He didn't stir from our voices. "Or what Harmony Grove is?"

My father agreed to close the dry cleaner for the rest of the day so that he could rest. Though he protested, I offered to close up for him; turning the open sign off and hanging the last of the day's orders. Even hours after he'd left, the smell of perchloroethylene was still heavy in the room, enough to make my head spin. I didn't know how he did it.

When I locked the front door, slipping the key in and pulling the handle to make sure it didn't budge, I spotted the black cat. She flicked her tail at me several times, blinking her large green eyes. Her ears perked up at the sound of the locking door. We held each other's gazes for a moment, coexisting like old friends. I took a deep breath and extended my hand, stepping toward her. Her small body shifted intermittently in place. As I drew closer, she sprung up and disappeared into the bushes. I didn't follow.

Matis was sure my father had a heat stroke, exacerbated by the chemicals in the dry cleaner and dehydration. When he told me, guilt sat heavy in my stomach. I'd been so absorbed in Dove's writing, I'd completely forgotten to be more attentive to him. My father was like a puppy, incautious and unassuming. If I didn't step up, he was going to continue to get hurt, I knew it.

Matis brought home fifteen bottles of clean water from campus after I called him and told him what happened. Our kitchen was covered in water bottles, filling the fridge with more on the counter. Matis wouldn't take any money for them. I'd never seen that many bottles of drinkable water at one time unless there was an expected shortage and Dove had been proactive about going to the store. My father and I were never as prepared.

Matis hesitated for a moment before answering. His eyes flickered back to the map. "No, I don't."

After I'd had enough of fighting myself on it, I decided the only person that had any chance of understanding Dove's journal was Matis. He was quiet when

I showed him, not commenting on any of the information Dove had left behind, even on the details related to the early virtual trials of the medication. He only read over each page and flipped to the next one, never rushing. I studied his face as he went through the journal, seeing where his eyes narrowed or jaw tightened, but he said nothing, only taking in the information as he read it over.

Matis treated Dove's notes with the reverence you'd lend to a classic novel, slowly making his way through the pages. I fought the urge to thank him, in fear that acknowledging it might ruin the moment, and I'd be back to my own thoughts, circling questions I didn't have the answers to.

Matis' hand brushed mine as he shifted through the pages. I felt safe, seen. The world felt fuller, smaller. I studied the intensity in his gaze.

Matis reached the second of Dove's drawings and flipped back and forth between the drawing on the first page and the second the same way I had.

"Doesn't it sort of look like the 2100 Florida model? Here?" I ran my finger across the sections of trees that seemed to go on endlessly, all the way to the borders of the page.

"It does, a bit." Matis stared at the drawing, puzzled.

"It doesn't make sense why she would go through the trouble of sketching this in such detail if it wasn't important. And—" I took the journal back from him. "What could these buildings be?"

Matis pressed his lips tightly together, a habit of his I noticed whenever he was thinking intensely. It made his mouth look like a small zero underneath his nose. "I don't know. Really, I—"

My father stirred from the couch and Matis stopped himself. His eyes wandered the living room. Matis lowered his voice. "I wonder if we should go out there and try to see it for ourselves."

I felt the color draining from my face, the tingling in my legs. Every part of me swore off ever going to the Wekiva River and getting close to where they found Dove's body. The weight of her spirit loomed like smog. Nothing in my conscious mind wanted to see it, to know that was the place it happened in. It would make all of this too real.

But still, there was something to the notion of finding out, of understanding why she'd sketched the Wekiva River in her journal, only to die beside it.

"Do you want to go?"

I stared at the journal, still open in Matis' hands, studying the lines from Dove's sketch, every intentional curve of the landscape she'd sketched between the pages. If there was anything to be clear to me, it was this.

"I think we have to."

TWENTY-ONE

We left for the Wekiva River in early Friday morning. I set my father up with water for when he woke, keeping the blackout curtains closed. His forehead was still discolored with a gash and bruise, but was starting to improve. I left the TV remote near the table by his feet, trying to think about what else Dove would have done to keep him pacified. I settled on an extra blanket and a strawberry protein shake. He was snoring.

"He'll be okay," Matis whispered.

I took a deep breath and followed him out the front door.

The sun was rising, rolling higher alongside us as we pulled out of the driveway. I couldn't feel the heat yet, only seeing the daytime through the light.

I wondered if riding in a boat was similar to being in a car. Did they rock the same way? I didn't have a frame of reference.

Matis decided we were taking the back roads north, trying to stay out of the way of commuter traffic. These were roads I'd never seen, so out of the way of my father's errands or the local routes to the grocery stores. I quickly lost my frame of reference for knowing where we were, entirely untethered. I was a stranger in my own city. You could leave me out here, and I wouldn't find my way home. I gripped the passenger seat.

Orlando extended her arm in front of me, and we sped toward the inside of her palm.

There was so much to take in; the winding path off the carved, straight lines of the highway. It was all quickly becoming less defined. It felt good to move like this, to roam, further from definition. We raced past tucked neighborhoods like ours, houses with hoarded driveways and chickens roaming the front yard. Where one thing was different, another the same. An old man waved from his front porch. I waved back.

I couldn't sit still, running my finger up and down the edges of the paper in Dove's journal, over and over. My grip left an indent in Matis' passenger seat, nails leaving half-moons etched in the leather. I knew this was important, but I couldn't shake the feeling that we shouldn't be doing it. I tried to distract myself with the cold AC against my hands, breathing in, grounding myself in the car. I could turn back, but who would that make me?

Matis was surprisingly quiet. The radio was off, the car filled with a steady hum of the road. He was focused, lips pulled tight in that familiar zero, deep in thought. I didn't want to interrupt.

We reached a tall gate near the end of one of the back roads where several Augmistums waved cars through toward a sign:

STATE PARK ENTRANCE: 8 MILES

I focused on my feet as Matis waved back at the Augmistums and we continued down the road. There was a new hole in my left sneaker. I could see my toes. They waved through the gap.

The area surrounding the state park was cleared of all infrastructure and most of the remaining natural features; only shrubbery and scattered bushes. Otherwise, it was a world absent of green. I wondered if it was to deter people from living near the park. Perhaps the state needed the resources for something else. Or maybe they just wanted them out of the way; the trees, the people.

We continued down the empty road. Matis tapped his SubcutaLink, finally turning on the jazz station. His speakers hummed, harmonizing with the road noise. It brought me a bit of peace. My fingers eased the lock they had on each other, my hands wrung red from the pressure. I watched the flush recede.

There was a large fence in the distance. Just above it, finally, trees, the tops tall as mountains pressed into the sky. The closer we drove, the more of them broke through the flat horizon, reaching, cutting into the blue.

I pulled from the window, suddenly claustrophobic. It was one thing to see this kind of height on man-made structures like skyscrapers and apartment buildings, but knowing Earth had her own ways of building cities was something else. It lacked control. These were trees that would, in theory, outlive me and everyone else. It was striking to see that kind of strength, especially with how little of it was left.

The sky gradually disappeared under the canopy of tree leaves, engulfing the car. Sunlight flashed between the gaps between branches, dancing shadows teased the world above. How small we were. It got darker. My eyes wandered out the windshield, seeing the lush, deep green world enveloping us.

This didn't feel right. I was a fish that preferred plastic castles to coral. I'd learned to love what I had. What would I have done with a whole ocean to hide in? How would I know which trees to cling to?

Matis slowed the car and I peered out the passenger window to a small brown sign a few feet off the ground.

We'd arrived.

It was still early, there were just two cars were in front of us. Matis reached out across the center console and tapped my knee. His hand was warm. I reached for Dove's journal, running my finger over the top.

Matis pulled forward. An Augmistum in the booth took our park fee, $105 per car for a day pass, and gestured toward the parking lot. The rock crumbled underneath our tires. No wonder it was almost impossible to come here anymore.

Matis rejected the $20 from my wallet when I tried to hand it to him.

The Augmistum whirred, instructing us to stay on the designated paths and kayaking routes.

"A reminder that there is no swimming allowed," the Augmistum beeped and then opened the gate.

Matis rolled the window up and placed the parking ticket on the dashboard. A family unloaded their two small children from the back seat. The little girl screamed as her father ignored her protests against sunscreen. The older boy opened the SubcutaLink on his wrist, tapping into a game as he leaned against their car.

We found a spot near the back of the lot, and Matis swung open his door. I heard the hymn of insects, wind whispering through the palm fronds. Paralyzed, I stayed in the car, peering out the windshield.

"Hey!" Matis tapped gently on the glass. "You coming?"

I closed my eyes. There was no escaping the event horizon.

I nodded and pulled my bag on my shoulder, getting out of the car. The weight of Dove's journal bounced against me, helping my heart rate settle.

The air was what hit me first, in all of its richness. The clarity. It was so clean it ran like a salve across my throat and lungs, dissipating the burning in my chest. After a few breaths, I barely remembered it at all.

We walked toward several signs and a small wooden bridge leading down the hill and into the park. My ears were ringing. A bird circled overhead, slow and detached.

Near the end of the bridge, there was a dirt path that curved around the bluest water I'd ever seen. Not even Dove's drawing could capture the real vibrancy, paired against the deep green trees. You had to see places like this through your own eyes to appreciate the depth, the spectacle. It wasn't until then I understood what nature meant.

I was finally within it, having the experience, not parasocially with a stranger. This reality was mine to absorb, not to experience secondhand. No wonder it felt so surreal—I'd never seen anything like it outside of a screen.

"It's so beautiful," I whispered to Matis.

"It is."

I finally saw the bird as it landed on a branch in the distance. It tilted its head toward me, before leaping up to the very top of the tree. We shared a silent exchange, before I lost track of him between the leaves.

"Do you want to look at the drawing?" Matis asked.

I nodded, digging through my bag for Dove's journal and flipping open to the page. My eyes flickered between the sections of the drawing, following the river to the sketched brown buildings.

"I think we have to take a kayak to get over there," I whispered. "There's no way there's a path we can walk to get that far in."

Matis nodded, studying the map. His face was tight.

"Are you alright?"

Matis looked back over at me, smiling. The breeze teasingly lifted the brim of his hat.

"Of course."

Matis laid a hand on my shoulder, not too heavy. I didn't have to shrug him off.

We walked around the crystal water and toward the kayak rental station. I couldn't take my eyes off it, bumping into Matis back as we reached the door. The bell chimed as we walked inside.

Overpriced T-shirts and sunscreen lined the back wall, along with memorial photo books of the park through the years. Photographs of families in kayaks butt up against older photos of couples and kids in the water, before they'd stopped allowing it. Everyone was grinning, facing sparkling in the water. There was no AC in here, the room stuffy and dated. A sole Augmistum worked the counter.

I hadn't seen one human besides the family in the parking lot.

We stepped around the model alligator skeletons and stuffed animals. Matis handed the Augmistum $80 for the rental and it gestured toward a kayak for us to carry to the water. I tried handing Matis the $20, but he pushed my hand away without looking.

"You must stay on the designated kayaking routes. Only enter the water if there is an emergency. Do not touch, feed, pet, or photograph the wildlife of Wekiva," the Augmistum whirred, extending its arm with a virtual waiver and then gesturing toward the back door to walk the kayak to the water.

Matis grabbed the front of the kayak, and I grabbed the back. The hill curved downward to the water, the ground gradually becoming soft with water. My foot sank into the mud, the Earth pulling me toward her. I stepped up and shook her off.

We reached the water, and Matis and I lowered the boat in the water. Matis stood in the water up to his calves, holding the boat steady.

I stared at him from the sand, feeling some of the water soak through the top of my sneakers and into my socks. I wiggled my toes. I'd never been in the water before. I'd never dared.

I eased forward, letting my right foot slosh into the water and then my left. The water was cold, soaking through my socks to my skin. I wondered, though it was forbidden, what it would be like to sink completely into the water, letting the cold run over my face, encompassing all of me. Would I be transformed into someone new? Would I disappear?

Matis found my eyes, a tired warmth sewn across his face. He seemed surprisingly comfortable by the boat, steadying it against the small waves by the shore.

"Have you done this before?" I asked him, twisting my feet deeper into the sand.

"Maybe in a past life," he joked. "How hard could it be?"

The water splashed my ankles, reaching all the way up my exposed calf. It was icy, sending pins and needles over the length of my leg. I closed my eyes and took a deep breath, focusing on the breeze instead of the water.

You are on earth. You have not been swallowed up. There is no danger here.

I felt the Augmistum's hollow eyes peering into my back from the top of the hill. It must be observing me, my apprehension. I took a more deliberate step, as the water brushed below my knees and sent a chill up my back. I took a sharp inhale. The air was too clean. It was sharp in my chest.

Matis steadied the kayak.

"Swing your leg over and climb in," he whispered. "You'll be okay. I've got you."

I took another breath and put my right leg and then my left into the boat, sitting firmly in the front. The kayak rocked, and my hands lunged for the sides, willing it to stop. I fought the urge to shout, staring down into the water. This was nothing like being in a car. You couldn't do anything to stop the water. It surrounded you, so you were inherently held captive to it. You had to relinquish the control you had on land. Here, the water controlled you.

"You have to move with it," Matis insisted. "Flow with the water instead of against."

I nodded and made myself dizzy. Matis pushed the kayak from the shore. I could not will myself to look up, focusing on the small waves lapping against the side of the kayak. My fingernails left several nicks in the paint, revealing the kayak had once been a shade darker than the night sky, the lighter grey color it was now simply painted over top.

"You're gonna be fine," Matis called.

I couldn't breathe right, like I was drowning before I'd even hit the water.

"Savannah, you have to look up," Matis instructed. "You're my eyes."

As we glided forward, the forest went quiet. Truly quiet. We were far enough to no longer hear the road, the dull rumble of civilization disappearing into the background like a distant performance.

I heard Dove's voice in my head, and I closed my eyes. The sound of the water became more intense, but I only heard it instead of being overwhelmed with the sight of it. I heard rustling through the brush, crickets chiming together in a gentle choir, the screech of a hawk. The breeze rustled my hair.

My soul and body were no longer intertwined. None of this seemed real. I didn't seem real. I felt the familiar lump rising in my throat, the speedy beating of my heart, the uncanny notion I was being sucked away from the present and becoming a passenger without agency. Every nudge of the water pulled my further away, from here, from myself.

"Savannah—" Matis called again. He was so far away. I could not open my eyes. This was the only way I felt safe, this sensory deprivation, only in my partial interpretation. It was all my brain could take. The kayak drifted forward. I'd lost track of time. Time turned over in my head, I'd come unstuck. I could be anywhere now. I could be anyone.

Matis' hand grabbed my wrist. I tried to recoil, but he stopped me. Gently, he guided it to the water. The coolness tingled my fingers as they grazed the surface, barely breaking through. Matis pushed my hand further, till it disappeared into the water, for only a moment. It did not detach from me. I did not detach.

"Savannah," Matis whispered this time. "You need to open your eyes."

I took one more careful breath, then I opened my eyes. The light stung and the world came into focus. Trees encapsulated the space, so tall and dense that I couldn't see the distant fence marking the park's border. The water was darker, rich Florida black water against our pale boat. I heard less rustling in the bushes and more of the gentle lapping of the water on the side of the kayak. We weren't rocking anymore.

Finally, I peered out past the boat at the scene ahead of us.

The traditional Florida woods we'd been in when we entered the park disappeared. It had transformed into something different, more surreal. Emerging from the sandy, dry dirt ahead stood hundreds and hundreds of orange trees; more than I'd ever seen.

In the distance, the top of several earth-brown buildings, looming and rectangular.

"It's exactly like Dove's drawing," I said, the words barely escaping my mouth.

"How did we get here?"

"I followed the side of the river it said we shouldn't."

A breeze pulled the humid air from my face, shrugging at my disposition.

Matis paddled forward. I saw several *DO NOT ENTER* signs he had navigated past to reach this point. He turned back to look at me, holding the kayak steady in the water.

There it was in front of me. Just as Dove had said it would be. I felt my hesitation, the urge to return. The urge to forget this, and stop.

The designated kayaking route clearly split off from here and went around the opposite bend, sending you toward the rental stand. This was prohibited territory. My eyes flickered out to the building in the distance and then to Dove's journal in my lap. The wind rustled the pages, and I looked out from the drawing to the world in front of me.

"Fortunate are the gentle, for they will inherit the world."

"We have to keep going."

Matis handed me my paddle.

TWENTY-TWO

A few weeks after Dove died, I tried closing my eyes and walking toward the main road in our neighborhood again. I was sick with missing her. The grief compelled me to do it. Here was my desperate attempt to shake the disconnectedness and fog I'd been living in since she died. I'd disappeared too. I missed school for three weeks, floating around the house like a ghost while my father went to work. Eventually, an Augmistum from the school came to our house and threatened my father with prison time if I didn't return. He'd signed the acknowledgement without reading it.

Even in the heat, the outside was far more comfortable. How long could I linger than in the doorframe of Dove's room? I'd spent hours staring at her unmade bed and cluttered desk. Outside, at least, I could see that life was continuing. Whether or not I'd be part of it was another question.

On the curb, I told myself to trust the sound of the cars, to feel the vibration of the tires as making contact with the road. I would know how much louder the cars would be would become as I got closer to the road, and the feeling of the heat would be enough for me to recognize where I was. To stop.

I'd walked these paths enough with my eyes open. I was no stranger to this place. It should come back like instinct, even if Dove's voice was no longer there to guide me. I made it into my new private game, pretending I was a wild animal creeping through the swamp, relying only on my other senses. I was a gator sinking into Florida black water.

I was a rattlesnake, shifting through tall grass. I was a deer evading predators. I was an opossum that wouldn't get hit.

It was the way Dove had wanted me to understand the world around me, that I belonged within it the way these animals did.

Taking cautious steps forward, I turned all my attention to the soles of my feet and my ears, listening, feeling. The earth responded to my footsteps, buzzing beneath with presence. I pushed on it. It pushed back. Wind raced over my ears, pulling on my hair. I took several steps forward, listening intently, remembering not to hold my breath, to trust my judgment.

There was a roaring in my ears. I imagined a forest floor, crawling with insects, amphibians and mammals, all gliding past each other. I was not just a quiet observer, but as much a part of the tangled ecosystem as anything else.

Nature was as much me as I was nature.

Suddenly, my mind turned. I was in a body of water. A river. And I was not a gator or a fish. I was myself, somewhere unfamiliar. I didn't belong here. I could disappear. I could drown. In front of me, face down in the water, a body. My fingers reached out and pulled on a curtain of black hair with not Dove's green eyes, but my father's brown ones. Mine.

My eyes shot open. I was nearly in the road. But there were no cars. No people. The street was silent. The road by our house had been closed for work that had not yet started, routing traffic in a different direction. Everything I thought I'd understood had all been nothing but my imagination, my fear.

Florida taunted my misunderstanding of her. She cackled in the buzzing power lines, wind whispering between the buildings. My skin baked under her sunlight.

I had been so sure still so wrong.

I raised my fingers to shield myself from the sun; they glowed red underneath the light. My forehead was damp with sweat. I was still alone, like I had been, even though I'd nearly convinced myself otherwise that I hadn't been.

Maybe I'd learned nothing.

TWENTY-THREE

The only detail from Dove's first drawing I didn't see were the flowers.

I didn't see a single one as we continued up the river, only scattered small bushes laying low beneath the orange trees pushing through sand. My eyes darted between Dove's drawing and the landscape, wondering what would have made her draw so many impossibly vibrant flowers on top of an already surreal scene.

The flowers in Dove's drawing *did* capture the overall *feeling* from paddling through this place: utterly dreamlike.

I'd seen hundreds of photos of orange trees. They were on the pages of textbooks, plastered across billboards, and license plates, but I had never seen one close before. We were told about the importance of citrus crops in Florida, how they had been our main export until several unstable cold snaps had killed them off and major agricultural businesses divested from the fruit. Now, the intense summers had become too much for most of the orange trees. They were the kind of plant that needed things to be just right to survive.

Oranges had become more a symbol for Florida than something of reality. It was about what they *meant*, not if you could actually *see* them.

The trees seemed to go on forever. I pushed my paddle into the black water, my eyes drifting between the drawing and the landscape in front of us. Dove had managed to capture the essence of the place perfectly.

I wondered what this place looked like before the orange trees were here: higher water, knees of mangrove trees peeking out of the surface, the illusive alligator sunning on a fallen branch. The land between the trees was completely overgrown by brush and dense grass. Any remaining walking paths had long been grown over. Perhaps there had been people here once, traipsing through the woods, hearing nothing but the quiet rustle.

Would it have felt somehow more surreal? Or simply honest?

"What do you think?" Matis called.

"It's. . .unbelievable." I shook my head.

"Is it like you imagined?" Matis pushed his paddle into the water.

Two birds soared past us overhead, disappearing off into the distance and out of sight.

"I don't think I let myself imagine it at all."

I let my hand wander back to the water, skimming the surface. It was so dark, you could only barely make out the remains of fallen, ancient trees soaking in the bottom of the riverbed.

It felt like we had been rowing for hours, the brown buildings drifting farther and farther out past the trees. I wondered if it was some sort of illusion, a mirage playing on our exhaustion. My arms were starting to ache from the paddle, itching under the sun. Several birds sang in the distance.

"I get why they don't let anyone back here." I turned back to Matis.

"Kind of a shame that no one gets to see it though," he replied, looking toward the trees. There was an expression on his face I couldn't place, and I realized it was distance, or fear, from his thoughts or me.

My eyes followed his, and we watched the breeze pull leaves off the branches before they fell into the water.

"Do you think it would still look like this if everybody could?"

Matis stopped paddling for a moment, pulling on the tongue of his sneaker. "Probably not. Look what we've done to everything else."

I understood completely why Dove had come out here as often as she did.

There was nowhere else like this anymore.

When I looked back, I noticed Matis was laser focused on the buildings that were drawing nearer. I turned forward.

The buildings were earth-brown, like rich soil or the trunk of an ancient tree, just as Dove had drawn them. They were windowless, perfectly angular, looking both natural and wholly out of place. Quite like a coffin. Quite like a raised bed.

I saw a small dock and accompanying ladder beside a paved pathway toward the buildings. Uneasiness grazed her fingers across my neck. There was a strange energy to this place, the dreamlike feeling melting into a surreal disassociation.

"Stop paddling," Matis whispered, loading his paddle back into the kayak.

I did the same. Without the constant rowing, it became eerily quiet. Not even the breeze rustled the trees. Several leaves fluttered and landed in the water beside us, traveling beside our kayak in silent solidarity. I could just barely hear the water.

The current pulled us forward, closer to the edge of the dock. Matis grabbed hold of the ladder in front of us, using the strap of one of the life vests to tie us to the pole. He climbed on the dock and extended his hand, which I took and climbed beside him. Matis started walking the path toward the buildings, and I followed closely behind. The closer we got, the more I realized this place looked familiar for reasons beyond Dove's drawings.

"Doesn't this look like the 2100 Florida model?" I thought of the thousands of tiny orange trees, scattered across northern Orlando. Here we were in the heart. Dove was more entangled in this than I thought.

"Mmm-hmm," Matis said, nodding. He wouldn't look at me.

The buildings were even more angular and intimidating up close, alien against the rest of the landscape. I couldn't even see a door. Peering around Matis, I saw a sleek blue sign propped at the end of the sidewalk. It had a small metal emblem on one side, an orange tree extending leaves toward all corners. In front of the sign were two neat raised beds, full of a rainbow assortment of flowers.

Harmony Grove: A Qucore Ecological Death Care Center

I blinked, reading the sign again.

"Qucore built this?"

I stared at the flowers, in every shape and color, just like they'd been in Dove's drawing. They weren't arranged as if they were growing from the ground; instead, they seemed to spring from the sign itself.

"What does—"

Matis walked to the sign, staring at it. He reached the raised bed and picked a single flower from the assortment: orange with a myriad of petals. A chrysanthemum.

"What is an Ecological Death Care Center?" I finally found my voice, unsteady in the back of my throat.

Matis started walking back toward me, spinning the flower by its stem in his hand. He stared at the sign. "I think it's a human composting facility."

"What?"

He nodded, studying the flower. Matis stared at the building, not surprised, only assured, like seeing the building in person had confirmed a suspicion. I watched his eyes take in all of it, an ache growing in my chest.

"Why is it out here? And why would Qucore *have* something like this?"

"I don't know."

My eyes wandered to the rest of the woods, the orange trees, vibrant and healthy in a place they shouldn't be. "Does that mean the orange trees are grown with—"

"Bodies. Or least, maybe they're going to be."

Matis' voice was hollow as he lowered the chrysanthemum to his side, studying the sign. My hand flew to my mouth. Tight sickness curled up my throat. I wanted to throw up. I couldn't look at the trees anymore, their beauty colluded with their origin. Now, they were only haunting, like twisted fungi growing from the people below. Scavengers.

The wind pulled several flower petals off the chrysanthemum. Matis turned away from me.

"Savannah, there's something I—"

"STOP!"

A loud bang and sudden whir broke the quiet. I looked to see several drones looping over me and Matis, beady red eyes glowing against the blue sky. The roaring whir of their fan blades crackled in my ear, making me dizzy. To our left, two automated and armed park rangers raced out through the woods, weapons drawn. I shoved Dove's journal into my bag and lifted my hands, freezing in place.

One of the Augmistums raced toward me and Matis. It got close enough where I could see that its eyes were nearly all pupil, no whites, no iris. That was common among security-focused Augmistums. Their eyes didn't need to be convincing to humans. They just needed to observe us.

"You are trespassing on private property," the park ranger hissed, its mouth not moving while it talked, voice booming through a small slit in its neck. The drones continued whirring above us. I felt their red beams sting on my back. I could barely breathe.

Matis raised his hands. He glanced at me. My hands were shaking.

"We're so sorry," Matis said, clearing his throat and looking forward. His eyes flickered between the brown buildings and the Augmistum glaring down at us. "I'm an assistant of Professor Powell's. We were coming out here to see the final construction of the facility. I didn't realize we weren't supposed to get this close."

My eyes widened, but I didn't speak.

"Then you must know this area is highly prohibited," the park ranger hissed. It got closer to us, and I felt myself bracing, as if I was going to be hit. It smelled so metallic. I could hear the whir of its computer. Only its silicone skin created the illusion it could be human at all.

"Yes," Matis said. "I would hope so. Again, I'm so sorry about this."

The Augmistum whirred, and my body tingled with a new and unfamiliar heat. Its colorless eyes flushed a deeper green than the woods, before fading back to an empty pupil. It must have been checking for weapons. I kept my eyes low, watching as it stepped forward.

"Present your identification."

Matis nodded, slipping one hand into his pocket and pulling out his wallet. He handed the Augmistum his COF ID, and then gestured for me to take out my own. I could barely breathe as I dug into my bag, pulling out my ID and handing it to the other park ranger. I couldn't even look at Matis.

"Why is she here?" The park ranger glared at me, my ID indicating my undergraduate status.

"She's my research assistant," Matis lied through a tender, focused expression.

"An undergraduate?"

"Yes," Matis replied. "Professor Powell is aware."

The park ranger flipped my ID, scanning its authenticity. I couldn't help but stare, fixated on the darkness in its eyes. The absence of life. My head was whirring, and I felt like I was sinking into the twin dark pools, disappearing. What was Matis talking about?

Wind rustled through the orange trees, and I caught my first smell of orange blossoms. My nausea got worse.

The drones continued whirring, hanging over our heads like two ruthless angels. Matis didn't break his gaze with the Augmistum. I stared at the stains on his shoes and the ground beneath us. I looked for any excuse to look away.

The sidewalks were newly paved, a detail missing from Dove's drawing. Maybe they were too new for her to have seen. There was the disconnect again, drifting out of my body and into something else. Matis and I now superimposed on Dove's drawing, alongside the Augmistums and the drones. Only sketches, part of the landscape, part of the background.

Did Dove actually wanted me to find this place?

And had Matis known, and then lied to me?

Waiting for the Augmistum to scan our IDs and return them to us took a millennia. I didn't look up until I saw its silicone fingers extend to me.

"Don't come back here without properly registering." The Augmistum handed our IDs. "Next time, we'll have to issue formal citations and make arrests. Even if you are working at the university."

"Of course." Matis nodded. "We're sorry about the inconvenience."

The Augmistum waved its hand, and Matis nodded, led us to the dock and our tied kayak. I barely looked up, mindlessly lowering myself to the boat. I didn't flinch as it shifted around in the water this time. I was so unbound to my body I might as well have already been sinking. I didn't turn back to the windowless building, the modern burial site, wanting to do whatever I could to dissolve it from my memory. I couldn't. Of all Dove's journal entries, the drawing had become the most horrific of them all, because this one I could see.

Matis untied us and I started to paddle forward. I knew the Augmistums were still watching us, waiting for us to get out of range of the building. I felt the eyes of the drones falling off my back, listening to their whirring disappear. My stomach didn't ease. I tried to focus on the water, plunging my paddle deep into the water and pushing us forward. I kept waiting for the moment I would wake in my bed, but it didn't come.

I heard Matis breathing quietly behind me, my eyes stinging with tears. What a horrible dream. What a horrible trick. Qucore's logo burned into the back of my skull, Professor Powell's knowing gaze from just over the sign, every last orange, the flowers.

The flowers.

I thought of Dove's careful notes, her observations on shadows and light, the way she'd illustrated each petal and root so vividly. Her drawings had captured this place not as a sanctuary, but as a marker of the cycle she saw here—where people came to rest, to fade into the ground among trees as old as the state itself. Life and death, intertwined like the roots below.

A home for the inevitable.

Was Dove thinking about the end, about making herself some sort of contribution? Is that why she wanted to die here?

Or had someone made sure she had?

We paddled in silence all the way back to the kayak rental, my rage preventing me from looking back and saying anything to Matis. I heard him breathing. It made me angrier. When we arrived at shore, I stared out at the water. It lapped up against my legs and I started walking in. Staring down the river, the water twisted my reflection, and wrapping it in the water.

The brown buildings completely were concealed from view back here. I supposed that was the power of imitating the colors of the earth; if no one knew to look for it, it could disappear completely, sinking into the swamp.

I tossed my bag toward the dry sand and walked further into the water. I could feel Matis' eyes on my back, but I didn't care. I tipped my head back, letting the cold water envelop my hair, before I fell back and collapsed underwater. I'd never held my breath before, and the dark suffocation of my closed eyes and held lungs sent my heartbeat radiating into my head. I held steady for what felt like an eternity, waiting for the pounding to stop. It didn't. I rolled over and opened my eyes, into the blurry portal underwater, spying the grass on the sand bed floor, small dotted fish making their way upstream.

I held my breath, feeling my throat and lungs burn, my vision blurry. A fish bumped against the side of my calf. My body started to ache; I was getting dizzy. I held firm, pushing myself back underwater with my arms.

I wanted to stay here. It was so quiet. I could finally disappear.

I could find Dove. I wouldn't have to keep searching. This could all be over.

I felt a hand pull me back to the surface, Matis holding my arm. I shouted, trying to pull away from him, and he pulled back harder.

"Savannah, stop."

I coughed up water, feeling snot drip down my nose to my lips. I wiped it off on my shoulder. I wanted the peace back. I wanted the quiet. I'd peered behind the illusion. I knew there was no way of getting it back.

My vision was blurry when I looked up at Matis. He held me up from the water.

"It was an accident." I frowned, seeing as though he didn't have a problem lying to me. It felt good.

"Let's get you home and dried," Matis whispered, kinder than anyone had spoken to me in a long time.

It enraged me. The openness of his face, the sweetness in his words. How clean he was. How orderly. How he'd treated my grief like it was just another variable he had to take into account when he spoke to me, and not the only thing I had; the only thing tangible. But he could lie in my dead sister's room, and *right* to my face.

"Do you think Dove knew about that place?" I spit, unable to contain the words any longer. "Do you think that's why she was here all the time? Do you think that's why they found her here?"

Matis wouldn't look at me.

"Come on." I nudged him, shoving a wet hand into his side. "Tell me. You must know something. Clearly you did."

"Savannah, I don't think it's a good idea to talk here."

"Where is it a good idea to? Because you could've told me *days* ago you knew what Harmony Grove was and you didn't. What? Are you involved with that too?"

"I didn't know *what* it was. I knew *of* it—"

"Liar."

"I'm telling you the truth," Matis whispered, but his grip tightened around my arm. "I don't know any more about what happened to Dove than you do, I promise."

He kept his hand locked around my arm. "You're going to get us in serious trouble. I can explain, I promise."

"How do you expect me to trust you? You *lied* to me Matis."

An Augmistum peeked its head out of the rental booth, eyeing us. I pulled my hand away from his side and straightened. Even in the heat, I was shaking.

"I'm done talking to you. You may know Qucore and whatever this bullshit is, but you didn't know Dove, I *did*. And she's the only thing that matters to me." I hissed, and stormed up the hill toward the parking lot. I was soaked, my clothes stuck to my body, hair matted at the base of my neck. The roaring of the drones was still ringing in my ears, my nose clogged with river water, my mouth bloody from chewing on my own cheek.

All I had left was what I saw. And what I saw was the end of everything.

I turned around in time to see Matis drop the chrysanthemum into the water, catch the current, and disappear.

TWENTY-FOUR

Dove was asleep, hunched over our kitchen table. Her dark hair was in matted tangles over her face, an empty orange juice carton on its side beside her.

I needed her to turn on the stove because I couldn't reach it. School started in an hour and our father was already at the dry cleaner. He hadn't woken her. I'm sure he didn't notice she was asleep at the table, pouring himself some water and disappearing. I was becoming less and less surprised with what he didn't notice: the mounting clutter, the bugs in the kitchen, whether Dove and I ate. Dove probably looked at him like part of the furniture.

Dove was at the table when I went to bed the night before, and was still there in the morning, journal tucked underneath her arm. Her breathing was deep, steady, and consistent. I'd never seen her like this before, so intimately vulnerable and soft. Dove was always so intensely aware. Her stillness was jarring, her eyelashes floating over the tops of her cheeks, making the dark rims under her eyes even more hollow.

I neared her, reaching out and tapping her shoulder. She didn't move. I hesitated and then took another step forward, leaning closer to her face. "Dove?" I whispered.

Her teeth clicked.

"Can you help me make breakfast?"

She didn't move. My eyes darted toward the clock on the stove. I'd be late if I didn't eat now.

I found a dirty frying pan in the sink, washed it, and then put it on the stove. I stood on the tips of my toes, reaching for the burner. I leaned far enough that the exposed skin of my midriff hovered over top. I reached for the burner, small fingers grazing over the side. Without realizing, I turned the heat all the way up. Moments later, when I turned back, hovering over the stove, the heat struck my abdomen. I bit my lip fighting the urge to cry out.

I jumped away from the stove, slamming into the side of the table and jolting Dove awake.

"Savannah," she shook her head, pulling me back. "Don't play with the stove."

"I was trying to help," I mumbled. I could still feel the heat across my stomach, like a lash against my skin. Dove turned the stove off.

"You're going to get hurt."

"You weren't waking up."

Dove's face tensed. Wordlessly, she wrapped her arms around me, getting on her knees and pulling me in close. The smell of orange warmed the inside of my nose as she pulled my head above her heart. Her voice grazed the top of my head, her fingers pulling me in tighter.

"Let me do it, okay?" she whispered.

TWENTY-FIVE

I didn't speak to Matis for several days. I didn't speak to anyone for several days. I busied myself with my final exams, pouring over notes and textbooks in a futile attempt to drown out the questions swirling in my mind. The dry cleaner patrons passed in and out of the store, blurring together into indistinguishable faces. I couldn't remember if I attempted to make polite conversation or not; it didn't matter. None of it did.

I couldn't source the root of my anger. Trying to unpack any of it was overwhelming. Matis had lied to me, but there was more to it. Ever since we got back from Wekiva, a venom coursed through my chest, suffocating me from within. I felt it when I tried to engage with customers, each word thickening in my throat. I felt it when I stepped outside, the sun beating down on my back, another autumn spent unseasonably warm; the world indifferent to my turmoil. The world indifferent to everything.

I wasn't just angry at Matis; I was angry at everyone, even Dove. The more I thought about it, the more I craved answers, as if knowing the truth would somehow ease the weight of my grief. The curiosity gnawed at me, mingling with my sorrow. I hated how I was forced to wrestle with these mysteries alone. I hated even more that I had to confront them.

Matis had spent even more time at the Center of Research Development. Our paths crossed less often, and I was thankful for it. Sometimes I'd hear him leave early in the morning, making breakfast and then quietly locking the front door. I'd come out only after I was sure he'd already left for the day, peering around the corner to the bedroom door he continued to leave open. I know he wanted me to give him a chance to explain. I was past the point of thinking he was worth it.

My father recovered from the heatstroke, dove back into his work like nothing had changed. Patrons whisked in and out, leaving piles of clothing on the counter. He smiled at them, forever unfazed. But he was moving slower, taking longer to get things clean. The smell of perchloroethylene intensified, clinging to the air like a heavy fog, a constant reminder of the world I was trapped in.

One afternoon, in the dry cleaner, I was sorting through hangers and cleaning supplies. The rhythmic sounds of machines echoed, my ears buzzing. As I folded a stack of freshly laundered clothes, I glanced at my father, who was meticulously hanging a dress shirt.

"Dad," I started, my voice hesitant. "Do you think about Dove at all?"

The air held still. He looked up, his expression distant, as if he were gazing through me rather than at me. "Sometimes," he replied.

I closed my eyes, squeezing them shut.

"Do you miss her?"

I heard him laugh.

"How could you not?"

I opened my eyes. He was grinning, stacking the shirts into a pile.

"Maybe we should talk about Dove more," I finally said

He smiled but it didn't reach his eyes. "We could." His voice was even, almost cheerful. I wanted to shake him out of his indifference, to make him confront the reality we were both living in, but the distance was palpable, and I felt powerless to bridge it. We wouldn't.

The tension hung in the air, and I turned back to the clothes.

After my father left to run an errand, almost against my better judgement, I walked into the backroom. I moved toward the door, the creaking of the floor under my feet almost too loud. I peeked inside, just enough to see.

The room was cluttered, filled with containers of perchloroethylene and old cleaning supplies stacked in a corner. But it was the far side of the room that made my breath catch in my throat. There, in the corner, was a shrine-like structure, a makeshift altar to Dove. I recognized old photos, scattered and framed haphazardly, my father's private memorial. There were photos of us as children, Dove and me, laughing, playing in the yard— tucked into a secret space in the corner, where only my father would ever see them.

I heard the front door open, but it was too late for me to leave.

"Savannah, what are you doing?" My father's voice was sharp, pained. His face, once soft and unreadable, now had a rigid edge, his features tense. He finally looked real.

I froze, my heart hammering in my chest. "I—what is this?" I asked, my voice trembling. My mind raced, desperate for an explanation.

He stormed over, his hands shaking slightly as he grabbed my arm, pulling me away from the doorway. "Get out of here. I don't want you exposed to this, I told you that."

My eyes flickered back to his private memorial.

"I'm sorry."

Walking out, I tripped over the small bowl of cat food he'd placed by the door. The black cat was now a constant guest, prowling at his feet, curling around his legs as he worked. Sometimes I'd catch her roaming outside of my bedroom door or on the windowsill as I left each day for the dry cleaner. My dad was always looking for her, his little shadow.

When I let her outside, she'd walk with me for a moment before darting back into the bushes. She never hung out with me for very long. I was alone more than I'd ever been.

Trying to get sleep had also become even more difficult. Every time I closed my eyes, I saw it—the brown buildings, looming over the multicolored flowers that had absorbed the entirety of the forest floor. The orange trees had become impossibly tall in these visions, bearing too much fruit, tugging the tree limbs and falling down; so ripe they were already rotten. Professor Powell's looming gaze was omnipresent over the curvature of the earth, watching, knowing.

In all these nightmares, I was weightless, unbound to Harmony Grove or the planet, tethered only to whatever was in front of me, pulled into whatever got my attention. It could be the black sky, the park ranger's void eyes or uncanny voice, a rumble from the depths of outer space. They all absorbed me the same, taking me away, folding and shelving me within them. There was nowhere to shake out of, nothing to come back to in these dreams. It wasn't much different from having my head completely underwater.

I couldn't breathe either way.

Deep down, something in me feared what I might uncover from here as much as what I didn't. What if digging into the past led me to something I wasn't prepared for? Something much bigger than Dove and our family. The hole inside me kept growing, threatening to take all of me into it.

Giving up would mean more of the same. The house, the dry cleaner, the endless summer and waiting, just waiting, forever. My skin would turn to leather. The storms would take the roof. I'd be waiting until my father would inevitably end up in Harmony Grove. Until I would too. The dry cleaner would disappear, crushed to sand, astroturf rolled over top. And that would be the end.

- *Wildfire rips through Alaska, taking out several new housing developments and killing 216 people.*
- *Autonomous drone strike in New York City on Columbia campus in response to protest over rising rent. Six children are caught in the crossfire.*
- *There is a pounding in my chest. It's new. More intense than I remember.*
- *Qucore sets a 2060 target date for launch of their heat intolerance medication.*
- *Israeli occupation expands its reach into Lebanon and Egypt, US votes against UN call for intervention.*

I froze. Dove had never written anything in these notes calling attention to herself. I studied her handwriting, the intensity in the scribbles, the slanted loops and curves made tight by what I could only assume was fear, but of what?

Four full circles were at the top of Dove's list, all perfectly shaded.

TWENTY-SIX

Rain returned, wind and water pushed against the glass of the dry cleaner. Summer storms had never usually lasted this late into the fall. No matter how much water came, the heat never seemed to lessen.

I'd done enough studying for the day, so I started sketching several characters around the corners of my notebook, giving them wide swirling eyes and angular mouths, as if they were going to suck all the information in my notes and then the whole page. I drew flowers too, hundreds, all shapes and sizes around the borders. Without the color they were more haunting than vibrant, nothing compared to Dove's drawing, let alone what we'd seen at Harmony Grove. My pencil snapped in half.

I'd barely made any progress. After the drawings and Dove's initial note, the last dozen entries didn't give me any information on Qucore or Harmony Grove or Dove. It was just more pages wrought with grief. I was coming up empty and didn't feel any closer to understanding what to do.

The front doorbell jingled. Lauren pushed through the dry cleaner door, carrying a pile of suits and dresses that she plopped on the counter. She grinned when she saw me. I hadn't seen her since our fight or spoken since I texted her an apology. Her face was wonderfully tan.

"Hey, Savannah," she said, laying out the various suits and dresses on top of the counter. She wiped the sweat off her forehead.

"You okay?" I asked her, reorganizing her piles to pair up the suits and dresses, then reached below the counter and grabbed an order form for her. Her father's Augmistum usually brought the family clothes in. I didn't think Lauren had ever come into the dry cleaner by herself.

"Exhausted," she said, tapping several buttons on her SubcutaLink. She pulled two silver dots off from behind both of her ears, conduction headphones, and slid them into her pocket.

"Do you think we can get all of these cleaned before next Friday?"

I assessed the pile. "Probably. I'll have to ask my dad, but it should be okay. I can always call you and let you know if it's gonna be longer."

"Cool, thank you."

Lauren started filling out the information on the order form, tapping the pen against the desk.

"I haven't handwritten anything in forever," she said, laughing, her handwriting squiggled and shaky. "I'm so used to auto transcription or typing it if I really have to."

"My dad still prefers everything on paper."

"It's so vintage."

I nodded, putting one of the suit jackets onto the rack to bring it to the back. Lauren's fingers slipped out from around the pen, streaking through her signature.

"This is an awful lot of stuff." I turned back to the counter, lifting a red dress and tucking it onto a hanger.

"We just got back from Curaçao," Lauren said, grinning. "My dad has been wrapping up his meetings prior to the election. We got back late last night."

"Are you on dry cleaning duty?" I raised my eyebrow.

Lauren straightened. "I volunteered, actually. I'm hoping I can help reduce his dependence on using his Augmistum for everything."

I caught myself before the smirk bloomed over my face. "Your mom couldn't take care of it either?"

Lauren's lips pressed tightly together. She rubbed her fingers along the hem of one of her mother's dresses on the counter. Her face fell. "No, she couldn't."

"Okay," I replied, lifting two more dresses to the rack. "Maybe you just wanted to come see me."

Lauren's face reset back to gentle exhaustion, eyes fawned open. "Maybe I did."

Lauren dated the bottom of the form and slid it across the table toward me. Her nails were a pastel pink, like strawberry milk. A singular flower was drawn near the tip. I stared at it.

"How was Curaçao?"

"So spiritually fulfilling," she said, pushing her hair back over her shoulders. "You should see the ocean there. It's so beautiful."

The thought of the water, expansive and unending, made my stomach churn. I thought about how filthy the oceans were at this point, everywhere. Dove had written about it in her journal. I could only imagine how much worse they had gotten since then.

"The ocean isn't really my thing." I shrugged, feeling the dirty water all over my skin. My mind drifted back to the springs, the clear cold water, the drones, the flowers. My head spun.

"You'd have to see it to understand." Lauren folded her hands together.

I didn't push back.

I ducked under the desk in search of another slip to write a note for my dad about expediting the clothes. Because it was Lauren's parents, I was sure he'd do anything. He'd seen her father on television, or in the photos I occasionally received from Lauren on their trips. I don't think they'd ever met. My father greeted Lauren's father's Augmistum at the door of the dry cleaner. I watched him peer outside to catch a glimpse of their sleek car rolling out of the parking lot. I knew my father held out hope that for whatever reason, they'd find common ground to be friends.

That's how my father felt about most people that considered him invisible. Like they should be idolized *because* they considered him to be nonexistent. Like that proved something about their own value and said less about his own.

"There's a lot going on right now. I wish I'd been able to enjoy it even more." Lauren frowned.

"You seemed really happy in all the photos."

Lauren laughed. "Glad you couldn't tell I was overwhelmed." She tapped her pink nails against the counter. "There's a Qucore press conference coming up soon that my parents and I are attending." Lauren leaned her hip against the front counter. "It's for the medication they've been working on for over a decade or something. There's a presentation for donors on the status of the trials."

Lauren delivered this information like she'd never said anything more boring in her life. I couldn't imagine anything more earth-shattering.

"Really?" My heart jumped to my throat. I felt the whirring of the drones at my back, saw the Harmony Grove orange trees extending in the distance. Qucore was getting everything they wanted. But Dove had wanted this too, the moment her work would actualize. Maybe Matis meant it when he said that we would all be thankful for her, even if she wasn't here to see it.

Matis was the only one that could help me put the pieces together.

"The Kettington family is supposed to be there too, so my dad wants him and my mom to try and get as much face time with them as possible. It seems like my dad's work can really turn toward the *next* election. 2060 seems handled. This fall is going to go perfectly. 2064 will be here before we know it!"

Lauren folded her hands on the counter. I still couldn't name a single candidate for the 2060 election this year. Rodger Kettington never missed a chance for airtime.

"I don't know what my parents are so antsy about," Lauren continued. "It's not like we're going to get access first. It's getting distributed to low-income people before anyone else."

She stared at me, and I watched her eyes drift over my head to the inside of the dry cleaner; the peeling paint, low ceilings, and cold fluorescent lights. My hand was inches from hers on top of the counter, mine sunburned, red, and blistered with calluses from rowing in Wekiva; hers a smooth, warm shade of golden brown. She looked so much younger than me, brandished, nourished by life. I wondered if she saw that when she stared at me, the way I noticed it when I looked at her. I wondered if she felt pity where I felt anger, and if she sat with it the way I did. Or if she felt nothing.

"It's still definitely a good thing to get it to the people that need it first," Lauren said, trying to recover the air in the room, pulling her hand from the counter. "I just hope we don't have to wait very long."

I thought about Dove, hunched over our kitchen table, papers strewn around her. Wiping my father's blood from the tile. I'd been drinking the tap water, letting it leave a metallic taste in my mouth. I kept forgetting to buy clean water.

"You've never come *in* here, have you? Hell, you don't even drop *me* here." I spit at her. The words came out before I filtered them the way I always did for Lauren. Before I put on the character she found the most palpable. "You've never set one *foot* in here, even though you know my father and I are here almost every day."

Lauren's eyes flickered from the floor and to me. "Savannah, I didn't mean it like that. I'm sorry."

"I know you didn't." I grabbed the rest of her father's expensive suits and shoved them on the rack. "But your intention isn't attached to your words the way you think it is. Sometimes you sound like a pompous jerk."

I could see the sting on Lauren's face, but she didn't move.

"I'm sorry. I know how important the drug would be to you and your dad. I shouldn't have said it like that."

"No, you don't, Lauren." My heart pounded in my chest. I swore I heard Dove's laugh tumble out of the machines in the back, whirring and then disappearing. "You have no idea what it would mean to us."

Lauren glanced at the floor and tapped her toe against the linoleum.

"You know I feel incredibly guilty for the way my family and I live," she whispered. "I know it isn't fair. I know that nobody else I know gets the privileges I do. I'm not blind to that Savannah. I just—" She fiddled with the strap of her bag. "I don't know what else I'm supposed to do beyond being sorry about it."

"Maybe you should try and figure that out."

Lauren nodded, crossing her arms at her waist.

"I'm sorry I've never offered to drive you home from the diner," she whispered.

"You can owe me a ride then."

We stood there for a moment, with the machines and their quiet rumbling. A faint smile came over Lauren's lips. She reached into her bag and handed over a small wad of cash and ration cards.

"For the dry cleaning."

I counted the money in my hands. It was more than double what the cost was. Lauren said nothing.

Neither did I.

TWENTY-SEVEN

I stayed late that night at the dry cleaners, looking out the front doors for Matis. He disappeared for more time each day. With Lauren's news, I wanted to talk to him more than ever, to understand how Dove, Harmony Grove, and Qucore's medication all seemed to be so intrinsically connected.

My father had already left for the evening. I told him that if any last-minute customers came in I would set their orders aside for him to take care of in the morning, gently rushing him out the front doors. He was uneasy on his feet. I didn't take my eyes off him until he was out of sight and around the corner to the house. The empty dry cleaner grew quiet. I hoped that the last few feet wouldn't overwhelm my father entirely before he reached the front door. I tried not to think about it.

The silence was actually nice and the rain had let up, which meant that the outside glistened under the last rays of sunlight and then with the flickering streetlights. The reflection of the water made even our road take on a cinematic appearance, something out of an old movie. If you caught it on camera, in isolation, it was as if the world hadn't changed at all.

I understood now why Florida had once been the primary destination in the United States for vacations. Now that I had seen Wekiva, drifting quietly through the river underneath the canopy of trees, the allure had begun to make sense. I knew the theme parks had always been the draw, but there was more to it than that. Florida had once bustled with life all across the state. There had been animals you couldn't find anywhere else in the country, plants that grew and thrived in impossible heat and humidity, untouched swamp. I didn't think it had ever been about Florida being *solely* beautiful, because I didn't think that it ever was *just* beautiful. It had been untamed. Undeveloped. The southernmost state tucked away from the growing metropolises of the north and west, a uniquely unconquered oasis people could slip into and sometimes disappear in. That's why people loved it.

Florida had always danced on the edge of being uninhabitable, we'd just pushed it over the threshold instead of maintaining the balance. That was what Dove had wanted me to learn when she made me read the books written about the ecosystems or the old ways of living. Floridian wide-open doors and front porches, the animals, the buzzing woods. I didn't hate Florida, I hated what we'd done to it.

And maybe, I hated what we'd done to everything. Perhaps, I always had, but it wasn't until Dove's journal that I realized the extent of everything that had been taken and changed, for all of us. Not only the landscapes or the policies, but how we as people had been transformed forever too.

Two of the streetlights twinkled and shut off, leaving a dark gap between the sidewalk and road. Two cars drove past, and the gap swelled with light bouncing off the slick pavement before it emptied and disappeared.

I closed my notebook and reached in my bag for Dove's journal, sliding it open on the counter.

• *Twenty-five people are killed in an apartment collapse in Miami after sea level rises cause a fracture in the foundation.*
• *West Virginia declares a state of emergency over coal mine runoffs from a collapsed mine. The federal government rejects the request for additional support.*
• *Harmony Grove increases planting of orange trees around the foundation of the property to support the 2100 Florida plan.*
• *Psychologists report 45 percent uptick in cases of post-traumatic stress disorder, anxiety, and depression in New England. Most relate their symptoms to the failing ecosystem.*

I'd been right. Harmony Grove had been part of the 2100 Florida plan. Dove's note confirmed it.

In the corner of this page, Dove had left more fully shaded neat circles. The number of circles on each page was growing at a much faster rate now, only two or three pages before another full one was added.

I ran my finger over the circles, studying where they grew and shrunk, perfectly in the same place on every single page of the journal. She'd notated them all so perfectly, the most steady part of the whole journal.

I put it back in my bag and gathering the rest of my things. The rain had restarted, casting heavy drops against the dry cleaner windows. I neglected to bring an umbrella, so I folded the top of my bag and tucked it under my arm as I walked over to the front door, scrambling in my pocket for the key.

There was still no sign of Matis.

As I turned around and locked the door, I felt the rain slide down the back of my neck and soak through my shirt. It was cold at first, warming against my face as I stared the storm right in the eyes.

I wondered how acidic the water was.

I glanced at my phone. There would be another bus to the research lab departing from here in a few minutes.

I started walking.

TWENTY-EIGHT

My skin was ripe with goose bumps against the blaring bus AC, the rain leaving a strange slick on my skin even after it dried off. The bus was empty. I closed my eyes and felt the hum of the wheels buzz against the road and my skin. The rain pelted against the bus, blurring the lights from the highway into a cacophony of color, streaking over the dense rain and darkness.

We eased onto the main highway, the distant billboards blurry against the rain, smeared against the storm clouds. The streetlamps cast their light against a nearly drained Lake Underhill, and I spotted several stray herons half-heartedly carving their beaks into the sand, more mechanical than instinctual.

In the low light, against the pavement, I saw Orlando was nothing but a wasteland. There was nothing to distort it. Nature fought against the far corners, clawing to get back within the parameter. The heat no longer broke, not even rain or darkness an escape. There was never a reset, only a constant boiling. No escape. Uninhabitable without intervention.

I closed my eyes, and let myself feel the movement of the bus on the road, the lights flashing against my closed eyelids before they faded into the humming darkness. My head bounced against the cool glass on the window. I pressed my tongue against my gums, rolling back my shoulders. I could almost rest.

The bus slowed, making a turn, and my eyes fluttered open, spotting the COF building in the distance. The Augmistum turned back and gestured for me to exit.

"Last bus comes in an hour," the Augmistum whirred as I brushed past it and out the door. "Don't forget that ID."

I stopped, turned around. Its eyes were lifeless, locked on the roadway. It couldn't even rotate its neck to stare back at me. The doors slid closed and the bus pulled away from the curb, leaving me alone with the lights in the parking lot. I heard the distant trees shifting in the wind. I tightened my grip around the top of Dove's journal in my bag, pulsing my fingers against it two, three times. The pages scratched against my fingernail.

What was I missing?

"Miss Alonso?"

Professor Powell stepped outside through the sliding doors, insulated cup in her right hand, binder tucked under her left arm. Her eyes gazed forward, like they had every night in my dreams, against my being. The wind pushed her hair across her glasses, but her focus remained undeterred. I heard drones whirring in my head.

"Professor," I said, nodding. My chest tightened.

"Mr. Wallace left twenty minutes or so ago. You just missed him." Her tone was indifferent. I felt the fear in my stomach, wondering if she'd ask me about our trip to Harmony Grove.

"Ah, that's my mistake then. I can wait for the next bus."

Professor Powell shook her head, turning back into the glass doors. The wind pulled the hair back from her face, streetlight against her nose casting a shadow on her cheek.

"You're more than welcome to wait inside if you'd like. I was getting ready to leave for the evening."

She stepped into the building. I let go of the spine of Dove's journal, and followed behind her. Inside was eerily quiet, the only light coming through the tall glass windows from the moon or streetlights; none of them flickered. The 2100 Florida model was barely illuminated, but I could still make out Harmony Grove's orange trees extending across the northern part of the state before disappearing into the distant shadow.

Professor Powell stepped toward the front desk and then sifted through some paperwork. I inched closer to the 2100 Florida model, my eyes falling back onto the space where our house should have been. I wondered what Dove would think about the forecast that our safe space wouldn't exist in the next forty years, if she'd known that this is what everything was really leading to.

"Your sister really was an exceptional person," Professor Powell called from the front desk, still focused on her papers. "I was. . .very distraught after her death."

I looked over. Professor Powell was staring at the 2100 model.

"It was hard to move forward without the person that made so much of this possible. There was a point where I almost gave up after Dove died, but I—" Professor Powell set down the binder. "I knew she wouldn't have wanted us to change course. I think she knew how much of a mistake it would be."

"That sounds like Dove."

Her shoes clicked against the tiled floor, easing behind me.

"I have a theory there are two types of people in this world—some set the stage for circumstance, others must ride out the situations as they unfold. Sometimes setting the circumstances for the right outcome requires sacrifice, both minor and major. Sometimes they are good. Sometimes they are not."

Professor Powell sat down next to me, her shoulder brushing mine as we looked at the model.

"Either way, there are only so many chances to find out which type of person you are. What you do when those choices are in front of you is how you find out."

Dove's journal weighed heavily against the outside of my leg. There was a moment of quiet. I heard Professor Powell breathing.

"Dove wanted you to see this someday," she continued, looking at the model. "She knew it might be hard at first, but maybe as you got older, you might grow to understand how important it was. I'm sorry that she couldn't be here to show you herself."

My mind wandered to the flowers in front of Harmony Grove, hundreds of them in all varieties; the lush garden Dove had drawn on the first page of her journal. The world she'd known about and what she'd hoped became of this one.

"Thank you," I whispered. "It feels like I hardly knew who she was."

Professor Powell locked on the curvature of the glass. “I think you know plenty. Probably as much about her as she did.”

A cloud rolled over the distant moonlight, darkening the atrium. I lost track of where our house would have been on the model, the curved greenery and winding sidewalks of the redefined neighborhoods blurring together in an indistinguishable collective. It was more comforting to see it this way, half obstructed. You could believe this was a model of anywhere, perhaps some distant landmass or a civilization already lost to time. It didn’t have to feel like I was peering into some kind of fortune teller, brandished by spirits that could only hold up their intentionality, not the outcome.

The soft hum of the evening settled around us.

“Professor Powell,” I started, letting Dove’s journal lean against my side in my bag. I settled on a half-truth. “I found some of Dove’s old notes at home. There were these half-moon and circle tracking dots in them. Do you know what they might mean?”

Professor Powell didn’t look up immediately, her gaze lingering on the model, as if she were taking a moment to choose her words carefully. She turned to me, her expression soft but unreadable.

“Dove was always very thorough,” she said, her voice even. “Those circles. . .they were probably part of her process—tracking things, patterns. It wasn’t unusual for her to use symbols like that. They’re all over her early notes.”

“But you don’t know what she was tracking?” I pressed, a knot forming in my chest.

She paused, the space between us thickening. "I think it's more about understanding the process. Dove didn't always share everything she was thinking. Sometimes, things don't have an easy explanation."

I nodded, looking back to the model.

Professor Powell rested her insulated cup on top of the model. The cup was covered in quickly sketched flowers and trees, small birds and animals soaring over the sides before disappearing around the bottom. The drawings were crude, but honest and imaginative. A world so unrealistic, it could almost be part of the 2100 model itself.

"I like your cup," I remarked, as the clouds let several streaks of moonlight collapse into the atrium.

Professor Powell tapped her fingers against the side. "Thank you. My niece made it for me. She passed away a few years ago. One of the flash floods in 2056."

"I'm so sorry," I replied.

Professor Powell nodded. "We all have the people we carry on, right?"

She took a sip from the cup. As she raised it to her lips, I could smell it clear as day: orange juice.

"Dove loved orange juice," I quipped, almost laughing.

Professor Powell's lips parted into a semi-smile as she lifted the cup off the top of the glass, wiping the small circle of condensation away with her sleeve. Being this close to her, I could see the deep wear lines in her face, the freckles on the bridge of her nose. She was almost human, like a boring, everyday office worker.

She pressed her lips together.

"I can say it's become a favorite of mine after knowing her."

Beyond the doors, I could hear the rumble of the bus tires against the road.

"Thank you for letting me stay inside," I said, nodding to Professor Powell. "I hope you have a good night."

Professor Powell nodded. "I'll follow you out to the lot."

She retrieved her binder from the desk, followed me toward the sliding glass doors, and tapped her ID against the scanner to secure the building.

"Nature infrequently favors intervention." Professor Powell stepped out into the parking lot, walking over to a sleek automated car parked in the first row. "There are things that have to run their course. The middle between two outcomes is no place to get caught." Professor Powell gave me a curt wave. "Goodnight, Savannah."

"Goodnight."

The Augmistum pulled open the bus doors, its fixed neck forward, glazed eyes on the road. Professor Powell's black car departed into the night before I got the chance to see it leave. I turned back, watching the COF building disappear behind me.

For a moment, I swore I caught a glimpse of Dove sitting on the bus in the rearview mirror, but it was just a trick of the light. Underneath the faded billboard lights and flashing advertisements, against the clearing storm clouds of the night sky, I realized I was looking at myself.

TWENTY-NINE

• $150,000 is defined as the new lower "middle" class.
• Wildfire tears through the remnants of the Amazon rainforest, putting some of the final acres at risk for total destruction.
• As the coastline recedes and orange crops decrease, Florida becomes more reminiscent of Orange Island.
• There's never enough water to drink at home. Supplementing with orange juice isn't working anymore, not even the additional Vitamin C and the sugar ease my exhaustion.

I'd been up late for the past two nights, skimming Dove's journal, Professor Powell's careful stare embalmed in my brain. I was sleeping only a little better, with one hand curled around the spine of the journal. I felt more at ease that way, less lonely. If the medication was as close to being done as Matis and Lauren had said, I wanted to finish reading Dove's notes and move on with appreciating the work she'd done, not wading through her memories.

I ran my finger across Dove's scant writing. I didn't understand her last note. Maybe she'd been ill. I sensed her sickness in the scribbling of her writing, the force she pressed from pen to the paper, leaving small indentations around the ink. No matter what Professor

Powell had said to me about Dove's hopefulness and desire for better, there was something on Dove's mind causing her immense distress. The journal only further proved it. I knew my sister.

At least, I hoped.

Only a few pages were left, but I'd only grown more hesitant the closer I got to the end.

I was excited about the medication being released. That's what I had to keep telling myself. I should be the biggest supporter of Dove's work reaching the masses. It seemed like the only *real* good news that had happened in a long time.

I just wished she was here to see it.

I still needed to draw the line between Harmony Grove, Qucore, Dove, and the medication. The constant search for answers had left me with a sense of not only recklessness, but deep apathy. And there was only one way through it.

I had to make sense of this. I had to talk to Matis, but every time I found the courage within myself to walk across the hallway to his open door, he was gone. By the time he'd get home, early in the morning the same way Dove had, I was teetering too close to sleep to bother having the conversation. I'd watch as he'd walk into his bedroom, toss his backpack to the floor, and pass out, the streetlight shifting across the side of his face until the sun streaked through the windows.

Standing from my bed, I peered out the window toward the dimly lit street, watching a stray car pass down the road and disappear. My eyes flipped to the clock on my computer. It was 2:30 a.m.

My restlessness got the better of me. I pulled on a pair of pants over my pajamas and walked to the kitchen to get some water. There was a throbbing pain in my head. The kitchen was hot and humid, even in the dead of night, Florida reaching her dull fingers through the walls. I pulled my hair off the back of my neck, tucking it under the shoulder of my shirt.

I saw Matis had brought home some more clean water, the bottles lining the counter. Guilt sat like a pit in my stomach. How long had I let us go without?

I reached for a bottle as the front door quietly squeaked open, accompanied by shuffling feet. I set my water on the counter as Matis came around the corner.

"Oh—" I hardly managed to get out.

This was the first time I'd really seen him in weeks. His eyes were lined with exhaustion, much of the light stripped from his face entirely. Matis looked like a ghost version of the person I'd met in the dry cleaner for the first time months ago, the warmth reduced to a small glowing ember I only caught again when he smiled.

"Hi, Savannah," he whispered, setting his bag on the counter. "You're up late."

I nodded, fiddling with my water. We sat with the low hum of the refrigerator. There was a dull ringing in my ears that almost harmonized with it. Matis cracked open a water bottle and took a slow sip. My unwashed face felt sticky. The silence was deep, and as we stood together, I'd forgotten the bridge I was trying to build. I squeezed the water bottle in my hand.

"I'm sorry about what happened at Wekiva," Matis whispered. "I should've been honest with you from the beginning."

"Listen," I started, ignoring the lump rising in my throat. "I—I don't know—"

"No, you didn't know. And I could've told you, but I didn't." Matis sat on the counter across from me. "Ask me anything," he said, nodding and resting his hands in his lap.

"How will I know you're not going to lie to me?" I swallowed, my heart pounding in my chest.

"I promise." He extended his hand out toward me.

I hesitated. "What happens if I find out you're lying to me again?"

He took a sip of his water, his eyes wandering to the back of the kitchen and then back to me. "I'll make sure you never have to see me again."

The small flame in his eyes jumped between the exhausted shadows of his face. My mind whirred.

"Okay." I reached forward and shook his hand, his skin warm against my own. "How did you know about Harmony Grove?"

Matis nodded, taking another drink of water.

"I saw the emblem on paperwork I was filing for Professor Powell." Matis tapped his heels against the cabinet before crossing them over top of each other. "I didn't know what it was or why Qucore was building it. I knew it was in Wekiva, and when you showed me the map in Dove's journal, I felt like we had to go see it."

"Why didn't you tell me you knew what it was?"

"I thought it would scare you out of going at all."

I frowned.

"I mean it," Matis continued. "I was afraid if you let yourself get anxious about what Dove might have known about or what could have happened, you wouldn't go try and see it for yourself. I thought it was more important for you to face it than hear the information from me."

I set down my empty water bottle. "But you knew there were going to be Augmistums and drones?"

"Yes, but you were with me."

"How were you sure it was going to be okay?"

Matis grinned, deepening the lines around his eyes. "Right now, Qucore has to stay all bark, no bite. Or they'll lose their funding." He folded his hands back across his lap.

"You knew more than you let on," I said slowly. "Not just about the place, but about why Dove would have known about it."

Matis exhaled sharply through his nose, looking away before meeting my gaze. "Yeah," he admitted. "I did."

I waited. Matis set his water bottle down.

"I knew Qucore was working on something *like* Harmony Grove. I found reports, buried under layers of approval processes and university research grants, about how Qucore needed to start growing oranges. How certain areas had been marked to 'observe the viability of long-term agricultural habitation through human composting.'"

Live data. Viability. The words sank in, heavy and suffocating.

"Are you saying this was all part of the research plan in tandem with the medicine?"

"I don't know how connected they are, just that Qucore has been pitching them in tandem for a long time."

My pulse roared in my ears. "Did Dove know?"

"Maybe she suspected," Matis said quietly. "Maybe she saw something she wasn't supposed to." He sighed. "That's why I never told you everything. I didn't want you to think—"

"That they had something to do with her death?" My voice came out colder than I expected.

Matis looked down at his hands. "I don't know. I don't want to believe that. Especially of Qucore. Or Professor Powell."

The house vibrated with the sound of my father's snoring, the hum of the fridge, the distant murmur of wind through the broken screen in the kitchen window.

I curled my fingers against my knee. "You should've told me."

"I know."

Matis crossed his arms over his body.

"I don't know if Harmony Grove is why Dove was in Wekiva when she and Carter died. I can't pretend to know your sister enough to guess her intentions. All I know is that the work Dove knew she was doing with Qucore was dedicated to building a better future. Everyone that's working on this project is. In life and in death even."

I sank into the kitchen counter.

"I don't understand why Qucore would be focused on stuff surrounding death if their goal is to keep people alive. What's the point of this medication if they're still building a. . ." I choked on the words as I tried to say them.

"That's the thing, Savannah." Matis leaned back. "It's about both. The people passing on support the people still here. The people still here can give honor and reverence to those that are gone. You know better than anyone how horrific the world has gotten. Wouldn't it be dark to think that there isn't peace in death either? Cast aside and wasted, the same as in life. The medication isn't designed to make you live forever."

"It gives me a bad feeling," I whispered.

Matis hopped from the counter and walked to where he'd set his backpack. He sifted through the notebooks and pulled out a manila folder. I watched him flip through the contents and he handed me a piece of paper and a photograph.

The woman in the photograph was a spitting image of Matis, deep skin and braided hair that fell past her shoulders. She sat on a park bench, several palm trees framing the background, the sunset disappearing into the distant horizon. She had the same warmth in her eyes he did.

"This is my mother," Matis began. "She was a nurse. She died of heat stroke three years ago when the AC went out in the hospital. She was taking care of thirteen patients by herself and passed out. She never woke up."

"I'm sorry, Matis."

Matis ran his finger around the edge of the photograph.

"I know you are. You're the first person I've met that could really understand why what we're working on is so important. For my mom. For Dove. The people that gave everything to others, and saw nothing for it. That's why this work matters. That's why I need you to trust me."

Matis looked at the picture before moving it behind the paper. At the top was the Qucore logo, and a printed version of the 2100 Florida model. My eyes fell to the dense orange grove. I could see it extending from what I now knew was the Wekiva River and all the way north. It was even more surreal when confined to a single piece of paper, rather than a standing model. The print made it feel like it was something tangible to follow, to chase. Not something imaginary confined to a sterile university atrium.

"Something like this can only be possible if the right people are working together to actualize it," Matis said. "And it can be. The world will change, forever, once this comes to fruition. That means something. It's coming, a chance for a new beginning."

I folded my arms low across my chest. I wanted to believe him wholly, forget my own doubts, let whatever fear dissipate and believe that the world wasn't as fucked as everything was painting it to be. I wanted to let that be reassurance enough. What else was there? Indifference? Would hope make me feel as powerless as the absence of it?

"I saw Professor Powell, when I went to the COF building for you the other night," I replied. There were three cracks in the tile. "She spoke highly of Dove. Of the project. Of needing to set circumstances to ensure the right outcomes. All very clinical. She also didn't seem to be too bothered by the fact I was on the campus without you."

Matis gathered the photograph of his mother and tucked it back into the folder. The map stayed on the counter, perfectly smooth around all four corners.

"I think she sees a bit of Dove in you."

I laughed. I couldn't help myself. "I am not a *fraction* of the person Dove was."

"Maybe a fraction is all you need to be." Matis slung his bag back over his shoulder.

"Do you know anything about *why* they want to plant the orange trees?" I asked Matis, staring back at the map. "They could be planting anything there, but why oranges?"

Matis shook his head. "No idea. They're not really natural for so much of that area either. But, maybe they're trying to change that."

I nodded, taking another drink from my water bottle. I glanced at our kitchen table.

"Dove loved orange juice. It was the only thing besides water I ever saw her drink. Professor Powell had some the other night too, oddly enough. There was a moment where I...almost felt like I was talking to Dove again. Like I could feel her presence with me."

I scoffed. "I know that probably sounds insane."

Matis was unphased. "Maybe the orange trees are for Dove then."

This time, I laughed. "Hilarious."

"Hey, it's just a theory." Matis shrugged. "Maybe she gets to be part of all this after all."

My face felt hot. I uncrossed my arms. "Thanks."

"You don't owe that to me."

"Maybe not yet." I pressed my lips together.

A small grin came over Matis' face. "Maybe not."

THIRTY

I woke from a nightmare complete with whirring drones from Wekiva flooding the skyline until they swooped down and swallowed Matis and I whole. I was drenched in warm sweat, shaking.

I sat up and realized my bedroom was cold for the first time in months. The heat had finally broken by the third week of November. It was a new record, for the eighth year in a row. Only two sweaters were in my closet; one was much too small for my arms, and the other one of Dove's.

I stood from my bed and walked to the closet, staring at Dove's old sweater. I couldn't remember when I last saw her wear this. I only knew the day I'd taken it from her closet and tucked it in the back of mine. It was a few weeks after she'd passed. I pulled the dark blue sweater over my head, feeling the scratchy fabric rubbing against my skin.

I'd gotten so used to my bare arms in the heat that the feeling of the fabric on my skin felt constraining and unfamiliar. The sweater smelled like mildew, with the faintest note of orange. It itched.

The house was quiet when I left my bedroom. Matis had left for campus, my father for the dry cleaner. The black cat sat quietly in our living room, large green eyes peering at me from the couch, bouncing her tail against the cushions. I grabbed a bottle of water from the fridge and stepped outside, letting the cool air brush my face.

It was usually too hot for habitual walks. Today, however, the cold air brought a renewed desire in me to explore, and I set off down the road. The street was quiet just before the morning rush. Scattered cars raced past toward the main road, and I followed their path, running underneath the flickering streetlights. My heart pounded in my chest, legs burning, waking up.

Coming to the corner, I saw the beginning of dappled sunlight breaking through the low-hanging clouds. Everything was scattered in pinks, oranges, and reds. The air didn't hurt to breathe. Not today.

I felt the desire to close my eyes. I thought of Dove. There was hardly a sound to be outside my heartbeat and the quiet clicking of my shoes against the sidewalk. The world was standing still, holding its breath too.

My eyes fluttered closed, the world shrinking and expanding. I stepped forward, inching into the city. The noise increased, more cars, buses with their whirring engines and squealing brakes. I heard muffled music, loud phone call conversations dimmed by the whirring street noise.

Undeterred, I felt my way forward. I knew this place. I'd lived beside these same buildings for as long as I'd been alive.

This was the only place I'd ever known. This was home.

My hands felt around lampposts and the cracked pillars of buildings, down glass storefront doors. I made my way past the mailbox, the long black fence in front of the used car lot, with snake vines crawling over the top reaching for the roadway. My shoes kicked against stray grass. I caught myself from tripping on a cracked lip in the sidewalk, cut through by deep weeds. The breeze beckoned me on, a gentle hand against my back, a marching order.

I knew I'd neared the last intersection before the turn onto the larger road. I heard the car horns blare, smelled the gasoline. I quickened my pace, joy leaping from my throat in a laugh, the first real one in a long time.

My fingers slid across the cool metal of a lamppost. They buzzed with the cold.

Suddenly, I heard the sound of another pair of shoes across the pavement. My eyes fluttered open, seeing an old woman unlocking the front door to the electronics store on the far corner. Inside, hundreds of TVs were already on and broadcasting, all facing through the large window. I nodded in her direction and she frowned, stepping inside.

I clasped my hands against my face.

I'd done it.

I'd seen without my eyes. I'd made it to the edge of the road, and stopped. I'd understood the boundaries, where they ended. Where I began.

Several cars raced down the stretch and turned onto the main street, joining the flow of traffic toward downtown. The noise didn't bother me anymore. It was a reference instead of an inconvenience; a marker, not an abrasion. All of those cars had people in them, going somewhere. Small ecosystems played out inside the metal frames, crossing their world lines with mine once and probably never again.

The glow from the televisions caught my eye, and I turned and saw the tail end of a commercial for the latest SubcutaLink model. The design was cleaner, the distinction between machine and skin harder to distinguish.

In the last frame of the ad, I saw the journalist from the Hurricane Barbara broadcast staring into the camera with a jarring pink lipstick and a vibrant orange shirt. Her eyes were overly bright, the way an Augmistum's were. Not a single vein in sight.

She tapped her wrist, extending her hand over her shoulder and winking before the ad cut to black and she disappeared. The broadcast returned with a man younger than my father with a fixed, straight line expression. They were arguing the gender identities of recent mass shooters before another story about increasing climate migrants from the southeast.

A graph popped up, demonstrating the number of migrants moving to the Midwest and New-New England was expected to increase by forty-five percent in the next eight years. The broadcast went on to interview several families fleeing north, citing the rising temperatures and increasing storms as their reasons to leave. The people on screen had weathered faces, crinkled eyes, and sunspots all over their skin. Their hair was whipped wavy by the humidity or the growing ocean, small children clung to their mothers' necks. One of the girls had startlingly green eyes. I blinked back at her.

We returned to the anchor, and in the captions through the glass, I could barely made out the text.

"The upcoming initial distribution of Qucore's revolutionary heat intolerance medicine, Forticlime, is expected to commence after a press conference in two weeks."

Forticlime. There it was.

Dove's work had a name. It had a release date.

"Now, heat intolerance medication?"

I saw the anchor laughing through the glass.

"Explain that to this cold front—"

THIRTY-ONE

"Can you believe it?" I screamed to Dove, throwing my head back, watching two vultures circling above our neighborhood. They were the first birds I'd ever seen in flight—dark and magnificent, looping in perfect coordination.

We'd had an awful rainstorm the day before. Flood waters whipped through downtown, pulling squirrels from their hiding burrows in the abandoned buildings and tearing through any low-lying brush to wash away the occasional snake or rat. The air smelled distinctively moist, the sun glowing against the strewn grass. I watched carefully as the ants returned to the mounds, pushing the dirt against the water, creating a wall. The earth ached with water, runoff, and blood.

"They're so beautiful!" I shouted, laughing, waiting for Dove to get closer so that we could stare at them together. Seeing birds was such a rarity. More often than not, the sky was dead space beyond the seeded clouds or private plane.

Dove walked over, squatting next to me and resting her head on her knees. Her eyes flickered to the vultures, blinking them in. Dove's arms were flushed red and sunburned.

"What are they doing here?" I jumped against the fallen foliage, accidentally pushing into the ant mound.

Dove only leaned over and rested her head against my shoulder.

A stray ant crawled on the base of my ankle, biting into the side. I started to cry.

Dove studied the circling birds, letting me cry it out. I reached my fingers down my leg, scratching the place the ant had been until my fingernail nicked into my skin, blood rolling down to my sock and staining it pink. I pressed the sock against the cut, trying to stop the bleeding. Dove's focus remained constant.

One of the birds departed. The other continued to circle. The wind rippled. I almost swore I heard a gator mating call, bellowing deep from the flooded roadway. That would've been impossible. I had no idea where any water was.

Dove kissed the top of my forehead, and I wiped my fingers across her shoulder, leaving a bloodstain on her shirt. The vulture extended its loop.

Dove carried me inside.

THIRTY-TWO

• Canada announces it is closing its borders to climate refugees.
• Qucore's heat intolerance and climate resilience medication receives further funding, making it the largest project in the College of Florida's history.
• I can see it now, as intended.
• The Global South requests another thirty years of guaranteed oil and coal usage in retribution for the Global North's role in ecological failure.
• For the first time, six million people in the United States are classified as homeless, many of them victims of forced migration due to climate change.

The cold front held steady, bringing a vengeful wind. Trees were torn out of the ground, garbage spilled from the tops of open cans and blew into the street like leaves spinning around concrete trees. I hadn't taken Dove's sweater off, the musty orange smell becoming a comforting relief in the unfamiliar weather. I hadn't felt the need to shower. There was no sweat to rinse off.

Dove's cryptic notes were increasing over the last few entries, her handwriting more disheveled. I could see smears in the ink where her hand had brushed through the previous line, leaving faint black smudges of her fingerprints all over the paper like wet shoes on carpet.

Everything was happening at once; the conclusion of the Forticlime trials and the medicine's initial release, the break in the heat, and reading the last pages of Dove's writing. My desire to understand made me paralyzed with want, and I didn't know if my avoidance was in preservation or pursuit of my understanding.

My final exams approached. The insistent beeping of my computer's ancient battery and the whirring of the automated attention response became dull noise in the background of every test I took. I cared less than ever about finishing my degree, about doing much of anything. All I wanted to do was read Dove's journal and see through the Forticlime release. The closer both became, the worse the feeling got.

I went on another walk in the morning, trying to catch the day again without cars on the street and persistent noise. I hoped the clearer air would somehow wipe my brain too, taking the stagnant feeling with it.

I rounded the corner to see "Paul Smith" back on our doorstep, in the same sweat-stained button-down shirt he'd worn last time. Even from a distance, I noticed the emptiness in his expression, the lack of blood or light in his eyes. When he spotted me walking over, his face stretched into a smile.

"Miss Alonso, nice to see you again." "Paul" grinned, making a quick scratch across the notes in his hands.

I ignored him, reaching into my pocket for my keys. "Paul" shuffled his stack of paper.

"Is your father home?"

"I don't know," I replied, pushing the keys and Dove's journal down into my bag. The bag hugged my hip; the weight of the book embracing my side.

"Paul" shuffled out of the way as I approached the bottom of the steps. "That's all right. I'm happy to leave some materials for when he gets back."

"I already told you." I frowned, walking up the stairs and back toward the front door. "We're not interested in an Augmistum."

"Paul" coughed, flipping through the notes on his clipboard.

"I really urge you to reconsider that." His smile didn't waver.

"I said, we're not interested."

"Like I mentioned, Miss Alonso, the Augmistum comes at no cost to your family—"

"Take us off your list," I huffed, clenching my jaw. He nodded, rolling his lips into his mouth.

"Even in your father's present state?"

My breath caught on the windchill. I was so unequipped for these temperatures that this colder weather had made me feel increasingly off balance. I was out of my element.

"What do you mean?"

He lifted his hands, my eyes flickering to the flier in his hand waving like a flag in the breeze.

"I know he's getting older. I'm sure the intensity of the heat this year hasn't been easy on his health."

He reached out to me without taking another step forward, extending his hand with the papers clutched within it. I took them.

"This program *was* designed with people like your father in mind." He smiled.

My eyes wandered to the printed fliers, bright in color with large font across the top:

Boost Your Well-Being with the Assistance of the Automated!

The photograph to the right of the text was a woman about the same age as my father, grinning inside of a small bakery, two Augmistums bustling between the different dessert cases. Though meant to be cheerful, the scene came off as utterly eerie, the uncanny lack of light behind the Augmistums' eyes the centerpiece. It looked AI generated, a half-ditch attempt at depicting what life actually looked like.

"Paul Smith" watched me closely. I could see there were new lines on his face. I felt deeply that he had to be an Augmistum himself. Perhaps there were ways to make Augmistums age too, to ease humans from the persistent uncanny feeling as the automated ceased to age around us.

I felt the other flier tucked behind the first one and slowly pulled it to the front. In this one, a man and woman were seated together on a park bench, staring at a distant orange grove. Their hands rested together. Below, tiny medical fine print. The couple's backs were turned to the onlookers. I felt my face get hot.

Resilience has never been this easy.

"I thought I'd bring a copy of that one, too," he continued, looking at me. "Florida House Bill 76-B93 is also allowing for select low-income communities to get initial access to Qucore's new Forticlime medication." He grinned. "I'm sure you know a little bit about that already."

The Forticlime poster was somehow more comforting and haunting than the Augmistum one. If I hadn't known better, the long black hair on the faceless woman could have been Dove, with Carter beside her. The ad was even more unnatural, the orange much too vibrant, the picture even more surreal. It was that sickly, unnatural orange, so painfully warm on the eyes that it stung cold.

"Maybe that one piques your interest more." He nodded, his eyes flickering to meet mine. "Or your father's."

I took a firm step toward him, tightening my grip on the fliers.

"Don't come back here," I said, frowning. "I'm serious. We're not interested. Leave us alone."

He held up his hands. "Heard loud and clear."

I felt the anxiety in my chest rising, making my head feel dizzy and disconnected. "My father is doing fine." My voice shook.

He was unblinking. I didn't owe him anything. "He has me."

"Paul" nodded. "That he does."

From behind the front door, I heard the gentle scratching of the black cat against the front door. I could almost see her green eyes blinking at the door handle, waiting for me to free her.

The wind picked up, rattling the side of our house. I heard the wood creaking. "Paul" and I watched as one of the ancient hurricane shutters my father purchased from the family fleeing north swung out, detaching partially from the house. One of the nails broke and rolled across the ground. The shutter tilted inward, leaning across the window like a cross. The house continued to creak, even as the wind stopped. With the blackout curtains closed, I wasn't sure my father would even notice it. I didn't know, if I hadn't been out here, if I would have either. The black cat meowed.

"Good luck, Miss Alonso." "Paul" gave a curt wave and returned to the sidewalk, walking with his back to the house and down the road before disappearing.

I opened the door, and the black cat wrapped her tail around my legs and sat on top of my toes. She didn't leave the porch.

THIRTY-THREE

I needed to talk to Matis again, but the upcoming Forticlime launch made him impossible to catch. He was beyond exhausted every time I saw him lately, dark circles under his eyes carved deep into his cheeks like twin canyons beside his nose. His cheeriness, however, hadn't wavered, and now that Forticlime was so close to being finished, he promised the work and sleep deprivation would be worth it. I beat myself up for not being able to find the right words to say. To tell him about my worries without making him hopeless. To not bleed Dove's world on him too.

The truth was, every time I stared at Matis, the only person I could see looking back at me was Dove—the worn-down, tired Dove I knew right before she passed. I was worried about him.

The two fliers "Paul" left sat undisturbed on the counter. I was sure my father must have seen them, but he hadn't mentioned anything. Maybe he hadn't. Maybe he didn't care. Maybe he didn't understand.

I was desperate for normalcy, real or perceived. I had a feeling normalcy as I knew it was coming to an end.

I decided to cook dinner for me and my father that night. Not from a can or the microwave, but fresh. I scrounged together any extra cash and ration cards we had and prepared pasta, with real tomato in the sauce and seasoned chicken, trying to retrace the way Dove had always cooked for us. The musky smells of the kitchen and living room were replaced with sizzling garlic, and after begging a woman at the store to let me purchase the last one on the stand, zest from a single orange. We wouldn't have fresh vegetables again for almost a month with what I'd spent today, but I convinced myself underneath the harsh light of the kitchen and through the steam rising from the stove it was worth it. Anything for a moment of normalcy, or what I'd always been told normalcy might feel like.

When my father got home, he sat at the table as if this was our nightly routine. Entirely normal. He folded his paper towel across his lap like it was a fine linen napkin, and then cut into the chicken and took quick bites. He ate so fast I wasn't sure he tasted anything, the food disappearing in a fraction of the time it had taken me to make it. I watched him hurry across the plate.

Part of me wished my father would savor it, like the people did in books or on TV. That would feel normal. They'd talk about the flavors between bites, taste the moment they were sitting in. Share stories. Share a future. Meals were always painted as sacred things when I watched actors play families on TV, or the influencers dining in large restaurants with hundreds of people in expensive clothes. To think about food as an experience.

My father coughed, not making eye contact. "Lauren came to get the dry cleaning today," he quipped. "She rolled down the window to wave but didn't come inside. Had an Augmistum do it."

I hadn't heard from her in weeks. Maybe it was my fault. I'd been so caught up in everything, I hadn't bothered to make small talk. I hardly had the energy to survive. Besides, I'd felt like I'd exhausted everything I could possibly say to her. The divergence I sensed, with the way the world was unraveling, didn't feel like something I could solve anymore, among everything else.

My fork caught on the edge of my plate, rattling some of the sauce onto the table. My father didn't react.

When was the last time we shared a meal? The hurricane? Did sliding half-full cans of beans across the tile toward each other *count*?

What *could* I talk about with my father at this point? The state of the world? The fear that I experienced every time I read another page of Dove's journal? The way I felt like I was always looking for answers in people, places, and things that never came?

I studied the outline of my father's face and in it I saw my own. The identical width of our noses, shared mole. Did I tell him I knew the starvation in his eyes, even in the mundanity of eating dinner together, more immensely than I could ever explain? The want for things that would sooner kill us before ever coming back?

The TV hummed, and out of the corner of my eye, I caught that SubcutaLink ad, featuring the former newscaster and her brightened eyes. My fork clattered as it caught the corner of my plate again, bouncing off the table and to the floor. The tomato sauce stained the ankle of my only pair of jeans.

My father finally laughed.

"Don't waste a meal this good." He tapped his plastic fork and knife on the top of the plate. "Shame to let any of it go."

"Serves me right for being clumsy."

We stared at each other, and just for a moment, the world was only this big. It was complete. Neither of us dared to look at the third empty chair, imagine the fourth. I felt the weight, clear as ever. This was just an attempted replication; nothing would ever really be what it was again. It was bound to be something else, forever.

My dad took a deep breath.

"Now I really miss your sister."

My father grinned, but his eyes were hollow underneath the fluorescent light in the kitchen.

"Me too." My voice came out in a whisper. I barely heard it.

He picked up his fork, swirling it absentmindedly through the remaining pasta. I could see the pieces I overcooked, mushy as they slipped back to the plate. The room went dull, only the television buzzing.

I wasn't hungry anymore. I'd put all of this in the fridge. The broken hurricane shutter rubbed against the window frame outside.

"Dove never struck me as the suicide type," my dad murmured, studying the wall. He wouldn't look at me. "When the police came to the house and told me they'd found her and Carter in the river, I—" His lips furrowed. "I didn't believe them. I thought there was no way that my daughter would ever take her own life if it meant she'd be leaving us alone. Especially, leave *you* alone."

The shutter groaned against the window. I didn't take my eyes off my dad.

"I'd been . . . worried about her for a while, but I didn't say anything. When kids are that age, hell, *your* age now, they think they're at the top of the world. Solid. Unmovable. Perpetually resilient."

He tapped his fingers on the top of the table, tracking a small circle with his index finger.

"I saw these empty bottles in her trash can. She'd torn the labels off. I didn't think anything of it at first, maybe it was counterfeit birth control."

My father frowned.

"I don't know . . . It wasn't till the number of bottles I was taking out of her can each week kept stacking. There were so many of them, nothing else would fit in the trash can."

I heard the distant call of a faraway bird. Maybe I'd imagined it.

"Prescription bottles?"

He took a bite of the mushy pasta, unfazed.

"I figure she and Carter must have been into something. Whatever it was, they couldn't pull anything from her toxicology report in the autopsy. So they told me in all likelihood, she'd probably drowned, even though there was one thing your sister knew how to do, survive. I guess I . . . I figured she would have known her limits."

My heart pounded. The food I'd eaten threatened to climb into my throat and empty onto the table. I saw that my fork had done more than stain the hem of my pants, but had splattered across the tile, leaving a dark trail of red. My head was spinning.

Had she been taking—

"How come you never told me that?" I stood from the table and my father finally made eye contact with me. He looked far away.

"What good would it have done? What would you have thought? That your sister was some addict?" His face drew tight. "Sometimes you have to leave some things buried." My father took another bite. My brain was winding.

"You didn't think I'd want the choice?"

My father looked at Dove's empty chair, wilting.

"You were only a kid. I look at you and still see my ten year old daughter without a mother or a sister."

Tears fought their way out of my eyes and I wiped them away. I was sure my father wouldn't have noticed, but they stung on my cheeks.

"But what about seeing things as they are?"

He looked at me, younger, almost the way I'd known him as a child.

"Savannah, that's the hardest part." My father looked out toward the television. He was gone.

The black cat slipped out from under the table, watching me. I looked away from my father, wiping my nose on Dove's sweater and crouching down toward my fork on the floor. I fought the urge to cry.

The cat's green eyes were fixed on my outstretched hand. She walked by my hand, her warm fur tickling my fingers. I petted her for a moment, before I pulled the fork quickly from the ground. Suddenly, the cat bent back, her back and fur fanning out in a combative arch.

"It's okay," I hummed, for both her and myself. I'd never seen her like this before. "There's nothing to worry about."

As I pet the top of her back just before her tail, I felt a sudden, aching sting. Yanking my hand away, I glanced just in time to see a faint glimmer of exposed metal reaching through the spine of the cat's back, sharp and reaching through the surface of its skin. As quickly as it appeared, it retracted back into her. The cat's face intensified and then relaxed, sinking its body toward the tile floor. My hand was bleeding.

My heart climbed to my throat, but I held as still and nonreactive as I could. I couldn't believe it.

The cat was an Augmistum.

It must have thought I was going to attack it when I pulled the fork off the ground and it triggered some kind of defense mechanism. The cat was back to normal just moments after it happened.

This could only mean one thing.

Someone was watching us. And it had to be Qucore.

The nausea in my stomach compounded, but I stepped back from the cat without reacting. I didn't know what had triggered in the cat beyond the slight attack, let alone what would be done if whoever was watching became aware that I'd noticed.

I had to find Matis. Immediately.

I left my crumpled napkin on top of my plate, stepping back from the table.

"I'll be right back."

My father was long disengaged. He'd cleared his plate. The TV flashed before him.

I swallowed the urge to race to my room, stepping carefully to not raise any more suspicion. I opened the door to my bedroom, reaching immediately for Dove's journal.

There was one page left.

I'd been avoiding this moment, hoping that by some unknown power I would read the last page of this journal and Dove would appear in the hall, knock on my bedroom door and apologize for being gone so long. She'd tell me I'd been paranoid this whole time, my grief warping the world into something she'd always known it wasn't. She'd ask me to believe people were good. Maybe she'd have several gray hairs snaking through the curtain of black down her back. I'd ask her why she'd let so much time pass.

Maybe she'd apologize, or try to. I wouldn't let her.

I would've let it all go if when I turned this page, she returned and this journal wasn't the only thing left. Her archive of apocalypse. I'd forgive everything, whatever Qucore was doing or had done or would do. I'd release the fear that permeated every facet of my mind and body. The way I felt myself falling apart with the planet. I'd forgive every horrible thing I'd read in this journal, if it meant I had her.

But when I turned the page, looking at the faded ink smeared and clearly rushed, Dove did not appear in my doorway. There was no magic, no lessons, no news to recount, no bullet points, no last message to me. No directions. The house creaked with the wind.

At the top of the page, eight shaded circles, and one line of text across the middle.

INHERIT 999

That was it.

Nothing pointing me toward something else to read or observe. Just her scrawled, frantic handwriting and the blank back cover.

I felt myself desperate to scream. I wanted Dove to turn in here so I could grab her and tell her charting out all the fucked up shit that happened while I was too young to realize that the world was falling apart had done *nothing* but make me afraid. That she hadn't given me anything but new worries and rage with her notes. I wanted to push her. To tell her what a shell her death had made my father. What it had made me.

I wanted her to hold me.

But it didn't matter what I wanted. This is what it was. I knew what I knew, and now, I had to guess what I didn't.

And for whatever *Dove* knew or whatever I knew, Qucore was watching us because of it. That I didn't have to assume.

I couldn't linger, so I grabbed the journal and tucked it in my bag. In the corner of my bedroom, discarded since my dad first gave it to me, I saw Dove's bag and my princess crown poking out of the top. I picked up Dove's bag and shoved inside mine with the journal, taking out the crown and leaving it on my desk. I needed as much of her as I could get.

I had to go to campus and talk to Matis. That was the only place I was going to get any closure, to rid myself of this. Dove had no more to give. I was on my own.

As I came out of my bedroom, the black cat watched me, fixated, but went back to wrapping her tail playfully around my father's leg. He grinned, patting the top of her head. The metal had completely disappeared. She was almost real, but now I couldn't unsee it; the uncanny green in her eyes, the fur too black, enough to be artificial. An impossible Dove. Designed specifically for us, our grief, and our sympathy.

"Savannah," my father started as I came back into the hallway, my heart pounding. "Did you put orange in this?"

"I did."

My father scratched the cat under the chin, and she closed her eyes. "It was delicious."

My throat burned, but I smiled at him. "I'm gonna go for a walk."

My father stacked his plate on top of mine, and tossed them both in the trash. I faintly tasted the orange zest on my tongue.

"You turned out good." My dad grinned, walking past me and tapping my shoulder before he eased into the couch. "I think Dove would be really proud."

He flipped through several channels of news, away from coverage of the recent flood in Trinidad, the additional drilling project opened in Alaska, the deaths of four thousand more children in the Middle East. He settled on a rerun of a movie I was sure I'd seen him watch three other times while he was resting after his heat stroke.

The tragedies he'd flipped through on TV were things I already knew about but didn't realize I'd become hyperaware of. I'd started logging them in my head too, everything happening that indicated things were falling apart. Where greed had gotten out of control. Where we'd failed to prevent the unforgivable. I was seeing the tragedy in everything now, I realized. In everyone.

Even me.

Maybe that was Dove's point.

The cat hopped on the couch and sat beside my dad, her green eyes wide as they flickered between the TV and me, her stare distinctly colder.

"Thanks, Dad." I waved and closed the door, tucking the fliers from the counter into my bag.

THIRTY-FOUR

As soon as I reached our front door I was running. Traffic buzzed in my ears, my heart pounded against my ribs. I started to sweat for the first time since the cold front started, the salt stinging the edges of my cracked lips.

I don't know what it was, but something in my bones pulled me to turn back to the house. I nearly rolled my ankle, but I stared back at the leaning old building, crooked and misshapen like a thumb pressed into the earth.

My dad had let the black cat back outside. She watched me, patting her tail against the sidewalk. We looked at each other for a moment, before she disappeared into the brush. I didn't have a lot of time.

I ran the rest of the way across the main road until I could see the bus stop. When I approached, the Augmistum closed the doors, and the bus pulled away from the sidewalk, tumbling off into the distance. They'd left without me. Maybe intentionally.

The putrid air beside the road stung the inside of my nose. My lips buzzed, my legs aching from the run. I was both within the world and outside of it all at once.

The cold bit at my exposed neck, and I wiped my nose on Dove's sweater. I was panicking. The road noise made my head spin. I swore I could hear Dove laughing in the rumble of the passing cars. My chest tightened. I reached for my phone, scanning for the number.

Lauren's voice was groggy when she answered. "Savannah?"

"I need a ride, please."

There was movement on the other end. Lauren yelled something muffled. I heard her running on the stairs. She set the phone down. Several seconds of rustling followed before I heard the sound of a front door closing and a car door opening.

"I'm coming."

The streetlights flickered on, their glow casting elongated shadows on the pavement. I heard the buzzing from the dated electric lines, a dull reminder of decay lurking beneath the surface.

I felt smeared into the background of a reality written hundreds of years before I was born. I was a set piece, a conduit now for stories that flowed through me but weren't mine. The things I'd learned, the tragedies that had unfolded had nothing to do with me and everything to do with everyone. We were all within and without this future that the people before us created, but were now reaping the consequences. I wouldn't call that a hero's journey; it felt more like a function of circumstance.

There was a reason Dove had left that journal in her bag—maybe it was for me, maybe for my father, or perhaps for anyone she thought might read it. To make the reader into that conduit. To understand the gravity of what had happened, in the past, and in the future. To seek truth.

There was a reason Dove had been working on Forticlime, why she'd died doing so.

I didn't think I could live with myself if I turned away from this truth. Dove hadn't been able to.

Lauren's car pulled beside me moments later. This time she was driving and the Augmistum was nowhere in sight. Her eyes were wide, frazzled, hands shaking on the top of the steering wheel.

"Get in," she called over traffic, flashing her lights at several drivers backed up behind her. Their Augmistums didn't go around, calculating for the inconvenience but waiting patiently for me to load into the car. I watched several human drivers throw their hands up, screaming at Lauren as they pulled out and around her, flipping us off. The Augmistums continued, unfazed.

I loaded into the passenger seat and glanced at a frantic Lauren, her pale blue fingernails tapping anxiously on the steering wheel. I'd never seen her drive before.

"Where are we going?" She swallowed, her eyes flickering around the moving cars until she found a gap to pull into the traffic.

"Lake Delta," I murmured. "COF Center of Research Development."

Lauren tapped the name into a screen in the center of her car, and the route popped up, loading separately into her SubcutaLink. She turned the car sharply to the left and headed toward the highway. My head tapped against the cold window from the force. Moving this fast underneath them, you could almost think the streetlights were shooting stars. I made my wish.

"Thanks for coming," I looked behind us at the traffic. The sea of cars stretched out forever, sinking all the way back into the downtown.

"I haven't seen you since I dropped off my father's dry cleaning. When I came back to get it, your dad was up front."

"I've been busy . . ." I pulled my bag closer on my lap. The corner of Dove's journal pressed into the side of my leg.

"Is everything okay?" Lauren's eyes darted between the passing cars. She was changing lanes a lot more than she needed to, and ignored the car's warning to follow the flow of traffic. I watched as we tore through cars, racing away from the city.

Lauren dug her nails around the steering wheel and into her hand. Her eyes were frantic. She dismissed the "Elevated Heart Rate" alert that appeared on her SubcutaLink. Lauren took an uneven breath.

"I feel like I should ask you the same question."

Lauren dismissed a second "Elevated Heart Rate" alert. "I'm fine."

The car slowed. She stared at me. I closed my hand around the strap of my bag.

"I'm—" I caught myself. "I'm meeting with Matis. The guy that moved in with me and my father into Dove's old room."

"Someone moved into Dove's room?" Lauren's face softened.

"I thought I told you my father was struggling to make payments on the house."

Lauren tapped on the steering wheel. "No, you didn't. I'm sure that was...weird."

I folded my hands back across my lap. Somebody honked in the distance. "It was."

Lauren's eyes flashed up to her mirror. I tugged on my seatbelt.

"He works at COF?" Lauren frowned. I nodded.

"We were . . . supposed to get dinner."

Lauren stopped at the onramp. Several people on the street stared at us through her tinted windshield. There was a woman with one leg and sunbaked skin, holding a baby that couldn't be older than a few weeks. The man beside her had black-stained knuckles and track marks up the length of his arm. They didn't look like they were from here. I wondered if they fled here from the coast or from somewhere else that no longer existed.

I had two ration cards buried at the bottom of my bag, but as I reached for them, the light turned green and Lauren sped forward. The car lurched onto the highway, cutting in front of several others. I felt nauseous.

"Hey! I was trying to give them some ration cards—"

"Don't encourage them."

"To what? Survive?"

"Don't you have somewhere to be?" Lauren's jaw tightened.

"I don't think you have to be so callous." I shoved the ration cards back into my bag. "I'm sure they're not out there by choice."

"I just—I don't want to be involved."

The small family disappeared in our rearview mirror, sinking below the traffic. Lauren pressed her lips together, blinking. She chewed on the inside of her cheek. She looked thinner than the last time I'd seen her, hollow circles forming underneath her eyes. I could see the filler in her face as her face disappeared.

"What's with you?" I finally asked her, pulling my bag in tighter.

"Sorry." Lauren shook her head. "Tired."

Lauren swerved her car across the highway. My stomach lurched. I tried to study the sky through the glass roof of the car.

"I've been to the Center of Research Development a couple times," she finally said. "My father's been bringing me to the board meetings recently for the . . . Forticlime release."

I held my guard. "That's interesting."

The rigid pavement bumped beneath us. I could barely make out the top of the skyscrapers through the dense, dark clouds. It was going to rain. The neon lights made the black clouds glow faintly orange, like artificial daylight draped in fog.

"I'm glad it's almost ready." Lauren took a deep breath.

"Me too."

I nodded, unsure what else to say. I studied the sound of the racing wind from outside the glass. Lauren raised her chin, the streetlights rolling over her head and sinking back behind the car. She slowed down.

"My mother is sick," Lauren whispered, not taking her eyes off the road. "She has been for nearly a year now. It's part of why I've been traveling so much with my father, in her place."

Lauren squeezed her fingers around the steering wheel.

"I've heard a lot about Forticlime. They say it could help save my mother. Her body can't handle the heat, no doctor has been able to solve it for her, and her organs are failing."

Lauren bit her lip.

"People like that family are going to get access to Forticlime long before my mother will. Long before *you and your father* even will. Is that fair? People that can't contribute. And people like my mother will have to wait . . . maybe even years before they get access to it."

"I don't think there's anything wrong with that." I sat up in the passenger seat.

"Are you kidding me?" Lauren turned toward me, away from the road.

"Lauren, they're on the street. They're out in the sun every single day."

"You can't tell me you think it's fair to *my* mother and *your* father—"

My face burned. "Lauren, you have always had access to anything you wanted. You're the only person I know that's ever left the country. Hell, the only person I know that's ever left Florida. I thought your dad's whole mission was making voting more accessible. Making *democracy* more accessible. Doesn't that extend beyond a fucking election? What are they supposed to do? Just die?"

Lauren's foot got heavier on the gas pedal. My hand reached for the handle in the passenger door. She slid over to the far left lane, breezing past the other cars, with controlled, automated drivers. The car gave her a speed warning, which she rejected. I watched as the "Elevated Heart Rate" warning flashed again on her SubcutaLink.

"I know. I know it's the *right* thing. It's the *just* thing. But goddamn it, am I going to lose my mother so that some . . . fucking addict can take the pills *we* helped fund?"

Tears formed in the rims of Lauren's eyes.

"I don't know. Savannah, at that last board meeting, the head researcher with the university, Powell or something, she . . ." Lauren trailed off, shaking her head. "She mentioned Dove Alonso came up the bill on who would get access to the medicine first. She had a serious influence over all of this."

Lauren sped past another car. My heart pounded.

"Can you slow down?" I asked. "You're going really fast."

"How come you never told me Dove worked on Forticlime research?" Lauren ignored me, and turned her eyes away from the road to look at me. She was still speeding. I felt my stomach tightening, but I knew I couldn't break eye contact with her. Not now.

"I didn't know until recently."

"Does it mean you're getting early access to Forticlime?"

"I don't know."

We whirred past several other cars on the highway. Our exit was approaching. Lauren needed to get over. The cars we passed appeared like intermittent flashes of color, fading into my vision as quickly as they faded out. "Lauren—"

"Because you would tell me if you *were*, right?" Lauren's voice caught in her throat. "Because between Dove and Matis it seems like you have a lot of ins at Qucore, and it doesn't seem to matter who my father talks to, *no one* can seem to get moved up the fucking wait list and I—"

The car took over with an emergency brake right before Lauren nearly slammed us into the back of another car. I held tightly to my bag and turned to see Lauren's eyes widen in shock, her hands clasped over her ears. She'd let go of the wheel entirely. It had been entirely up to the car to save us. The Augmistums in the surrounding cars were reactionless. The car steered itself, returning to a reasonable speed and moving toward the exit.

Both of us froze, feeling the force of the stop gradually melt off our bodies. I stared at the glass roof of the car, trying to sink into the black. I could taste my heartbeat.

"I can't lose my mom, Savannah," Lauren whispered, folding her hands together. "They told us if she dies before she can get on Forticlime, we can donate her body to this Harmony Grove place to help support the people that *will* get to use it. Whatever that's supposed to mean."

My eyes narrowed.

Lauren breathed shakily as we rolled off the exit ramp, and she pressed on the top of her SubcutaLink as she took several labored breaths in.

"Isn't that fucked?"

Lauren finally tapped on the "Elevated Heart Rate" warning, using the SubcutaLink to steady herself. She blinked back tears. I knew this fear. The desperation, the desire for control of things that extended far beyond what humans were capable of. Death was the one thing Lauren's father could not pay to prevent. Money could not salve the sting. There was nothing *anyone* could do to stop that pain. I knew that too well, and in some twisted sense, that had made me hollow to it.

"I'm so sorry, Lauren," I finally whispered.

Lauren stared at the road. The Center of Research and Development building glowed faintly orange and blue in the distance. She rested her hands on the steering wheel, rocking it back and forth gently. The car did not respond to her motions; she had no control with the autopilot on. Her movements were infantile, absent of intent.

"If you can help me get Forticlime faster . . . please. I'll give you anything. I'll let you fly with my father to Asia. Anything you want. Savannah . . . please."

The car rolled into the parking lot, and I unclicked my seat belt. The door unlocked by itself. I took a deep breath.

"I . . . I don't think I can," I answered.

Lauren sat up and wiped off the smeared mascara from under her eye, which had exaggerated the misplaced filler in her face. Her expression was hollow, but without anger. She looked like a stranger. I felt present in a way I hadn't in a long time.

"I don't want you to think I'm a bad person, Savannah," Lauren whispered. "I want everyone to be saved, I mean that. I . . . don't think the people that have given the most should have to suffer, you know? I'm sure Dove would've believed that, too."

"Depends on what you define 'the most' as, doesn't it?"

Lauren rubbed her hands on top of the steering wheel.

"Thanks for the ride."

She didn't wave. Dove's journal leaned against my hip as I stepped toward the front door of the research center. Lauren's car disappeared back toward the highway.

Something clicked.

THIRTY-FIVE

Familiar cold air met my face as soon as the double doors opened. The atrium itself was more crowded than I've ever seen it. Students and staff weaved through the hallways, rushing between the different classrooms. It was surprisingly lively for a room so otherwise sterile. There were new chairs populating the room, arranged in more collaborative circles, all a deep, vibrant shade of orange.

Several students brushed past on my way inside, my eyes scanning over the frenzy looking for Matis. The 2100 Florida model loomed in the center of the crowded room like an altar, the glass picking up the light and hurried expressions before throwing them back and around the room like a prism.

To the left of the model, a new addition: a table with a stack of dark orange pamphlets, advertising Harmony Grove.

"Assure Your Future: Why Harmony Grove Is the Right Choice for Post-Mortem and Supporting Future Generations."

The pamphlets were stacked several high and mostly undisturbed. I took one in my hand and flipped it over, spying the Qucore logo in the bottom right corner. Smiling faces surrounded the body of text detailing the importance of human composting for reducing your carbon footprint, even after death. There was a tiered pricing model for different composting types based on the preferences of the deceased, and a note near the bottom.

"Qucore will use the composting from Harmony Grove for the continued growth of the Florida economy and people, through community investment and projects to make life better, even in death."

I touched Dove's journal in my bag, my eyes darting to the ceiling and the cameras perched in every corner. If I was right that it was Powell's team behind the black cat monitoring the house, I knew I didn't have much time before I'd be confronted.

I caught my reflection in the 2100 Florida model, finding the new rings around the bottom of my eyes, the deepening folds around my nose. I could see my father's face in my own clearer than ever, the heaviness in my cheeks, the jagged edge of my jaw. The last few months had aged me. I felt it as much as I could see it.

"Savannah?"

Matis came around the corner with a clipboard in his hand, backpack slung over one shoulder. I caught his face parallel to mine in the reflection of the glass before he inched closer and it sank into the floor.

"What are you doing?"

"We can't talk here," I said, lowering my voice, trying to mask it under the shuffling of feet circulating the building. "Something is happening and I don't know what to make of it."

I watched Matis' eyes scan my face, before he outstretched his hand and took us down the corridor and outside. I was searching for anything that could eavesdrop on our conversation, and Matis stepped farther into the parking lot. I followed him, watching a pair of girls walk toward the front doors.

"Someone is spying on the house. I think it's Qucore."

Matis lowered his voice. "What are you talking about?"

"That black cat is an Augmistum."

Matis took a deep breath. "Really?" I nodded.

"Why do you think it's Qucore?"

"Wouldn't they be the only ones with animal Augmistums yet?" I whispered. "I couldn't believe it till some defense mechanism kicked in and she cut open my hand."

I held up the bandage for Matis. His eyes widened.

"Savannah, I had no idea, I mean it. If it's Qucore, I wouldn't know anything about that." His eyes were tired. I had to trust him; I'd promised I would. If I didn't, there would be no other tether for me to grab.

"The cat showed up only a few days before you did. And then it was that fucking government solicitor that I'm almost sure was an Augmistum. Now these—" I dug around the top of my bag and pulled out the advertisements for Forticlime and Harmony Grove. "Advertisements. And the way Dove's writing ends in the journal, none of it makes any sense unless it's—"

I gestured at the clear glass doors with the Qucore emblem. My face felt hot. I could feel the tears pooling in my eyes. I couldn't will them away.

"Ever since I started reading Dove's journal, I've been on edge, and I can't shake this feeling like—" The "COF" logo at the top of the building caught my attention, looming over the parking lot like a distant god. I looked at it, willing it to tip over and fall on top of me. To break the illusion that my anger and this quest to understand have somehow separated me from the confines of reality. "Something is completely wrong. And there's something fucked up about Forticlime and what Qucore's goal is with it going out. I think they might think Dove had told me something she wasn't supposed to."

"Did she?"

"I...I don't think so. At least not directly? I don't know."

Matis didn't react. Several students walked back to their cars. The sound of the buses rolling down the road barely registered. Matis' hands were wrung out, constricted around each other. He looked exhausted. Honest. Human.

"What do you mean?" Matis lowered his voice, taking a step toward me. "Savannah, the drug is safe. It's been tested. It—"

"I don't think it's ready. What if . . . what if it—" My mouth went bloody from chewing my cheek.

"Hundreds of people have been working on this medication for years. Decades. People that really want to help others. People that have been trying to find some kind of solution for the *mess* of a planet we have left. Good people. Like Dove."

"But what if Dove *wasn't* good?"

The words fell out before I could catch them. Matis' eyes widened.

"Why would you—?"

"What if none of this is good? What if it's all . . . fucked in a way I can't explain."

The ache in my stomach was back in full force as soon as I said it, the weight of Dove's journal heavy at my side. I could almost see her. The pain made the vision even clearer. I felt her hand across my eyes, willing them to close, see the curtain of black hair, smell the oranges.

"Why would you think Dove wasn't good?" Matis frowned, confused. "Do you know what she probably sacrificed in order to help get us to where we are today? What she must have understood in order to make this real?"

"But that's exactly it, Matis." My heart pounded in my chest. "I think she understood everything she thought about the world, and that's why she wanted Forticlime to exist. Because the world is so past the point of no return. Because of the suffering. Because of what it could mean to escape it."

"What do you mean?"

"What if Forticlime is a clever way out, rich or poor, ending the numbness, escaping when there's nothing left to push for? And Harmony Grove is just some twisted cover up for where everyone goes. That's why Dove was in Wekiva when she died."

Matis shook his head.

"Savannah, Dove would never—"

"But you didn't know Dove!" My tears were hot and visceral as they poured over my cheeks, tingling against the cold air. "And maybe I didn't either."

I heard the sound of the front doors opening and glanced over my shoulder to see a mousy brown ponytail peaking past the bushes.

Professor Powell's footsteps cemented me still in the parking lot. I took an uneasy breath and straightened up. My ears were ringing.

"Miss Alonso," Professor Powell said gently, tucking a folder underneath her arm, her painted insulated cup in hand. She looked bored. "Good to see you again."

I willed myself to nod, wiping off my face. Matis took a step beside me.

"You must be incredibly proud of your sister. I can't imagine how excited she would be to know that we're so close to realizing her work."

The humidity was still palpable, even through the cold. The urge to cry again was crawling up my throat. Professor Powell's disinterest only made me feel worse. My mouth tasted like salt.

"What do you want with me?" I stood up straighter, swallowing back the ache in my chest.

"I don't want anything from you, Miss Alonso," Professor Powell said, nodding. "I thought our conversation the other night made that clear."

"Why were you watching our house?"

"Why does anyone watch anything? To understand." Professor Powell took a sip from her cup. "It was remarkable to me how two girls born from the same parents under identical circumstances a decade apart, could be so similar and so different."

"You don't know me," I hissed, my throat tight.

"I think I do, Savannah. I think I do." Professor Powell's owl eyes flickered between me and Matis, lips pressed together.

"You know, Dove would probably be disappointed that the low-income distribution for Forticlime isn't going to be as expansive as she originally proposed," Powell continued. "She was very adamant about making sure people like you and your father could take the medication with support, given she knew how expensive it would become."

I didn't move.

"We've had so many requests from the board to expand the distribution to higher wealth tiers, and the sponsorship funding program from the state only lasts so long. Unfortunately, Forticlime is the kind of drug that requires buildup in your system over time in order to be most effective. I'm hopeful, though, that expanding the program will help get us a little closer to the retribution we're all in need of. Perhaps the drug in the hands of our donors is a worthy sacrifice."

Professor Powell's eyes wandered toward the "COF" sign on the top of the building.

"Dove's willingness to support Carter in his development of the algorithm to test the effects of Forticlime, no matter what, was the only reason we've been able to get this far to begin with."

The streetlight made the rims of Professor Powell's eyes so dark they pulled nearly all the light from her face, making her features gaunt and hollow. She was as plain as I'd ever seen her. I couldn't have picked her out of a lineup. That gaze couldn't permeate into my dreams anymore. She was just someone with power. She could have been anyone.

"Dove was willing to do whatever it took to get the outcome she thought was right. And deep down, you agree with her. What she wanted for the world, what she believed it had become. And how she could make what she wanted happen. You want what Dove wants, don't you?"

Time stopped. The Earth continued to rotate. I could feel it, even if I didn't believe it. The ringing in my ears grew louder. I could hear Dove laughing, bright and clear, like just over my shoulder. She was different now in this delusion, green eyes wicked and dark, though her face was still soft. I saw it so clearly. She should've been here, with me. She shouldn't have left me to figure out her mess alone.

Professor Powell lowered her voice. "There is a chance to drink from the gauntlet of life again on this planet. To face the elements instead of brace for them. Do you know what happens to mortals who drink the blood of gods, Savannah? Only the worthy ones survive."

"How do you decide who's worthy? Who made you into a god?" My whole body hurt.

"There are no gods, Savannah, and no monsters. Only humans and circumstance."

The ringing in my ears was more persistent than ever. I had nothing else to lose. "Why did Qucore build Harmony Grove?" My whole chest burned.

Professor Powell smiled, unfazed. "How else would we have enough orange trees?"

"What are you talking about?" She did not look at me.

"When Forticlime finishes its initial trials with lower-income communities and becomes unaffordable, only the wealthy will still be able to take it. As space opens—whether the planet becomes too hot to survive, or through more deliberate means—we'll make our way to Florida 2100."

I took a step toward her, daring her to look at me.

"Forticlime will kill people, won't it."

She does, unmoved, like we'd been discussing the weather over dinner. "But so will the planet. So will people." She lifted the folder from under her arm, tapping it with a finger. "Some bodies will handle Forticlime, and others . . . won't. Ichor wasn't meant for the masses. But the research says it's all inexplicable anyway—so why waste time finding out?" She raised her cup to her lips. "You know it makes you crave citrus, don't you? Luckily, we're in the right place."

Professor Powell swirled her cup in her hands, full of orange juice.

I dug my fingernails into my wrist to stop my stomach from unloading its contents on the asphalt. I closed my eyes and I was a kid again, and Dove was screaming at me for drinking her last orange juice. I was taking out the trash and the orange juice cartons were everywhere.

I smelled the orange juice in Dove's breath as she rested her head on my shoulder at the theme park. It was in her skin. It was all I had left of her.

It had been her salvation, her freedom from a world rotted out.

And it was her poison.

"I think you deserve to know that your sister's life wasn't a waste. Without Dove, the dream of a healthier, more egalitarian Florida wouldn't exist. The dream of a healthier *Earth* wouldn't exist."

I wanted to kill her.

"I've never thought Dove's life was a waste." I feel my heart pumping in my chest, so fast I'm almost dizzy. "I only thought her death was."

Professor Powell grinned, shaking her head. "I can promise you, Savannah, that wasn't a waste either."

Two other students came out of the front doors, and Professor Powell turned back, catching their attention. "You're making a lot of noise out here. I suggest you head home," Professor Powell said, stepping back toward the front doors. "You too, Mr. Wallace." She gestured toward Matis. "You've done an exemplary job, but your work at the lab is finished. It should never have been reported to me that you took Miss Alonso to Harmony Grove, when you yourself have never been approved to be part of that project."

Matis didn't move.

"If you can make it, you should come to the press conference. I think Dove would have wanted you to be there. Maybe your father can take some time off from the dry cleaner and come too. Especially since he won't need to feed the cat anymore."

My heart pounded, and blood rushed to my head. I felt dizzy. The world had stopped spinning, but it did not end. There was no boom, no mass disruption, just a professor, defending her work, bored and unfazed by my grief, numb to guilt.

"Why are you telling me this?" I was twisted with rage. Grief so tangible it tasted like metal. Professor Powell didn't flinch, her wide eyes blinking slowly, waiting.

"Because I think you agree with me. Part of you wants the world that Dove did. One free of chaos. Of hurt. No matter the means. And this is the only way some of us will get it. You're soft, Savannah. The hurt of this world tears through you. Don't you think there's something natural about closing your eyes and starting over? Letting go?"

Professor Powell tucked her hands in her pockets. My vision turned to streaks and shapes, like looking ahead through glass.

"Remember what I said. There are only so many chances to find out who you are, Savannah. I think I know already. Maybe soon you will too."

Professor Powell walked toward the other students and disappeared into the building. The doors shut behind her. I stared at the closed doors, the tightening in my throat the only thing stopping me from screaming. I knew I couldn't. Not here. Not anywhere anymore.

Matis and I stood motionless, listening to the slow ripple of the breeze through the palm fronds. I heard bugs chattering in the distance. The humidity stirred. I heard my own breathing as clear and distinct as the wind.

I swore I could hear Dove talking, somewhere in the roadway or the street noise, or maybe within me.

THIRTY-SIX

"I shouldn't have come here. I'm sorry." My words caught on my tongue. I could barely hear myself over the ringing in my ears. My mind wandered to the shrieking cars on the highway.

"No. Don't." Matis pulled out his car keys. He didn't look at me, brows furrowed.

"What do we do?" I felt untethered, weightless, unbound to time or the planet itself. The journey that had tied me together for the last few months was over. I had hit the wall. There would be no more clues.

Matis stared at the COF building and then me. "Let's go home."

Dove's voice grew distant and eventually disappeared. The streetlights came up and hummed in quiet sympathy. Above the car one light flickered for a moment and then went out, like it had never been there at all.

I followed Matis toward his car and slid into the passenger seat, resting my bag on my lap. I peered inside, staring at the spine of the journal, and the strap of Dove's bag tucked within mine. The edges were fraying. As Matis reached to start the car, I pulled Dove's bag out, peeling back both sides like the skin of an orange.

The last refuge of her things. This was the only corner of her life I'd yet to peer into, the last hiding place.

I saw her wallet, folded doodles, discarded gum wrappers, and several pens. The bag was mildewed, worn with time, with the faintest smell of orange and river water. I pulled out a worn book, the cover and text lost to water and time, and another pen, before I saw it.

Buried in the bottom of her bag was an empty pill bottle, the label still hanging on the side, yellowed and smudged.

My hands scrounged for the bottle, lifting it to the light. Matis started to back up the car but stopped, his gaze drawn to the orange hue. Dove's name was on top, above a code: 99999-060-99.

"Do you know what this is?" I turned to Matis, rolling the bottle in my hands before passing it over. He stared at the numbers, not saying anything.

My heart hammered as I reached into my bag, pulling out Dove's journal and flipping to the very last page.

INHERIT 999

I traced the swoop of Dove's handwriting, then glanced at the pill bottle in Matis' hands.

"This is a code from the National Drug Directory," he said slowly, tapping on the bottle cap. "It's how they track medications, like a data entry system." His eyes lingered on the label. "This is Forticlime's."

Silence filled the car, the shadows shifting as palm fronds blocked the light. The car hummed, and the thinning street traffic underscored the stillness around us. We couldn't idle here much longer without risking a fine, but the idea of moving felt impossible. A sick, coiled feeling tightened in my stomach.

I'd been right. Dove had been taking an early version of Forticlime.

I thumbed back through Dove's journal, my fingers brushing the small circles at the top of the pages. It had been right in front of me this whole time.

"Pill counters," I whispered, running my finger over each dose. Matis leaned over my shoulder as I reached the last entry. Eight full circles. "Don't you think?"

Matis flipped through the pages, pausing over the growing clusters of circles. I flinched with every page turn.

"Eight pills is too much, even for someone with a tolerance. We didn't plan for people to take that many until they'd been on the medication for years. No one's meant to need that unless temperatures are extreme. That amount would decimate your immune system."

"And you know that because..."

"That's what the tests say." Matis shook his head.

"With the algorithm that Carter and Dove built, right?"

He nodded. "Right."

"Do you think..." My eyes drifted to the looming "COF" sign, glowing coldly against the night. "Dove and Carter are how they figured all this out?"

Matis shook his head.

"I—I don't know. Forticlime is designed to work so that as the heat worsens, you need more, but you're supposed to build a tolerance."

"Maybe that's what she was trying to do. See how far she could push it."

I rolled the bottle over in my hand.

"What if the heat rises faster than the tolerance? What would kill you first?" My chest was heavy. "How could you tell?"

Matis leaned back in his seat.

"You probably wouldn't be able to."

The streetlight flickered. The sky rumbled. It would rain again soon.

"Maybe that's what Powell meant. It comes down to whether it's the climate or the medicine that kills you, or doesn't."

I shut my eyes, feeling the cool air brush my face. The faint citrus smell lingered on the journal pages and floated to my nose. I shifted in my seat and the Forticlime leaflet slipped from the journal into my lap. I stared at the neon orange.

"Maybe Dove didn't want people to face that choice," I whispered. Powell's indifferent stare burned in my memory. "She knew the medicine wouldn't keep up forever, that eventually people would be trapped between heat stroke or overdosing on Forticlime." My throat tightened. "She could have been trying to prove it before it was too late. To leave something behind so no one could say they didn't see it coming."

Matis was silent. The car buzzed. "Are those really the only choices?"

Matis turned on the radio.

There was a tsunami in California. Eleven thousand dead.

I let myself cry.

THIRTY-SEVEN

My father was asleep when we got home, wearing one shoe, the other foot bare. He looked more worn than I'd ever seen him, age permeating through his face. So much of his hair had turned gray and there were deep-set creases around his eyes and mouth. I hadn't realized how much time had passed. He'd gotten so much older while his life moving in a loop between our house and that dull back room. That was his world.

The TV flickered, flashing across his sleeping face. I caught the tail end of the former newscaster's new SubcutaLink ad again, her face painted across my father like a mask. His sleeping face looked hollow underneath hers.

The news returned with a report on rising assault cases in Orlando, brushed over California's latest tsunami, then ended with the announcement that the population was up for the first time in six years. I wondered if my father would notice the black cat's sudden absence, or if she, too, would fade like another memory he'd be forever unsure about.

Matis and I walked silently down the hallway toward our rooms. I glanced at Matis' SubcutaLink as it flashed with an email: his termination letter from the lab. He tapped his wrist to dismiss it, his face more sure than I'd expected.

"I'm sorry," I whispered to him. "This is my fault."

He shook his head. "You have nothing to apologize for."

We stood for a moment in the quiet hallway. The space between our two worlds used to feel so separate, but I realized now it had been blurred this whole time. Dove had tied us both together in ways we hadn't even understood a decade ago, when she was still here. There was a history neither of us had been around long enough to write, yet we could now quote as if we'd lived it. Matis' eyes softened.

"I'm sorry, Savannah. I . . . I guess I didn't understand all of this the way I thought I did."

"Take your own advice," I whispered.

Matis leaned forward, and so did I, both of us clinging to this semblance of closeness. He kissed the top of my cheek, his lips wet with tears I hadn't known I'd been crying. His forehead pressed against mine. An understanding. A consensus. Something I'd spent my whole life searching for since Dove's death.

"Where am I even supposed to go from here?"

Matis held my face in his hands for another moment. "What else were you looking for?"

"An answer. Something to do, a sign, a path, a next step..." My heart ached in my chest, the hallway shrinking as if pushing the air out of my lungs. I gripped my bag. "No one told me to do anything. I don't know what I'm supposed to do, what we're supposed to do, if we're supposed to do anything..."

Matis ran his hand from my cheek across the top of my head. "We do whatever we can, then, right?"

The air thickened. I longed for Dove's guidance, her voice echoing in my mind as I faced this alone. My heart tightened as I thought of Professor Powell, who had sent the cat to see if I was as desperate and hopeless as Dove had become. Was that what I was destined for? The despair threatened to swallow me whole.

Matis' voice broke through my thoughts. "Sometimes I think you look too much to Dove to make your choices. You're your own person, Savannah. You have to decide what's right."

I blinked, fresh tears blurring my vision, hot as they tore down my face. I let my shoulders relax, my arms finally falling to my sides. The AC hummed, and the light slipping between the curtains cast narrow shadows on the floor. Matis' face split through the middle.

"That's all we can do."

He tapped my shoulder and slipped into his room, closing the door behind him. I stood frozen in the hallway before retreating to my room. Now I was alone.

My room felt tight, too small for me. I dropped my bag, kicking my shoes into the pile of clothes against the wall. My bed was unmade, sheets balled in a corner against my pillow. I still felt Matis' lips against the top of my cheek. They'd been warmer than any day all year.

I couldn't tell if Dove wanted our liberation or our demise. What else would have been the reason for ensuring Forticlime was going to be as destructive as the state of the world? She'd known things were dark, even then, and maybe that had been enough to fortify her decision to push the limit on Forticlime. To find out where the line was so that someday, people could find their way out.

Or maybe, it was to ensure that we could force our way out of the mess we'd created, instead of facing the consequences. It seemed they would come either way.

Professor Powell's knowing gaze pressed against the inside of my skull, blurring my thoughts. She was unimpressed. There was something honest about it, not calloused or even really evil.

Mostly, bored.

Bored in the sense of boardrooms, and numbers and figures. Quantifying risk versus benefit in the number of displaced, wrapped in the flurry of academia and an allusion to some past folklore most of us didn't know anymore.

But maybe that was the evil. The boredom. The solution searching we were all doing. The contemplating of the sky as it fell upon us. Taking the coward's way out because if nothing, it was comfortable. It kept us from facing the humiliation ritual we'd made of reality and ourselves.

Dove had been Professor Powell's perfect experiment, or maybe, her perfect volunteer. Dove with her spirit to do what was right, her unbridled belief that there was a way to take care of everyone. Dove, acting as my mother when no one asked her. Dove with her books and her beliefs and my princess crown in her bag, wrapped up in something that had outgrown her and that she had further facilitated with her demise.

Was tragedy required for things to be better? Was intervention? Was resolve?

There were no more pages to ask.

The wind rustled my window screen, gently scratching as if begging to come in. Palms in the distance waved against the dark overcast clouds rolling low over the road. I could sense the air without being in it. It was something you understood with enough time in Florida—there was weather you only had to sense in order to know it was coming.

I opened my laptop, trying to distract myself. I absentmindedly sorted through the internet and the tiny "AI-Generated Content" warnings in the corners of nearly every video and advertisement. Sponsored videos about body lotions made from snails, a dress that transformed your figure, egg donation, or animal adoption dispersed themselves between desperate videos of people asking for money to move from their hometowns. An unexpected snowstorm in Missouri had caused a large pileup of cars on the road. Drones had been used to directly target civilians using facial recognition technology from social media posts. A flood had decimated half of the year's wheat crop. An eight-year-old girl spent fourteen days trapped in the shell of a car begging for rescue before she died from dehydration and heat exhaustion. Crops were failing, and people starved. But hey, a potato chip company was sponsoring a pop-up wedding venue in Las Vegas.

My brain may have been scooped straight down the middle, hollowed out into fragments I hardly recognized. The world in front of me though, I did.

I caught a warning in the corner of my computer screen that I had another overdue assignment for school. The final exams were so close. I'd forgotten entirely about them, the final hurdle before the real world. Tapping my keyboard, I turned back to my scrolling. I didn't even know why I was doing it. It didn't make me feel any better, but then again, Dove's journal hadn't either. Nothing was.

I stood from my bed, pacing the room, memorizing the number of steps it took me to reach the door to my window and back again. I sipped from the stale glass of tap water on my desk. I pressed my feet into the floor, then my hands. I tried memorizing the color of the carpet, the way it felt against my fingers. The way my hands could change the shape of it by pressing into it.

I wanted to be here. I didn't want to feel this way anymore.

For the first time, I let myself scream. I screamed until my throat was raw and my mouth tasted bad. I screamed without fear of waking my father, of disturbing Matis, of scaring any of the neighbors or passersby.

I screamed with conviction. I screamed for my mother. I screamed for the other mothers. I screamed for the barren planet. I screamed for a version of myself that didn't know the things I knew now. I screamed for the heat.

I screamed for Dove. I screamed at her.

My father did not stir from the living room. Matis did not knock.

Dove's journal was still tucked in my bag, where it had lived for months, infiltrating my every thought. I reached for the bag in my fury, dumped the contents on my mattress, and pulled the journal out with greedy hands.

I went back to the first page, the only letter Dove left, before the bullet points, before the mapping of the world that existed today and the one she thought would be right; the one she thought would liberate me and my father and all of us. I looked at the page of her conviction, the belief that all sacrifice was worth it, even if someone, anyone, was left to see it through. The sweet poetry, the swirling cursive.

Why did we have to be the ones who choose what should and shouldn't be saved? Hadn't we done enough to make the world bend to our will? Why did she believe that destruction was the path to reconciliation? Why did any of us?

I would not.

One by one, I pulled out the pages from the spine, shredding them with my hands, with my teeth, crushing them between the bones of my hands until they were all before me in various states of tattered, the spine bare. I tore the journal in half, feeling the seams pop and rip apart from each other, then bent each cover in half.

My princess crown was still on the desk, plastic and persistent.

I held the journal scraps in my hand, wiping the snot from my nose. My throat burned. From the corner of my eye, I caught a glimpse of the streetlight flickering out and then on again, reaching all the way out the window toward the road.

Two people walked side by side, their forms impossible to make out underneath weather-worn clothes.

One extended an arm, handing the other an orange. The other person took the orange, peeling it and halving it through the middle. They handed one half back to the other person without conversation and kept walking into the dark. I watched their wordless exchange until they disappeared.

I gathered the scraps of Dove's journal and brought them to the trash can.

THIRTY-EIGHT

Florida was the paradox of transformation and stagnation. A parable for dialectics, perhaps.

The heat, and unchanging seasons faded into each other until June and January were nearly identical. The violence of temporary storms, but the persistent palm trees, their long tendrils our evergreens. The quiet reckoning, the bellow of the people, the animals, the air, the call in all of us to something consistent, something reckless.

I heard once that any photo you take in Florida, you could tell it was in Florida. I didn't remember if it was Dove that told me that, or my father. I didn't think it mattered, but it was true. There was always something distinctly Floridian in the feeling of every shot, whether you were pressed against the city, the coast, or deep in the wilderness. It was the way the scenery looked like nothing else in the United States, the power lines hanging low across the palms, brush and black water that couldn't be mistaken for anywhere else.

Though the sea had reached into the Florida coastline, pushing us deeper into the past as the future arrived, I still recognized this place. This was the only home I had ever known. I would die here. But it would go on, in its own, reshaped and transformed way.

And so would we.

THIRTY-NINE

- *Someone I've never heard of became president. I don't see much of him because the news is overrun with advertising for the 2064 election candidate Rodger Kettington, who I expect to see at the Qucore press conference today.*
- *Desalination technology is helping combat the water crisis.*
- *Russia announces the first case of the Russian Plague in 288 years, likely from bodies emerging from rapidly melting ice in Siberia.*
- *The Ozone Hole has finally sealed.*
- *New advancements in farming technology are creating healthier, drought-resistant crops and fighting famine.*
- *Halley's Comet returns in six months.*

I closed my notebook and tucked it against the window. The sun warmed my hands against my desk. Several cars sped past the house. I took a deep breath.

Matis agreed to come with me to the Forticlime press conference in a silent shoulder brush down the hallway. We'd never verbally agreed to attend together, but when I woke up this morning, his bedroom door was open again, like an extended hand across the hallway.

I didn't really know why we'd both decided we had to go. I couldn't explain it, but I'd felt a deep sense of urgency that had startled me in the middle of the night. It had pulled me by my wrist toward my bedroom window to watch the sunrise. It was the same force that had compelled me to flip the pages in one of my old school notebooks, and begin a bulleted list for myself, tracing events the way Dove had, like coordinates on a map. My goal was to log everything, bad and good. Not one or the other.

I laid a dress in the corner of my bedroom, one of Dove's old ones I found buried in the back of my closet. It was dark purple. I knew it would've been better against her skin, jewel-toned against her curtain of dark hair. I don't ever remember seeing her wear it, but it smelled like her.

The fabric was surreal against my skin, the aged crinoline underskirt scratching my thighs. I saw my father's eyes staring back in the mirror. A strange feeling of peace washed over me. I knew that person looking back. I knew where she'd been and where she was headed. I finally liked seeing my father's eyes in my own. It felt, for the first time, like I got to carry him with me, not just that his burdens were mine too.

When I stepped out of my room, I saw Matis moving several textbooks and binders over to the far corner of his room. Not since he first moved in had I ever seen his room this messy.

When Matis saw me staring, he paused, setting the papers in a scattered pile in the center of his bed.

"I've been going through my notes, trying to understand where I missed something." Matis stacked one binder on top of another, shoving them both into the far corner of the bed.

"Maybe there wasn't anything to miss."

Matis looked down at his pile. "I would hate to think I didn't understand everything."

"I don't think anyone can."

We stood together. I could barely picture what Dove's room used to look like. Her unmade bed and scattered desk were the only details my brain still clung to. Otherwise, this space felt entirely rewritten. There was new history to be made, the past no longer the book I had to confine myself to reading.

I looked at Matis.

"I think Professor Powell sent the black cat Augmistum to see if I've lost all hope like Dove did. That's what she must have meant when she was talking about 'finding out who I am,'" I said, finding my footing. "To see if I'm in the same place mentally as Dove was. If learning everything Dove knew would make me want the same world that Qucore does. As Dove did."

"Well, do you?"

"No."

I noticed one of the exposed thumbtack holes in the wall, counting several evenly spaced around the window in a circle. I forget what Dove used to have hanging there.

"I think this is a reminder that we can't halt the consequences of what we've done. There's no easy fix. There are consequences, but there also has to be a way through."

Matis followed my eyes to the wall.

"Do you really think Dove would have wanted this?" Matis tugged on the sleeve of his shirt.

"I can't pretend I really knew what Dove wanted anymore." I ran my finger over the holes in the wall, the ghost of her lingering in the air. "I have to do what I think would be best for us. The people still here. I think we both have to."

Matis' nodded. "What do you want to do?"

"I want to see if Professor Powell is right about me." I stepped away from the wall.

Matis studied me. I held his gaze, watching as a passing cloud shielded the window and pulled most of the sunlight out, before the room flooded with warmth again. He nodded, then pulled one notebook off the foot of his bed. He opened his backpack and slipped it inside. He took a deep breath.

"I'll meet you by the car?" Matis nodded, pulling his backpack over his shoulder.

"Sounds good," I whispered as he walked out the door.

Alone in Dove's bedroom, I felt strange. I still wanted to be angry, though I knew I'd been angry for a long time. Dove had put a preconceived idea of the future ahead of what it would mean for her to still be here with me and my father. She must have known the outcome of taking that much Forticlime. By then, the notion of dying had become abstract for her, martyrdom in the name of research and discovery, and left people to interpret her actions.

How was she supposed to ensure that Professor Powell and even myself didn't misinterpret what she had wanted: to free people from their misery. Professor Powell only sought to cruelly hunt for a Florida with a clean slate and would use what Dove had discovered about Forticlime's effects as the perfect scapegoat. Dove had failed in that way, to be understood.

Professor Powell didn't grasp Dove's vision, but really, neither had I.

I couldn't swear on her ghost any longer.

A weight settled in my chest; it was clearer now that my sister had become a victim of someone else's ambition, left to navigate a cruel world that had turned its back on her while she begged for reasons to stay. The same way I'd begged for her return.

I hadn't heard from Lauren. Maybe I'd see her today.

I heard the front door open and saw my father slump onto the couch. His hands were ragged and trembling, eyebrows more gray than brown. His breathing was labored, and he hardly acknowledged me when he stepped into the living room. I watched as he reached for the remote, turning on the TV and flipping through the channels before landing on a shopping infomercial. I wasn't sure if he was really watching.

The air hung heavy, the silence between my father and I thick. My father sat, his body worn and fragile, face etched with the kind of exhaustion only time and regret could carve. The years were obvious.

I knelt beside him, my fingers tracing the edge of the couch as I tried to find my voice. "Are you okay?" I asked, though I already knew the answer. I didn't need to hear it, didn't need the confirmation. His stillness spoke louder than words.

"I'm fine," he muttered. His gaze drifted, never really landing on anything. He was breathing shallow, tremulous.

The infomercial on the TV flickered, the voices a distant hum, but neither of us paid it any mind. There was nothing left in that world that could distract us.

"You need to stop working so hard in this heat," I said, my voice soft, a last attempt to pull him from the edge. "You're going to get hurt. Can't you see that?"

He didn't respond right away, his eyes unfocused, as if he could still see things that weren't here. "It's never been just the heat, Savannah," he said after a moment, eyes curling toward the TV.

His hand gestured vaguely toward the kitchen, the old familiar motion, as though the answer was already written in the corners of the room. "Water," he rasped, his voice just above a whisper. He finally turned to me.

I stood, my feet dragging across the worn floor, moving quickly. The weight of his eyes on me, even as they never quite found focus, was enough. I handed him a bottle of water.

"You know," he said quietly, setting the bottle beside him, "I've been thinking it might be time for me to get myself an Augmistum." His eyes were clear for a moment, almost hopeful. "You're nearly done with school . . . You'll be out on your own soon . . . Maybe I shouldn't be breathing that stuff anymore in that backroom all by myself."

His voice trailed off. I looked at him.

"Why did still use it?" I asked softly. "Really."

He closed his eyes. "Better the devil you know than the devil you don't," he murmured, a thin, tired smile curling at the corners of his mouth. "But it was my devil. Not Dove's. Not yours. Maybe it's time it's not mine."

The living room was already getting hot from the mid-morning heat. My father looked back at the TV.

I grabbed my bag off the counter, lighter since Dove's journal was no longer in it. There was an ease pulling it over my shoulder. My bag looked dull against the fabric of Dove's dress. Somehow, the combination made sense.

I turned down the hallway and headed for the front door, hearing the monotone dialogue onscreen echo through the hallway. I pulled back the curtain in the living room, enough to let some of the natural light in without the full strength of the heat.

"You look just like Dove in that dress," my father called, his voice crackling over the blurred noise from the television. "She'd be happy it fits."

"Thanks, Dad," I called back, softly opening the front door. "See you later." I swallowed, pulling the Forticlime ad out of my bag and leaving it on the table by the entryway.

Laughter roared from the TV screen as I closed the door.

Daylight flooded my vision as I stepped outside. I saw Matis sitting in the car, his notebook pressed against the steering wheel, writing. The sun prickled the back of my neck, searing its fingers into my skin. Cars on the road rumbled, and the breeze shifted between the buildings, whipping through my dress. The power lines whirred. The digital billboard shifted and sang between advertisements. I raised my chin to the light.

Out of the corner of my eye, I spotted it. A black cat, perched at the edge of the sidewalk, almost daring to walk out into the streaming flow of traffic. Its tail bounced on the sidewalk, eyes closing sleepily as it leaned toward the road, unafraid. We locked eyes, her black pupils perfectly centered within the widened green abyss. I froze.

I hesitated at first, waiting to see if I could catch the lack of light across the pupil, a skewed hue in the iris that revealed an artificial nature, but I didn't. I stepped toward her, and she didn't flinch, bouncing her tail passively on the ground, once, then twice, never breaking my gaze. I towered above her, making a shadow across where she sat. Her fur was dark against the sun-bleached sidewalk.

Slowly, I reached my hand out toward her, gently pushing my fingers into her fur and then picking her up in my arms. There was no sting, no defensive evasion, no strike, no blood. She was soft, her sides squishy, the heat of her body organic. She purred.

This wasn't an Augmistum, a tracker, or a device meant to monitor my descent into despair. She was real.

This cat was alive and unguarded. I felt a flicker of connection. I could still reach for something genuine amidst the chaos. We all could.

I stood still, holding her in my arms and watching the traffic go by, feeling the burning smoke through my nose and into my throat, the heat prickling my skin, the weight of the world outside of me. The black cat kneaded her soft head into the crook of my arm, her claw catching the neckline of my dress. Carefully, I walked her toward my front door, unlocking it and letting her step inside. My father wouldn't notice the difference.

"You ready?" Matis called from his car, tucking his notebook into his bag.

I felt the sun against my shoulders, rolling down my arms. My father had not seen the hurricane shutter, still crucified across the front window. I'd just have to fix it.

"There's somewhere I'd like to go first," I said, lowering myself into the passenger seat. Matis slipped the keys into the ignition and pulled out of the driveway.

I turned back to our small house as its slanted form disappeared behind us. Our crooked thumb. My world. I didn't feel Dove here anymore. There were no more ghosts—just me, my father, and Matis. I'd renounced my living death. I was here now; I had to be, to make anything better, to live with hope in a way Dove couldn't. I had to be the difference.

Maybe that's what she would have wanted. I knew it was what I did.

As best as I could remember, I pointed Matis toward road signs and back streets, down neighborhoods I could only recall from a distant memory. I told Matis to keep driving straight.

With my eyes open, I recounted every detail I could until I knew we were in the right place.

The roads had gotten older, some of the houses were worse for wear, the streetlights in some sections crawled with vines. Nature had invaded, without pushback. It was a welcome harmony. As we drove, the houses grew and expanded, pushed out and away from the main roads and tucked themselves into more trees. The canopy was almost enveloping, but not quite. There wasn't enough green for that. Maybe someday there would be.

The sidewalks grew wider. The temperature fell with the increased shade. I heard several scattered birds somewhere in the distance. We were close. I felt it.

I rolled down my window, leaned out of it, and breathed in the earth, eyes opened, toward the oak trees.

"Slow down," I called to Matis. "It doesn't last for very long."

ABOUT THE AUTHOR

Vanessa Frances is an Orlando-based, award-winning writer whose work blends the intimate and the uncanny, exploring what it means to be human in uncertain worlds. She works across theater, film, and fiction. *Orange Island* is her first novel. When she is not writing, she is biking, kayaking, or slipping into the water, drawn to quiet, in-between places where stories take shape. Find her at https://vanessafrances.me/

RED ROOK STAFF

Red Rook Press is a student-run literary press from the University of Alabama

Acquisitions

Oliver LaRose (liaison), Alex Demuth, Charlotte Diel, Richard Dixon, Malik (Karsten) Erskine, Brea Gaillard, Kaira Harper, James Huntley, Scarlet Jacobson, Isa Matson, Aidyn McKinney, Marshall McGahey, Megan Millar, Mia Mittag, Ainslee Monroe, Nathan Neugebauer, Veronica Oehlers, Ava Rudd, Cooper Smith, Scarlet Sodergren, Ellie Spohrer, Kiley Stevens, Saadat Tayyibah, Alyssa Wallner, Mae Webster, Maggie Welch, Madelyn Woods

Audio

McKenzie Knight (liaison), Alex Demuth, Joie Ingram, Ava Rudd, Vaughn Taylor

Design

Anna Cobb (liaison), Anna Luis (liaison), Sam Brown, MiKayla Davis, Elizabeth Golembiewski, Andrew Kelley, Adyson Keough, Karliegh Plank

Fiction Editing

Jack Armstrong (liaison), Hannah Mauck (liaison), Alex Demuth, Charlotte Diel, Jordan Earnest, Malik Erskine, Audrey Faircloth, James Huntley Andrew Kelley, Dante Larkins, Mia Mittag, Ainslee Monroe, Cooper Smith, Saadat Tayyibah, Noah Thompson, Cannon Williams

Promotions

Maya Mungo (liaison), Sam Godwin, Kaira Harper, Adyson Keough, Dante Larkins, Megan Millar, Evelyn Moran, Tavetta Moton, Averi Obrien

Special Projects

Wrenley Brown (communications liaison), MiKayla Davis (children's book liaison), Livi King (P.R. liaison), Ever Wood (zine liaison), Jane Champ-O'Connell, Bee Hydrick, Dante Larkins, Mia Mittag, Aidan Strebel

Website

Ansel Smith (liaison), Jordan Earnest, Sam Godwin, Adyson Keough, Megan Millar, Tavetta Moon, Swastee Regmi, Saadat Tayyibah

Faculty Advisers

Paul Albano, TR Brady, Sarah Cheshire, Josh Dugat, Merrill Lee Girardeau, Stephanie Marker